The Ronald Reagan Murder Case

A George Tirebiter Mystery
by David Ossman

The Legends of Filmland depicted in this work of fiction
are almost entirely fictional themselves, and their fictional activities
herein are meant only to entertain.

The author gratefully acknowledges untold
contributions to the Legend of George Tirebiter
made over the years by
Phil Austin, Peter Bergman and Phil Proctor,
his companions in The Firesign Theatre.

For
My wife
Judith Walcutt
yes I will yes

THE RONALD REAGAN MURDER CASE
A GEORGE TIREBITER MYSTERY
©2018 DAVID OSSMAN

Published in the USA by:

BEARMANOR MEDIA
P.O. BOX 71426
ALBANY, GEORGIA 31708
www.BearManorMedia.com

ISBN: 978-1-62933-284-0 (alk. paper)

DESIGN AND LAYOUT: VALERIE THOMPSON

TABLE OF CONTENTS

Chapter 1

A Day at the Beach

You can still spit on Gus Lemming's enamel-pink beach hacienda if you lean far enough over the edge of the Santa Monica Palisades. I spit at it frequently in the early Forties, when Gus was my boss at Paranoid Pictures. He was cruder than the four Warner Bros. put together, more powerful than a speeding Louis B. Mayer, and he owned me and loaned me for seven long years. In January of 1945, I still had three years to go. It seemed like a life sentence.

This particular Saturday, Gus was hosting a wrap-party for *Pardon My Pinup*, a sarong-filled B-programmer destined to be shown on oil-stained sheets hung between battered palm trees "somewhere in the South Pacific." I had been the unlucky director, my cast was strictly 4F, but we got through it on schedule in spite of Buster Bailey's Big Band collapsing with stomach flu, down to the last trombone. Buster thought it was tainted oysters from a wedding party at the Coconut Grove.

I had slept late after the usual excitement of my Friday night radio show, and Wilshire was unusually slow with beach traffic, so it was the middle of the afternoon as I drove down the Incline, which connects the middle-class city dwellers of Santa Monica to the millionaires whose homes stretch along the sand, and headed north on the Pacific Coast Highway. My radio was tuned to an Eddie Condon jazz concert, and my mind was empty of business, at least for a day.

You wouldn't have known there was a war going on only a few thousand miles west. Catalina Island loomed bluely on the horizon in the balmy winter sunshine, still the land of the free and the Home of the Cubs. The glittering Santa Monica shore had no webs of barbed wire, only high fences separating the recently rich from each other and from the mostly fatherless families gathered around their blankets and portable radios.

The American Way, for which we had been hard at war for three years, assured that everyone who tanned tanned equally, at least in California.

Gus's hacienda was only about a mile north of the Incline, and he had a couple of Samo High-school boys parking cars for his guests. I gave up my midnight-blue '39 Mercury coupe to one of them, along with a quarter.

"Yes, sir, Mr. Tirebiter. Thank you, sir. Say, I really liked your show last night. You sure made mincemeat out of that pickled Shakespearean ham!"

I was still trying to sort out the kid's menu as he peeled away into traffic. Since I wasn't going to get any new tires for the duration, I wondered how many miles he'd just left on the asphalt in front of me.

The wrought-iron gate stood open under a mission-style arch dripping with orange bougainvillea. The delirious combination of hot orange and shocking pink wouldn't be popular for another twenty years or so, but it reminded Adrian D'Excesse, a Metro set-designer who also did producers' houses, of *Summer in Sorrento*, for which he had almost been given an Oscar. Beyond the gate, I could see a sapphire pool surrounded by famous faces and infamous bodies, a long bar with white-coated Filipino waiters doing chilly things with good gin, and Gus himself, holding court with his stooges—the Three you know about and half-a-dozen others who ran Paranoid Pictures for him.

"Hiya, Georgie!"

Mae West sidled up alongside me.

"Is that a microphone in your pocket, Georgie, or are you just glad to see me?"

I gave Mae a twirl—Gus's big console phonograph was playing Cugat's new one, "The Walter Winchell Rumba," and passed her on with an exchange of sexy winks, to Jerry Colonna.

"I'm daring Dali to a duel, George," he stage-whispered. "Lip fur at twenty paces!"

Salvador Dali made a surreal pair with Alfred Hitchcock at the bar. The painter of soft women and soft watches was in town to dream up some nightmares for *Spellbound*, and his oiled mustachios vibrated like rhinoceros horns in the brilliant flashes of lightning from the pool.

"You can't win unless you melt his wax, Jerry," I said, taking Mae back for a spin that came so close to the edge of the deck that Chico Marx nearly pulled us into the deep end.

Mae said, "I like my lip fur shaved close and kissable." She spun back to Jerry and I was on my way to join Jack Houseman at the bar when Chico splashed past me out of the pool and settled into a deck chair next to Lemming.

"Hey, Gussa, baby!"

Gus loved it when Chico used his sliced salami dialect. "Wha'chu wanta me, Chic'?"

"Is ita true whata they say? You t'ought Georgie Tirebiter was Charlie McCarthy when he comina to see you on hisa firs' day ata Paranoid? Atsa gooda joke, eh, boss?"

"Ha!" Gus tried to laugh around his seven-inch Romeo y Julieta cigar. "George walks inta my office and I say, 'You the new office boy? Jeeze, didn't they tell ya I wanted an egg salad an' a lemon Coke for crapsake?' Right, George?"

"Right, Gus."

"An' the wastebasket is full again, I told him."

"And I said, 'I'm Georgie Tirebiter, Mr. Lemming. You hired me. From radio, remember?'"

"Yeah! An' I sez, 'You? I tell 'em to get me the new Awsome Welles, they send me the old Henry Aldrich!'"

The flacks and stooges laughed. Why not? I'd set him up for the punch line. My topper's timing was a steal from Jack Benny:

"So, I emptied the wastebasket . . ."

There's nothing like leaving on a good laugh, and I did, ending up clinking a cheery gin and tonic against Houseman's balefully pale Miller High Life. He had only recently returned from the Overseas Radio Propaganda Service and was producing an Alan Ladd quickie.

"How's the new picture coming, Jack?"

"You might like to meet the writer, before I kill him."

Houseman gestured toward a spectacled gent in a natty window-pane-plaid sport coat standing off to one side of the patio, puffing on a pipe and gazing toward the waves, where a trio of starlets were giggling at the edge of the chilly surf.

"That's Raymond Chandler?" I said. "*The Big Sleep*? *Lady In the Lake*? Not exactly Bogie, is he?"

"It's a matter of days before we lose our star, Tirebiter, the script's not finished, and the God-damn picture is half-shot . . ."

"So's Chandler, by the look of him."

Jack and I crossed to the patio wall and I was introduced. The famous writer of hard-boiled detective stories shook my hand with his small, cold cat's paw and murmured a greeting.

"Tirebiter . . ."

"I enjoyed *The Lady In The Lake* very much, Mr. Chandler. It ought to make a great film."

"Metro thinks so. I'm supposed to get to work on it as soon as *Blue Dahlia* is done." He took a gulp of his drink. "You don't think a wounded war vet with a steel plate in his skull could murder his army buddy's wife do you, Tirebiter?"

"Not in a musical."

Chandler located my eyes—with some difficulty, I thought—and seemed to be debating whether to take me seriously.

"There's an idea, Ray," said Houseman. "What do you think of my engaging Tirebiter here for a few rewrites? He could elbow all that dialogue aside, subvert the audience's attention with a hot musical number, and afterwards no one would remember who had done what to whom."

Chandler pursed his lips and returned his gaze to the starlets.

"Why don' t you put Marlowe on the case, Mr. Chandler?"

"He's been acting up on me. Doesn't like plots. Can't focus on the plots."

"Alan Ladd's due at Fort Dix in two weeks, Ray."

"To hell with plots."

Houseman shrugged at me behind Chandler's back and rolled his eyes.

Chandler's voice was barely audible, what with the waves, the girls, and the party music. "I think I'll have to get drunk, John. I'll figure it out if I'm drunk."

"The studio won't understand that, Ray."

"I think I'll start now." He held out his paw. "Good to meet you Typewriter . . ."

"Tirebiter," I said.

"Did somebody say something about another bourbon?"

He drained his glass and picked his way carefully across the dance floor, trailing pipe smoke. It smelled like Three Nuns to me. The record player paused between platters, leaving him alone, blinking in the sunlight. The music started again. It was "Brazil," a big hit. The dancers closed ranks as he reached the bar and I lost sight of him—for good as it turned out.

"A chill wind seems to follow him around, poor fellow." Jack shivered. "Well, I'm going to walk home while the sun's still up."

"I'll stroll along with you, if you don't mind company."

"Absolutely not. You can tell me about this next feature Lemming's given you. *Three WACS in a Jeep?*"

We walked on up the beach toward Malibu.

"There's been a title change. *First WAC In Tokyo*. If you can believe it, Gus wants me to work in a dance number for Charles Laughton."

"He can do it, but can you?"

"I've got our dance director working on a parody of this Captain Kidd picture he's doing next. Sort of cross it with 'Slaughter on Tenth Avenue.' We'll back him up with a lot of dancing seamen."

"He'll like that."

The Bay curves West, backed by a craggy line of mountain ridges. To the East, where the summits are higher, some snow glinted under the darkening blue of Southern California's winter sky. It certainly was an improvement on Elk Forest, Illinois, where I had lived nearly twenty of my twenty-five years. Houseman and I walked along in silence, the steady crash of the surf broken only by screams for help.

"Are those screams for help?"

"I thought I was having a Surrealist epiphany."

Off to our left we could see a figure in swim trunks standing in the shallow surf, waving.

"Good God, it looks like Ron Reagan."

"Who's that?" asked Jack, picking up his pace across the sand.

"Contract player at Warners—'Do it for the Gipper,' remember? He's been in the Army recently."

"All-American Boy. What's he got there?"

We were running now, toward Ron, whose wife Jane Wyman had been in *Smart Blonde* with my wife Lillie, and whom we'd entertained on a couple of occasions. He'd always seemed to me a level-headed guy and we could easily trade stories back and forth about radio in the Midwest in the Thirties.

A large red and yellow object was washing sluggishly in and out of the waves. Ron was tugging at it with one hand and waving at us with the other.

"Help! That you, Tirebiter? Help, for heaven's sake!"

"What have you found, Ron?" I kicked off my loafers and waded in to help beach the thing.

"It's a duck! It's a dead duck!"

"A dead duck? On Malibu Beach?" Houseman stayed above the water line and clucked his tongue. "Bad for property values, I should think."

"Never happens at Arthur Treacher's parties," I riposted, helping to drag the monstrous, feathered thing out of the water and onto a pile of kelp. A cloud of sand fleas rose like a plague.

"Golly!" Ron Reagan stared down at the soggy mass. "It's a duck, but it's not a whole duck. It's just the top half."

Dexter D. Duck, Paranoid's trademark cartoon cross between Daffy and Donald, stared up at us from the kelp. The fleas settled back down on its bright yellow beak. A pair of naked human legs stuck limply out from the bottom of the costume.

"There's a guy inside! Come on, fellas!"

Ron pulled the legs and I pulled the head and the head came away in sodden cardboard chunks. What we saw was so unexpected, Houseman gave a little screech. It was a body, of course.

"It's a dead guy!" yelled Ron. "But, jeepers! The dead guy is me!"

He was right. Tanned, handsome and possessed of a small black hole right through the heart of his white bathing togs, Ronald Reagan lay at our feet, his skin beginning to pucker.

CHAPTER 2

I'LL TAKE MULHOLLAND

The three of us gazed down at Reagan's face. Had I been writing one of the popular radio melodramas of the day, I would have cued a portentous musical sting from the orchestra and a woman's hysterical scream from the sound man. Fade to black. Commercial.

However much the occasion demanded the disembodied elegances of my beloved medium, they remained uncued. Instead, the *actual* Ron Reagan (or perhaps not—I had no way of knowing at the time) kicked a rubbery frond of seaweed across the dead Ronnie's face.

"Looks like the duck forgot to duck. This is a whole new seventh inning." Ron gestured at Houseman. "Who's that fella?"

I made the briefest introduction possible under the circumstances. Jack closed his mouth before opening it again to say, "Pleased to meet—ah—both of you, Reagan."

"Ron," I said. "We're going to have to call the Sheriff. There's a party at Gus Lemming's place. I'll go back and use the phone there . . ."

"No, no Sheriff! And keep everybody away. Call PAcific 1-9-4-4. Tell whoever answers to get Col. Casey out here with a squad of MPs. This duck is a military secret, Tirebiter. The outcome of the war may depend on keeping him absolutely quiet."

"He looks quiet to me," murmured Houseman.

Reagan assumed the pose of calm authority he would call upon many times in the future. "Wellp, I'll stand guard until the troops arrive."

All I knew then about Ron's military service was that he was stationed at the old Hal Roach studios in Culver City, converted for use by the Army to make training films. Hollywood gagsters called it "Fort Whacky," but most of us, more respectfully, knew it as Fort Roach. (My bad eyes, allergy to feathers, and status as the sole support of my elderly mother had kept me out of the service, except to serve up our boys and gals a series of such harmless movie entertainments as were ordered of me by the studio, and to keep the homefront laughing with my "Hollywood Madhouse" radio variety show.)

Reagan, who had come out to the Coast from radio a few years before me, was employed by Uncle Sam as a film narrator, but, naturally I had never seen any of his finer efforts—"Rear Gunner," "For God and Country," and "Mustangs Over Yokohama."

Jack and I hotfooted it back to the party, which was still in full swing. "Rum and Coca-Cola" was blaring out of the phonograph, Gene Kelly had arrived, sporting an entirely new look for *Anchors Away*, and Leo G. Carroll and Leon Ames were in the middle of a martini-fueled game of cut-throat shuffleboard. While I found a free phone in Gus's Olde Englishe "library," Houseman regaled the revelers with an elaborate rumor—a Japanese spy had washed up on shore from some one-man sub lurking out in the Catalina channel. Lt. Reagan was in charge, he cautioned (which got a horselaugh from Lemming and a general chuckle from those who were acquainted with the mild-mannered young actor), and no one was to go anywhere near the corpse . . .

The patio emptied immediately. I was watching the stars stagger in a celebrity parade up the beach as my call went through. A voice that sounded like a toad with a frog in its throat belched, "Casey."

"Tirebiter."

"So the hell what?"

"I'm calling for Lt. Reagan. He's dead."

"Say that again. Twice."

"Ron Reagan gave me this number. He's out on Santa Monica Beach with a body. The body looks just like him. He said you should get right down here with a squad of MPs."

"Gotcha."

The phone went dead. The phonograph outside on the patio gave out with amplified ka-chunks from the run-in groove of "Besame Mucho." I watched as one of the Filipino house-boys took the needle off. The pool was empty except for a Roman-nosed older man with a straw hat shading his face, floating in a life-preserver, his eyes closed. He was a silent-movie has-been whose name escaped my memory.

I ran my hand across the beautiful leather spines of a full set of Victor Hugo that filled one of the library shelves. As I had suspected, there were no books behind the spines. The entire unit had come from one of Paranoid's classier efforts, where it had been authoritatively lounged against by Charles Coburn. There was a washroom behind the bookshelves, and I used Gus's personal bar of Lifebouy to freshen up. After a few minutes I heard sirens blasting past up the Highway, and decided to redeem my automobile and drive back home before the rush began.

The high school car jockeys had either gone off duty or were part of the curious crowd gathering a few hundred yards north. I could see a couple of khaki-colored sedans and a pair of uniformed sentries with rifles at port arms standing in front of a narrow walk between two houses—an elegant Robin Hood

Tudor and a grey shack with driftwood siding. The U. S. Army seemed to have things under control on the homefront as well as on the banks of the Rhine.

My coupe had been parked on the far side of the Highway, headed in the wrong direction. I got in, found my keys under the floormat and U-turned toward the Pier. A Red Cross ambulance, its siren muted, flashed past me before I got there.

It occurred to me that I would never know anything more about the surreal activities of the day if I didn't push my acquaintance with Ronnie beyond the bridge-party stage. The Ron Reagan murder case was certainly the most interesting mystery I'd come upon since arriving in Celluloid City; Jack Houseman and I were the only civilians who knew about the double in the duck costume; I knew that it might be a story worth writing some time. I would evolve some plan to get back together with the Lieutenant as soon as possible.

Those thoughts took me east and north, toward the San Fernando Valley. Lillie and I had a small home near Bob Hope in Toluca Lake, which is next door to Burbank and an easy drive into downtown Hollywood, where both the Paranoid lot and the CBS broadcasting studios demanded my presence six days a week.

Lillie had stayed away from the Lemming party claiming a migraine. I knew that she preferred not to appear in public with me in the harsh sunlight. It might expose the ten years' difference between our ages. On radio, of course, I used the voice of an elderly gentleman to create the put-upon "George Tirebiter" of "Hollywood Madhouse," and she assumed a similar *grande dame* persona. Our publicity photos featured me in Monte Wooley-esque character costume, while Lillie's personal Max Factor makeup artist managed to re-create her as she had once looked playing Marie Antoinette in her final Broadway hit, *Vandals of 1934.*

As I wound up the Sepulveda Pass to Mulholland Drive, I evolved a double-headed scheme. First, I would suggest to Lillie she invite the Reagans over for a barbecue. Second, I would invite Ron to do a sketch on my show, which would give me another opportunity to follow up on developments.

Satisfied, I flipped on the Merc's radio. The unmistakable saxophone of Charlie Barnet, broadcasting from some Eastern hotel ballroom, filled the coupe with rhythm, and, in a minute or two, he was joined by Lena Horne, singing in that honey-colored silken tone she always had all to herself.

I crested the Pass and turned right onto Mulholland. Wartime had dimmed the lights of Van Nuys and Encino, but the vista of small towns, farmland and distant mountains was still terrific. Not many people had moved up to this part of the city yet, and only an occasional gate in an occasional low stone wall interrupted the view. The road wound in steep curves along the crest for a couple of miles and the music and the Merc moved perfectly together, putting me into the mellow mood I had felt a couple of times before, sharing a reefer backstage at the Canteen with Bob Mitchum.

George Tirebiter in costume for "Hollywood Madhouse" (1944)

Lillie Tirebiter, star of "Hollywood Madhouse" about 1944

The euphoria was broken by a news bulletin—the Nazi Bulge in Belgium had collapsed. General Patton's Third Army had taken 3400 prisoners. I hardly noticed the car behind me until its spotlight hit my rear-view mirror and bounced back into my eyes.

It would have been damn foolishness to pass in broad daylight, let alone in the grey, two-dimensional dusk. There was no shoulder, but I slowed, hoping the LAPD wasn't on patrol for speeders. The spotlight stayed on my head as the car pulled alongside. I hit the brake. My front windshield dissolved in a cloud of broken glass and my hat flew off my head. I felt a sharp nudge on my front fender, the wheel spun out of my hands and I was airborne. I caught a glimpse of Ventura Boulevard a few hundred feet below, then a brilliant, glittering rectangle of blue light loomed larger and larger in front of me and I was swallowed up in it, swallowing quite a bit of it along the way.

I was in no shape to realize it at that moment, but I'd just dropped in on a very exclusive pool party at Miss Linda Darnell's.

I had very nearly missed accomplishing what the Sioux had failed in—killing Buffalo Bill. Joel McCrea, the star of Linda's recent Technicolor oater of that name had just left the pool for the buffet table when I and my car did a belly flop into (fortunately) the other end. He told me later that he had been sure a Jap Zero had mistaken Linda's back yard for Lockheed's air terminal.

I shall draw a veil over the rest of that Saturday evening. Suffice it to say that when Dave's Towing lifted my once immaculate machine onto dry land and the water drained out, I found my favorite fedora resting mushily on the back seat. It had a single hole in it, the same size as the one through Ronnie's double's heart. The plot, I thought, was thickening. My blood, however, was turning to chlorinated water, and my one day of rest had drawn to a nearly permanent close.

Lillie had long since gone to sleep when Tony Quinn dropped me off on his way home from the Darnell affair. I sat up in the breakfast nook, nursing a cognac. It was more important than ever to find out what Reagan was up to, now that I seemed to be on the target list. "Madhouse" had already been cast for the coming Friday, but there was a guest spot open in two weeks. I would have a network V. P. call Ron's commanding officer and suggest something patriotic, a la Norman Corwin, to feature Ron's narrative skills. CBS was about to premiere a new Corwin series—somewhat lighter fare than his globe-trotting Free World portraits of the past couple of years—and perhaps we could actually interest our country's most poetic radio writer enough to come up with a short pageant projecting his dream of a post-war America. It was worth a try, and it would give me a good excuse to have Lillie call Jane and set up the cook-out for mid-week if possible.

My ability to think and the snifter of cognac came to an end simultaneously. I was still wearing borrowed clothes and my hair still stank of chlorine, in spite of Miss Darnell's perfumed shampoo. I showered again, dowsed myself with some lime-scented stuff from Bermuda and fell into a watery sleep.

CBS Radio City 1939. Scene of "Madhouse" Broadcasts

Chapter 3

Meet Me at Musso's

The work week of a radio player with thirty-two live broadcasts a year—and there were many of us in those halcyon days—was virtually unending. "Hollywood Madhouse" aired on Fridays. On Sundays I would meet with the writers to block out the comedy situations involving Lillie and myself and the "Madhouse" regulars—teen-age singing ingénue Rita Monroe; the phony Shakespearean ham actor "Sir Lionell Flynn," played by former vaudeville comic Phil Baines; our maid, "Porcelain," portrayed by a Black actress named Mattie Daniels, who was also a wonderful stride piano player; and announcer Ben Bland, whose mildly alcoholic ramblings were built into the Glamorama Soap commercials.

On Monday I would meet with the writers again, to punch up the sketches they had written in the meantime. Tuesday and Wednesday my producer-director, a grimly efficient New Yorker named Buzz Melnik, would put together the musical portions of the show, work with our sound-effects men, time out all the ingredients and prepare for full rehearsal. Thursday we ran the show twice, without guest stars, rewriting as we went along. Friday the entire cast assembled for a morning run-through. Then we did two complete live broadcasts—one at 4:30 for the Eastern and Central time zones, and a second at 7:30 for the West. I must say I loved it, even when I was directing a movie and my days lengthened to eighteen or so hours. After all, I was only twenty-five and full of youthful energy.

My writers and I usually met over Sunday lunch in the back room at Musso & Frank's—then, as now, my favorite restaurant in Hollywood. The fact that it still exists, and that its red-coated waiters still serve the best double martinis, grilled lamb chops and creamed spinach in North America, is a barely believable anomaly in a town hell-bent on demolishing the past while recreating itself in the worst possible taste every five years or so.

I met Pete Potash in the lot where I parked my radio-less loaner—a mid-Thirties Dodge sedan that had last been driven by one of the Dead End Kids in a serial called *Junior G-Men*—and we walked in together. Pete was twice my age and had been one half of a sometime vaudeville comedy act called Potter & Porter which had lasted long enough to play the Palace during the stage show between screenings of Gloria Swanson's last silent picture. Pete was a funny guy, a great gag writer and the head of my four-man writing team. He was also the last man I ever knew who wore a derby hat and detachable celluloid collar.

Manny, a waiter who looked and sounded like S. Z. "Cuddles" Sakall, showed us into the wood-paneled function room.

"Good afternoon, Mr. Tirebiter, Mr. Potash. It's a Martini-toony and a . . . ?"

"Sazerac, heavy on the bitters, Manny."

"That's right, sir. Mr. Murphy and Mr. Gibson have already arrived, sir."

Florida Murphy had acquired his first name, which he shortened to Florry, as a result of having been born during that state's land boom in the early Twenties. He was 4F'd out of the military for a glandular disorder, and weighed about 250 pounds. As usual, he was wearing a badly wilted seersucker suit and one of an apparently endless collection of aloha shirts. This one featured outriggers and purple ginger flowers. Florrie had a couple of credits for Abbott and Costello movies, and was a terrific ventriloquist. His dummy was named Senator T-Bone Culpepper and the two of them bantered about politics, which was a pretty rare thing at the time. CBS had taken him off a local daytime show and given him to me when we were in development on "Madhouse."

"Hiya, Georgie. How about this one? The bit where the kid sellin' the papers gives out with the headlines? He says 'Tirebiter Crashes Star's Pool Party! Read all about it!' An' you argue with the kid, like always—'It was an accident,' you say, and he says, 'Geeze, Mr. T., you shudda let the boy park the car for ya. It wouldda only cost a dime.' An' then you say . . ."

"He says, 'What the heck, kid. I got a free wash." Mel Gibson supplied the topper. Not the Mel Gibson who put Australia on the map a generation later. My Mel was a prep-school drop-out from Connecticut. His father, Dana Gibson, was a popular Broadway playwright whose biggest success, *It Happened in Philadelphia*, had brought the family to Hollywood. Mel could read *Ulysses* and pop punch lines at the same time, and frequently did.

"I don't think I want to bring up my little accident on this week's broadcast, boys. And come to think of it, how did word get around so quickly on a Sunday morning?"

Florrie said, "My phone rang at 7:30. Reporter at the *News* named Squeek. Gives me tips on Hollywood Park sometimes. Got the word from the overnight guy at the County coppers desk. Thought I'd dig the story."

"Great," I said. "I'll bet he didn't mention I was the bullseye for some gunsel's target practice."

Manny came in with our drinks, a tray of shrimp cocktails, and a couple of tall containers of bread-sticks. He raised his eyebrows at the overheard suggestion of gun-play.

"Say," said Mel out of the corner of his mouth, taking his Florsheims off the table to squint at me. "You in with gangsters, Tirebiter?"

Manny raised his eyebrows even higher, made a "tsk-tsk-tsk," and withdrew.

"Gangsters," put in Potash, "are a great comedy gimmick. OK. George, howzabout gangsters kidnap you on the way to the studio. Lillie calls up Jack Benny to go the ransom. Big laugh. So Sir Lionell gets the job of carrying a paper sack full of money to some boffo rendezvous . . ."

"Cucamonga," Florrie filled in. "Benny sure put that burg on the map last week."

"Whatever." Mel has the ball now. "So everybody's waiting for the phone to ring, only we have to get them out of the room somehow. Porcelain is there, and everybody knows how she garbles all your phone calls . . ."

"And the phone rings . . ."

Pete is interrupted by the phone ringing.

"Swell sound effects they got in this joint."

"Only the best for my writers, Pete." It's the plug-in phone at the table, of course. "Tirebiter here. Where the hell are you, Dave?"

The fourth member of the writing team was Dave Marmelstein, a nice Jewish boy from Los Angeles, whose father was my agent at William Morris. He was sort of "in training" with our show, and he was always late to meetings.

"You don't know me, Mr. Tirebiter, but I need your help." It was not Dave. My ear was caressed by a woman's voice, sultry as a Gulf Coast summer afternoon. I heard music—"Siboney," violins . . .

"Huh?" That was all I could manage. "Who is this?"

"I can't tell you now. Just do this. Drop into Pickwick Bookstore on your way out of Musso's this afternoon. Ask to see a copy of "Nightmare in Black Glass.""

"Nightmare in Black Glass?"

"That's all I can tell you now. Please, please do what I ask."

The phone clicked down on the other end. Summer was over and all the gardenias in the world suddenly turned brown.

"Business, George?"

"Funny business, Pete. That's the business we're in, isn't it?"

"We better be!" chimed in Florrie. "Look, here's another one. You get kidnapped and natch the show hasta go on. What happens is, all the rest of the kids hafta do your lines an' they try to copy Tirebiter's old goat voice, but the sponsor doesn't buy it . . ."

"Meanwhile . . ."

"Meanwhile this Grasshopper is starting to taste like the water in Linda Darnell's pool. Forget gangsters. There's a clause in my contract that says I have to be alive to pick up my paycheck."

"Pretty snappy comeback, Georgie. Lemme write that down."

The food arrived, along with another round of drinks. Even Dave arrived, with a pretty good sketch he'd written for Red Bunyun, our comedy guest star. I listened, laughed whenever possible and gradually the show began to emerge from set-ups, punch-lines and cigar smoke. I was only half in the room, however. To borrow Ronnie's most famous movie line, spoken in *Kings Row* as he discovered his legs had been amputated, 'Where was the rest of me?' Somewhere in the tropics, with a voice sweeter than mango syrup dripping in my ear, my head buzzing with honey bees, and the sensation of an electrical storm—just over the horizon, but coming fast on a hot wind.

CHAPTER 4

MR. PICKWICK'S PARADISE

Hollywood Boulevard was quiet on a Sunday. The Chamber of Commerce's glamour campaigns to the contrary, the "Main Street of America's Movie Capital" looked pretty much like any other American Main Street. For size there was the swanky Roosevelt Hotel; at Highland, a towered bank building where Philip Marlowe was supposed to have had his detective business; and a cluster of three multi-story offices at the intersection of Vine. That curiously famous cross-roads was, and remains, shabbily commercial. Musso's and Pickwick Books were located along a three or four block stretch of mostly single-story buildings, including a number of antiquarian book stores and modest eating establishments, the ubiquitous small-town line-up of drugstore, shoestore, *corseterie*, haberdasheries, and other specialty shops owned and operated by people who actually knew their customers by name.

For the benefit of Japanese tourists and Middle Western thrill-seekers, the Boulevard sidewalk is now punctuated with brass stars dedicated to both the celebrated and forgotten folk of show business. The Curators of Fame, for a handful of dollars, can arrange to include nearly anybody, including television producers and cartoon characters, in the tinsel panoply. My star is in a driveway next to a Middle-Eastern take-out stand not far from the old Egyptian Theatre. I try to visit it once a year and scrape off the chewing gum.

It was my habit in the Forties to take a stroll down the boulevard after Sunday lunch, browse the international newsstand on Las Palmas, and I often dropped in at Pickwick to find a new page-turner to occupy me in the dead spots of my working day. The bookshelves rose high enough to require a ladder, virtually every volume in print was available and there were always bargains housed higgledy-piggledy on tables in the back, at the top of a single flight of creaky wooden stairs. The front door even had a little bell which tinkled sweetly as I entered. The real world was once rich with radio sound effects.

"Good afternoon, Mr. Tirebiter. Can I help you with something?"

"Thanks, Grace. Yes. I thought I might pick up a couple of new mysteries to read on the set."

"Certainly. Dorothy B. Hughes? Cornell Woolrich? Of course we have all the latest Pocket Books if you'd prefer Christie or Gardner."

"Someone suggested a title to me—I don't know the author. It's called "Nightmare in Black Glass.""

"Oh, yes. S. S. Van Dyke. Halfway up the stairs, to your right, bottom shelf. Alphabetical by author."

"Thank you, Grace."

I squandered a little time looking vaguely at Travel, Poetry and First Editions, so as not to appear too anxious. There was a large display of paper-backs with the usual garishly graphic covers, bannered "Send A Book Overseas." The most popular titles seemed to be "The Pocket Book of Boners," "See Here, Private Hargrove," and "The Case of the Curious Bride." "The Thin Man" and Ogden Nash were also in evidence.

Van Dyke was near the end of the mystery section. I crouched and ran my fingers along the backs. There it was! Only one title, and only one copy. I made sure I was unobserved, slipped the book out and stared at the dustcover. The red-haired girl in the clutches of the shrouded skeleton was screaming horribly. She seemed unaware that her dress was being kept up only by prominent features of her remarkable anatomy. I whistled and, as if summoned, a folded slip of paper fell from inside the pages and fluttered to the floor, like a baby robin on its first flight from the nest. I caught hold of it softly, rose and ambled nonchalantly to the back of the aisle, pretending to admire the variety of Hobbies available to those with something called "free time."

I opened the paper, releasing a vaporous whiff of ripe gardenias which swarmed over me like white satin gloves on the dance floor of a Havana nightclub. The note was written in soft, inky curves, laid out as suggestively as a black negligee on cream-colored sheets. The stationary was monogrammed S. S. V. Her voice seemed to whisper to me:

"Dearest George. Thank goodness you came! I have good reason to believe you are in great danger. We are both being followed, and I can't risk being seen with you . . ."

How did she know I was being followed? *Was* I being followed?

"I'll be in the fifth row of Grauman's Chinese for the five o'clock show on Wednesday. Meet me in the dark and we'll talk. Come alone, please. Please!"

It was signed "Stella Sue."

The tango music and the flowery scent faded away. I almost expected the notepaper to flash into flame and burn to ash between my fingers, but it didn't. Soft and vulnerable, it rested quietly in my hand. I slipped it into my inside coat pocket and went back downstairs with the book.

"Oh, I'm sure you'll enjoy that, Mr. Tirebiter. His last one was thrilling—"The Groom Wore Red.""

"His?"

"Sure. S. S. Van Dyke." Grace flipped open the back cover and showed me the author's photograph. "Nice looking, if you like the Sunny Tufts type. See?" She indicated the short biography below the photograph. "He works in a defense plant on the graveyard shift and writes murders during the day."

"I don't believe it."

"I'm sure it's possible, Mr. Tirebiter. That'll be $2.95, plus 3 cents tax. Two-dollars and ninety-eight cents total. Out of five . . ."

She rang up the sale, gave me my change and slipped the book into a brown bag with jolly Mr. Pickwick's picture on it.

It gave me a creepy feeling to think that I was being watched, or followed. I walked back to the lot where I had left my borrowed Dodge, and decided on a cup of coffee at one of the local drive-ins. If somebody suspicious pulled in, I could keep an eye on him. Or her. Also, I could see if "Nightmare in Black Glass" contained any clues. Clues about what? Anything. I was a confused young man.

CHAPTER 5

THE EXTRA GIRL

Herbert's was a circular building set in the midst of an asphalted corner lot near Hollywood High. The lower part was all plate glass and glass brick, topped by a sort of sombrero roof fringed with spotlights and a tall, curvaceous marquee with H-E-R-B-E-R-T-S spelled out in flashing neon letters. A juke-box, piped out to the car-park through bullhorn speakers, played "I'll Be Seeing You."

The car-hops wore spotless white bolero jackets and white slacks with a maroon stripe up the side. They also wore roller skates. Some of them were better skaters than others. There was a minor crunch as my waitress rolled into the door. She saved her tray from flying through the window by setting it on the roof of the sedan.

"Can you roll your window a little way up, please?"

"Sure."

She fastened the tray in place. It had a heavy china mug, a cloth napkin, stainless steel spoon, two little pitchers of cream and a matching bowl of individually wrapped sugar cubes. You got a lot of service for a dime in 1945.

"Mr. Tirebiter?"

"That's right."

"Gosh, I thought it was you when you ordered your java? I asked Myrna to look at you, 'cause she was on the set with me? And she said it was you okay and to go ahead and say hello and maybe you wouldn't mind? Do you mind?"

"No, that's all right. Can I give you an autograph for your little brother or something?"

"Oh, no!" She laughed with her mouth closed and covered it with her hand. She had nice hands and good fingernails painted a red that Uncle Joe Stalin might consider a little gaudy for May Day. She looked around and stuck her head conspiratorially into the car window.

"Can I talk to you, Mr. Tirebiter? I'm on my break in ten minutes."

"Do I know you?"

"Well, sure. My name is Melody Jakes? That's my screen extras name?" She ended most of her sentences with a question mark, which I identified with being from Texas. "I guess you don't remember me, but I'm in that new picture of yours? *Pardon My Sarong*? I'm an extra nurse? In a crowd scene? I was sort of kneeling right near Dennis O'Keefe? Oops! I gotta go, Mr. Tirebiter, but I'll be back in ten."

Melody slipped her head out, barely missed knocking over my coffee cup with her pointy little chin, and skated away toward a beige Pontiac. There were not a lot of cars pulled in around the restaurant. A couple of teenagers in jalopies, a nice '37 Ford convertible a few spaces away with a uniformed guy and his date, eating hamburgers and guzzling a single strawberry malt out of separate straws. As I put cream in my coffee an early '30s Hudson Terraplane pulled in almost out of sight on the far side of the building. I opened my new book.

I don't usually go in for the prep-school sports and steam-room vulgarity of the Athletic Club, (it began), *but business is business and mine is usually murder. I dressed for the occasion in my new suit, the one with the barely visible burgundy check which matched the silk display handkerchief. My shirt was the pale blue of a new day in high mountain air and I'd got my shoes shined by the hunch-backed Negro boy in the Parker House lobby. My appointment with Wallace Colby was at 3 p.m.*

So far, so good. A little preoccupied with clothes, but that was understandable for a woman writer.

Colby is already the publisher of a big Los Angeles newspaper, but he has designs on the Mayor's job. I knew his face from the grainy photograph that headed his weekly column, "The Hot Seat," and his politics from the column itself. In it, he spilled dirty secrets, made friends and taunted enemies, and flattered himself by dropping the names of show-business types.

People drove in next to me on the passenger side. It was an older couple in a De Soto with a badly dented left rear fender and bald tires. I sipped some coffee and turned the page.

That was enough to make me dislike him, but not enough to turn down a job. When Lopez called to say he'd recommended me as hired protection for two days in Coronado I could hear my creditors sigh. I was supposed to pick Colby up at the Athletic Club and drive his Caddy south. It wasn't the dumbest thing I ever did, not by a good six inches . . .

My passenger side door opened with a throaty squeak. I jumped, and spilled a couple of drops of coffee on the upholstery. Melody got in, her skates clunking heavily on the floorboards. The juke-box was playing "It Had To Be You."

"Gee, I never thought a big movie director and radio star would drive a car like *this*?"

"My other car smells like a swimming pool."

"Really? Wow! Swimming pool? I wish I even had a car, let alone one that smells like a swimming pool! Holy cow! Excuse my skates, but I just work here as a hop to make ends meet, you know? And sometimes I fill in over at Western Costume, because I did costumes for that dumb play "Our Town?" At my High School? That was Boone High in Plano, Texas? Before I moved here? I mean my family moved here, 'cause my daddy does sheet metal work and he's indispensable for the war effort? Anyway, that's what I wanted to talk to you about!"

"The war effort? Or 'Our Town'?"

"Unh uh. Western Costume. I cut your picture out of the paper, see?"

She took a square of newspaper out of her bolero pocket, smoothed it out and handed it to me. The headline read, 'Unidentified Duck Found on Beach," and there was a gruesome photo of two attendants shoving a stretcher into an ambulance, human legs dangling from the feathery cardboard corpse.

"This isn't my picture."

"But the story says you were there? You were one of 'filmland's famous' who found it? Here's your picture, here."

She turned the paper over. It was me all right, standing beside my car like a deep-sea fisherman with a record-breaking tuna. 'Radio Star Drops in Unexpectedly on Film Queen.' Not reading the L. A. tabloids saved my ego a certain amount of heart-break, but I'd obviously missed what my writers had chuckled over that morning.

"That's me, I'm sorry to say. But I'm not sure my little accident has anything to do with the unidentified duck."

"Well, reet! But I know who the duck is, I mean I think I do, because like I said, I work these two or three evenings a week at Western? And last Monday— I know it was Monday, because the Teen Canteen is open Tuesday through Saturday, and when I'm between extra jobs, I have an act I do there with another girl? We're called the Four Bobby Soxers, which is a joke nobody seems to get, but it's because we have four feet, reet? We do some Andrews Sisters and Myrna does a magic trick which works sometimes?"

I felt like I had run a mile along the beach wearing Frankenstein's Monster's boots.

"Ah . . . Western Costume?"

"That's what I'm trying to tell you! Last Monday I rented out a Dexter D. Duck costume and it never came back yet! Well, I didn't rent it out exactly, but I went back in the racks and found it for Irv, who was actually doing the renting out, physically, if you know what I mean—except here's the weird thing—Irv says to this guy, 'So, are you in a movie or what?' You know, making gab? And the guy says, 'Surprise party.' And Irv says—he's such a dumbo—'Yeah, too early for Halloween,' and so the guy says 'Not in Hollywood,' and he picks up the package with the duck suit and walks out the door and maybe he's the unidentified man you found on the beach! God! Was it horrible?"

"No, it was very peaceful, actually, except for a chord of dramatic music and a woman's scream that seemed to come out of nowhere. But I don't see what I can do . . ."

"Well, his name and address are on the receipt and . . ."

"Ah, Miss . . ."

"Jakes? Melody Jakes? It's my screen extras name?

"Well, why don't you give your screen extras name to the papers, Miss Jakes? Give the renter's name to the police. They'll trace it, if they're interested. He—he didn't look like anyone familiar from the movies, did he?"

"Oh, no! He looked foreign. I think it's a gang, Mr. Tirebiter. An espionage gang? My sister—I have two sisters and we all came here from Plano? Princess works at a poker club in Gardena and Rosie works at Lockeed? But she's not a riveter if you know that song? And what if I told on this man who got rubbed out, then the gang that rubbed him out would kidnap me and Rosie would have to turn against her own country and steal bomber blueprints or something to ransom me? Or Princess would have to pick up the ante, or whatever they do in Gardena? I'd never get to be a movie star that way, so what if I just get the receipt for you and then we'd both be doing something for our country, reet?"

Working my way through the syntax, I realized that Melody had more of a point than she realized. I said, "I suppose it is really better if you don't go to the police. I can . . . well, I have channels—to pass it along. Reet?"

"I knew you weren't a sad-sack, Mr. T.! Rosie will never know what you've done to save our family. I'll get the receipt at the store tomorrow and you meet me, how about at the Hollywood Bowl trolley stop on Cahuenga at 10:15 at night? Where I transfer for Glendale?"

"I think I can manage . . ."

"And gee, Mr. T., if you need anybody to wax the jeep in your next movie, just call me."

"Wax the jeep?"

"Isn't it called *Four Waxing a Jeep*?"

"Not any more."

"Oh, well."

And with that she opened the door and roller skated away. I flipped my lights on and off and put a quarter on the tray. She was back in a flash, unscrewed the tray, raised it above her maroon pill-box hat and spun twice on her way back to the kitchen. My head was spinning too. "Clang, Clang, Clang!" went the juke-box. I ground the sedan into gear, backed out and was about to pull into traffic when I noticed the Terraplane pull out behind me. It cruised half-a-block back as I headed east on Sunset.

CHAPTER 6

THE TAM, THE PLACE & THE WIFE

The Terraplane stayed visible behind me as I cruised over the Cahuenga Pass, down Dark Canyon Road, crossed over the Los Angeles River, under the illuminated Burbank sign and past the Warner Bros. soundstages. This part of the city, where the river bed curves around the foot of Cahuenga Peak, never fails to remind me of the Old Hollywood I had seen on Saturday matinees at my neighborhood Odeon. Since the days of *Birth of a Nation*, the marshy river bottom with its craggy, chaparral-covered backdrop had been used for picture making. Cahuenga loomed over Western backlot streets, New England country roads and outdoor settings from Scotland to the Sahara.

More than twenty years after the adventure that was presently overtaking me, in the throes of my personal Sixties Revolution, I took up residence in a teepee built for me by a Mohawk Indian, hidden in a grove of eucalyptus trees not two hundred yards from the traffic-heavy canyon pass. I felt I was sleeping safely between the paws of the great bear which California's natives had once seen in Ca-hueng-na's hump-backed profile. Medicinal herbs, wild tobacco and crisp watercress grew in abundance, and my Indian friend took me to find a quiet clearing where a clear spring always bubbled up. This marked the site of the original native village, he claimed, and I have no reason to disbelieve him. Standing in that spot I could see the crumbling Himalayan lamasery of Shangra La, which rose for decades out of the Warner's lot, above the concrete river banks.

The Terraplane turned into the studio gate as I watched it in my rear-view mirror. I actually felt let down, having stretched my imagination as far as possible to make the old car into a physical threat.

Lillie and I lived in a patioed Spanish-style house with wrought-iron grills over the windows, a Mission tile roof and the usual variety of semi-tropical plants that had been tended, before the war, by a retinue of Japanese gardeners. Those horticultural miracle-workers having been interned for the duration in desert prison camps, Lillie spent a good deal of her time puttering in the flower beds, and the Guzman father-and-sons kept the lawns trimmed and abundantly watered. We had bought the house in the first flush of my Hollywood success, right after our wedding in 1941. I had married the boss's daughter.

Lillie's father, Albright Ames, had been a Broadway producer in the Teens, a partner in the Knox-Haymarket vaudeville theatre circuit in the Twenties, and a major owner of Mid-Western radio stations as broadcasting caught on big in the early Thirties. A child actor from the age of ten, I found myself appearing in radio dramas as soon as my voice changed. I had regular work on Ames' flagship station, WOP in Chicago. Poetry, commercials, prosperous young men-about-town, character roles, I did them all. I developed a series for myself, "Young Tom Edison, Electric Detective," and wrote each daily episode for three years. More writing jobs and network broadcasts came my way, and by 1939, only Jack Benny and Orson Welles were better known to radio fans than I was.

Under her mother's tutelage, Lillie had studied voice and gone to a Swiss finishing school. Her father's influence got her an audition for O. Z. Dillingman's celebrated review series, *Vandals*, and her career as a show-girl was launched. When we met, she was a glamorous thirty year-old New York sophisticate, nearing the end of commercially profitable youth, and I was a much too full-of-myself twenty year-old radio star. We thought we needed each other, courted via cross-country express trains, and finally married two days after I turned twenty-one and signed my Paranoid Pictures contract. Memorably, it was Pearl Harbor Sunday.

None of this history was on my mind as I pulled into the driveway of 105 West Wind Circle and turned off the shuddering engine of my borrowed sedan. No wonder. The tropical heat of Stella Sue Van Dyke's voice had once again begun coursing through my veins like 155-proof rum.

The front door opened and my wife stepped out, posed next to a burst of flamingo-beaked orange flowers in her dark blue Jean Louis suit, grimaced, and held her nose. I hoped it was her opinion of the vintage Dodge I was driving and not of me.

Sunday nights Lillie and I liked to have cocktails and dinner at the Tam O'Shanter Restaurant in nearby Glendale. The building looked like one of Walt Disney's more rustic Dwarf cottages, shingles cascading down the turreted roofs and a stuccoed exterior modeled to resemble quaintly half-timbered stone walls. A liberal use of neon to outline windows and ring chimney pots added to its humorous aspect, and we had started eating there because the place made us laugh.

Lillie usually drove us to the Tam in her own car, which otherwise stayed in the garage, given the scarcity of "A" gasoline coupons and other automotive necessities. It was a Lincoln, an early Continental model, and she had it painted platinum blonde to match her hair.

"I have to read about you in the papers, George," she said as we tootled toward Glendale through Griffith Park. "You might have told me about Saturday night before Louella called."

"What in hell did she want?"

"Anything Hedda doesn't have."

"No one has anything, Lillie. Jack Houseman and I were out on the beach by pure chance. Ron Reagan put military security over what we found, but I can tell you it was bizarre."

"A Dizzy Duck costume?"

"Dexter Duck. The thing had a body inside it that looked like Reagan's double. Nobody's supposed to know anything about that. I thought for a minute it was some practical joke, but if it was I don't know on who. The accident was no joke at all. A car pulled alongside me on Mulholland and put a bullet through my windshield and that dark green Stetson you got me for my birthday last year."

"Good God, George!"

"I don't think the body and the accident had anything to do with each other, but I can't be sure."

"What do the police think?"

"Not much, probably. Filmland hijinks. I thought I was being followed this evening on my way home, but the bozo turned off into Warners."

"What are you going to do?"

"Well, I'm going to offer Ron a guest spot on the show next week. Why don't you call Jane and have them over for dinner? Then I can pump him in a sociable way about his big military mystery. The other business, well, maybe it was mistaken identity. Anyway, I'm going to keep my eyes open. I'll borrow a revolver from the prop department to stick in the glove compartment."

"I'll give Jane a ring tomorrow. Gee, I'm glad you weren't killed, honey."

She leaned her cheek over for me to kiss.

A familiar profile under a tousle of white curls was set off by the indirect lighting as we entered the bar. It turned and nodded to us. It belonged to the silent film actor I had last seen in the Lemming swimming pool. I nodded back, but Lillie went over to him, clasped his hand and said a few words.

"Who is that?" I asked, as soon as we were seated in our booth and had placed our drink orders.

"Don't you remember him? Jesus, General Lee and the King of France? Basil Brewster. He toured in one of Daddy's shows—it was "The Vagabond King," that old chestnut—after his career went bust. I used to sit in his lap."

"I'll bet he enjoyed that."

"No cracks. He's a lovely old man."

"He was at Gus's party yesterday. I wondered why. He hasn't made a picture in twenty years."

"There's always a possibility. Besides, he likes to keep an eye on the younger talent. He congratulated me on you."

"Does that mean what I think it does?"

"Don't worry, honey. I'll protect my big, strong boy."

We ate our club sandwiches and drank our Bloody Marys. Brewster tipped his hat to us as he left. He looked remarkably fit for a man who had made his Broadway debut in 1903, Lillie told me, playing a Flying Monkey in the original production of "The Wizard of Oz" with Montgomery and Stone.

"Maybe he'd like a job in *First WAC in Tokyo*."

"That would be generous of you, George."

"Can he speak?"

"Of course. It wasn't sound that ruined him, it was the Taylor D'Arcy King murder." Lillie lit a cigarette—she smoked Marlboros when they came with a lipstick-red filter tip.

"Big Hollywood scandal? Director dead on his yacht?"

"It was Basil's yacht."

"Really! Who done it?"

Lillie smiled and waved at Brewster, who had lifted a glass of champagne in a toast to her.

"I'm sure I don't know. He was married to Mary Maple Murray then. It was a cover, you know, dear. She was a cocaine addict and a man-eater. Basil saved her from a scandal with Chaplin by marrying her."

"The Twenties must have been something!"

"Mary practically invented the Twenties."

"Colorful as hell. Maybe Brewster can play Judy Shay's banker father. He has a tizzy when she joins the WACS. It's a couple of pages. Has he got an agent?"

"He probably has a telephone. Probably still lives on Whitley Heights in one of those Venetian villas. He told me once he had the first swimming pool in Hollywood. An all-over tan means a lot to a guy with his interests."

"Done. If I don't meet these antiques while they're still alive, what's the point of being here?"

"The money, George. The point is the money."

I wondered whether she was right about that all the way home.

CHAPTER 7

RADIO PARADE

CBS, which still holds down the corner of Sunset and Gower with five stories of Art Moderne, was a magnet for tourists in the Forties. With half-a-
dozen or more live broadcasts every day, tickets given away at all the local hotels,
and a parade of talent otherwise available only on the silver screen, the building
was Mecca. A couple of blocks away, NBC's pale green prow anchored on Sunset
and Vine, and crowds lined up there to see Jack Benny, and the rest of
Sarnoff's comedy stars. In between, there was dining and dancing at Earl
Carroll's Theatre and big bands swung at the Palladium.

Radio was a public entertainment, a kind of three-ring circus act. All of us
thrived on pleasing the live audience while dancing the tightrope of Network
Time, making sure that families at home could follow the story while giving
them a variety of jokes and music both familiar and mildly surprising. And don't
forget the sponsor. We never did. Glamorama, a division of AAAcme Chemical
Corp. of Lynn, New Jersey, paid the bills. Their representative, a dour ad agency
lawyer named Morton Skully, also read our scripts, made sure that his Aunt Hazel
could understand and not be offended by any part of them, and insisted that our
endorsements of the boss's soap sound as real as if we actually used it.

Agnes Moorehead and Frank Sinatra were rehearsing an episode of "Suspense"
down the hall from my office when I arrived at Radio Center on Monday
morning. I could tell from the screams. She was being menaced, of course, as
usual. Frankie was the bad guy. Unlike "Hollywood Madhouse," which spread its
forces across the big stage of Studio A, in front of an audience of two hundred
people, "Suspense" could contain its stars in the confines of Studio C, with only
the sound effects crew and a small orchestra, heavily padded, at the far end. The
padding was for the screams, which were, as the joke went, "well calculated to
make you wet your pants."

My writers were in a good mood.

"We gotta do the spot," announced Florrie as I walked in. Today, his shirt had
Kodak views of volcanoes, one of which was giving birth to a blazing lava flow
across his stomach.

"They sent over one of those Mr. Announcer interviews-with-a starlet things, but it needs a twist," put in Potash, who was sitting behind my desk, his shiny shoes propped up on a pile of pink and blue script pages.

"I suggested something patriotic, George—like 'Girls, when your guy gets back from running the Nazis out of Norway, you want to look your swellest . . .'"

"Makes her sound pregnant, Dave," said Mel, puffing on his pipe, without looking up from this week's *Life*.

"How about it's an audition?" said Dave. Being the youngest member of the group, he tried harder.

"Howzabout it's an audition for an audition and we use Rita?" improved Pete.

"That's okay," I said. "What do we have her doing this week?"

"She's scoutin' the Ranch Market with Red," said Florrie.

"Lillie's teaching her to walk like a Vandals Girl," Mel offered simultaneously.

"At the same time?"

"The Vandals bit is at breakfast. You're trying to eat a two-minute soft-boiled egg and read your script. Rita's balancing it on her head."

"Rita's balancing the script *and* the eggs," put in Florrie.

"Good!"

"Rita's talked Red into using her in the movie he's doing."

"It's called *The Oasis Man* and he sells ice cream."

"Sells it to a Nazi spy, unless the war's over."

"It's in the can already. This is just promotion."

Red Bunyun was a brash young comic making his second movie. Rita had been a band singer at sixteen. She had a pleasant singing voice and a sexy naiveté, and I'd featured her in one of my Paranoid musicals, but otherwise her career had not really taken off. As a matter of fact, the running gag on the program was her constant auditioning, with the underlying (but naturally unspoken) suggestion that if she'd only take advantage of a casting couch or two, she'd be made. Pun intended. Such were the male chauvinist comedy standards of the time, I'm sorry to say.

"So there's a scene at the Ranch Market. Rita's getting orange juice and a bagel . . ."

"Too ethnic."

"A donut."

"Too fattening."

"Some pretzels."

"Too stupid."

"An American Cheese samwich."

"Too . . . maybe it'll work."

"Red delivers a load of ice cream bars, spots Rita and they do a number."

"Red wants to do 'If I Loved You' funny."

"Rita wants to do 'The Boy Next Door.'"

"That's not funny."

"What does the band want to do?"

"Ah, let's see . . ." Pete shuffled through a stack of mimeographed pages. "Ray's got in mind 'Full Moon and Empty Arms'. The other two band spots are 'Laura' and some real oldie . . . 'Darktown Strutters' Ball.'"

"Dey will if dey gets de chance."

"Badoom-bop!" Dave did Florrie's rim-shot.

"'Laura' I like," I said. "Weren't we talking about the commercial?"

"Sure, Georgie, sure. The commercial leads into the song." Florrie lifted his bulk to act out the scene. He looked like a walking post-card rack. "See, Red and Rita are strollin' around the produce stands, feelin' up the cantaloupes and pokin' the celery, and they run into 'Well, if it ain't Ben Bland. Fancy meetin' you here.' And he does the starlet interview."

"But it's gotta be just to audition her for the interview."

"Right!" chorused Florrie, Dave and Mel.

"Here's the bit. Ben says, 'Did you remember to buy Glamorama, Rita?' and she says 'In the three-bar Party Pac.'"

"And Ben says 'Three bars is a party as far as I'm concerned,'" Florrie added, sitting down again.

"Har har har."

"And *she* says she's got an audition coming up tomorrow for some picture and Red says are you going to do a scene from a play . . ."

"*I Remember Mama*," suggested Mel.

"Dot's right. Mit a Sveedish ac-cent."

"I vant to get a loan."

"See your banker twice a year!"

"And Ben says, 'Rita, do something you really believe in. Talk about Glamorama Soap."

"Oh, gee, Mr. Announcer, that's a swell idea. Can you help me?" said Dave in a quivering falsetto.

"Bang, we're there."

Pete made a couple of notes on his yellow pad. It was his job to decide when the boys had fixed the dialogue well enough to move on to the next beat.

"What about the song?" I asked.

"They need a dumb little duet. She can't hit any high notes anyway."

"'Two Sleepy People.' It was big for Hope," said Mel. He held open *Life* to a picture of Bob Hope and some blonde prancing around on a make-shift stage in Iceland.

"I like it."

"Me too."

"Okay. We already got the breakfast scene. You try one more time to get Sir Lionell to move out of the pool house."

"What do I do, burn it down?"

"How about you tell him he's got to go to New York to read for a big, big part in *Harvey*?

"Yeah. The title role."

"He doesn't even have to wear makeup."

"We could have some nice stuff at the Pasadena train station next week. Tearful farewells, et cetera et cetera."

"Then, Lillie's got some displaced Russian circus act dropping by . . ."

"Rumanian."

"Bulgarian."

"That's it. It's, you know, a Gypsy balancing act."

"Three big strong guys. Lillie's mad for 'em."

"Discreetly!"

"But suggestively!"

"They've got one of those spring-board things."

"Great! One of 'em goes right through the roof!"

"No!"

"Right! They send Georgie through the roof. Literally! Boinggg! Airborne!"

"Love it! Love it!"

"Bingo!" Pete made another couple of notes.

"The Noblemen sing 'Way Down Yonder in New Orleans' with Mattie sitting in for a piano break."

"Best thing in the show. Present company excepted, George." Mel was a jazz fan, with a great collection of obscure records. Casting Mattie in the show had been his idea, and had taken some considerable argument both with the bosses at CBS and with Mr. AAAcme.

"Back for Red's in-one with you, George, which I gotta draft of."

"Wind down with 'Laura.'"

"Then comes the Ranch Market spot."

"Commercial, duet and back to you, George, for the newsboy bit."

"Not that 'drops in on pool party' business?"

"It's better now, George. We'll read it to you."

"Let's go to Lucita's for huevos rancheros and those tequila things first."

"Buen idea, Senor Florida!"

The boys put their coats on, lit up, and stampeded out of my office. After a moment, I could hear Agnes Moorehead screaming. It was music to my ears.

CHAPTER 8

BACKLOT TO DANGER

The boys would supply me with a full script by the end of the day, and I planned to go over it with Buzz in his favorite booth at Nick's around six. Pre-production work on *First WAC in Tokyo* was on the schedule in between.

Gus's joke about taking me for the new office boy was true. I had been brought out to the coast with much fanfare by CBS, and Lemming wanted Paranoid to have a piece of my action. Movies based on radio shows and characters like "Blondie" and "Henry Aldrich" were a staple at all the studios. It was an inexpensive way to create and sustain a series of second-billed 63-minute features. Gus's problem with me was that I looked too young and sounded too old. I signed with the studio thinking I would be given a "Madhouse" series, learn the business and ultimately become what I imagined myself to be—an amalgam of Errol Flynn, Orson Welles and Preston Sturges.

Instead, Gus decided that I would "break in" by directing inexperienced young performers in the feel-good stories that spaced out the ballads, dances and swing band numbers in Paranoid's light-weight musicals. I was also assigned to co-write their dialogue. *Robin Hood, Citizen Kane* and *The Palm Beach Story* could come later, and better not at all, according to Lemming, who distrusted writers and made sure that his scripts were mostly collaborations between hacks and wannabes.

It was an odd combination, my radio success and my almost anonymous film work, but I got used to it. Six pictures had gone out with my name as director in the past four years.

First WAC was the last of a string of wartime vaudeville movies, where every name on the lot, plus a few we could buy cheap, would appear in specialty numbers. My WAC was to be played by Judy Shay, who could holler her way through a comedy song. Her love interest, an Air Force mechanic, was a Mickey Rooney look-alike named Eddy Boston. The plot allowed the two of them to airlift a B-17-load of entertainers to Hawaii, and thence on to whatever Pacific island had been liberated in time to get it written in. I had borrowed Sterling Holloway from Disney and located Cliff Edwards in a downtown hotel. They would duet in "K-K-K-Katy," a sweetly old-fashioned song. I had signed Charles Laughton to do a pirate bit, and his wife Elsa Lanchester to sing one of her not-very-blue cabaret songs. Now Lemming wanted Charles to dance as well. Whatever.

I bought a paper to look at as I walked the couple of blocks from Columbia Square to Paranoid's lot. The end-game of the war was being played out on all fronts—MacArthur's battle for the Philippines, Patton's GI's slogging through the snow toward the borders of Germany, the Russians "liberating" Hungary, V-2 rockets smashing into southern England, Air Force bombers over Japan. In January, of course, we had no idea what the rest of "Victory Year" 1945 would bring in the way of mega-death and destruction. The end of the war and the end of the world meant the same to most of the unlucky globe, that seemed clear enough.

The secretary at Paranoid had three calls for me. One was a sergeant from the LAPD, one from a Max Morgan at a westside prefix, and one from Basil Brewster. I decided to take care of Brewster first, since I had planned on calling him about playing Judy's father.

"Brewster residence." A voice I took to be Asian houseboy answered on the fourth ring.

"Mr. Brewster, please."

"He expecting you? Otherwise very busy."

"George Tirebiter, returning his call."

"Ah. So, Mr. Tirebiter, thank you for getting back to me. Lillie suggested I should call."

The faint Asian tone disappeared from the voice, which deepened and flushed with sincerity.

"You're Basil Brewster?"

"I am also my butler, cook and chauffeur, each with a distinct personality, suitable to the occasion."

"I'm interested in a banker, small town type, two pages of stern stuff with Judy Shay as your little girl, determined to join the WACS."

"Judy! Darn it now, girl!" Brewster's voice broadened into a likeness of Judy's twang. "Boys join the Army in this family! Girls stick to cookie bakin'!"

"I'll buy that. Two days at scale is all I can do. You know Paranoid."

"Paranoid didn't exist when I made my last picture, Mr. Tirebiter."

"That must have been the Golden Age indeed, Mr. Brewster. I saw you in Gus Lemming's pool on Saturday, didn't I?"

"I was there with a friend. There are some people of your generation who show kindness to my generation. Even affection."

"Even a job. You'll have to come in for a fitting this week. Someone from the costume department will give you a call."

"I appreciate this."

"Just do a good job, Mr. Brewster."

"I specialize in good jobs, Mr. Tirebiter." He rang off.

"I'll bet," I said into the mouthpiece.

The officer from the Valley Division wanted to know if I knew anyone who wanted to kill me. His dialogue could have been played by Harry Carey in any number of cops 'n' robber movies. I followed the script.

"Nope. I don't have any enemies. At least that I know of."

"Yes, sir. Well, we checked out the tire tracks on the highway, so we know you wasn't covering up for drunk driving. Big car plowed into your coupe. Rubber to prove it. I'm thinking you got a gambling habit you can't pay off and don't want to talk about it, right?"

"Wrong."

"Sure, Mr. Tirebiter. Let me know if you get any more threats on your life, OK? That might keep the file open a few days longer, Otherwise . . ."

"I appreciate your investigative efforts, Sergeant."

"Sure you do." He broke the connection.

So much for the hole in my hat. Any more threats on my life? I wondered what he had in mind. I opened my mail and none of it was threatening, except a bill from the Madrona French Cleaners which Lillie had refused to pay on the grounds that they had given us back someone else's paisley slipcovers, one size too small.

I looked at some costume sketches. Since almost everyone was in uniform except during their routines, I approved a lot of khaki, along with an extravagant Captain Hook's outfit for Laughton.

We were planning for the production numbers to take place on an outdoor platform copied from the ones that Hope, Crosby and the USO people actually used, set up somewhere in the tropical jungle which occupied half-an-acre of the Paranoid backlot. Bill Most, a set decorator, went with me to scout out the exact spot. Bill had been at the studio long enough to have planted most of the palm trees and elephant-ear that now flourished around a small lake. The area was used continually for the multi-episode serials that Paranoid ground out—*Manhunt on Hidden Island, Tiger Queen of the Jungle* and *Nick Carter in Darkest Africa* were the latest, all of them directed by my Toluca Lake neighbor, Spencer Bennett, for whom no situation was too absurd or cliff-hanger too unlikely.

The *Tiger Queen* set was still up—a plaster rock wall with built-in throne for Ruth Sterling, two big masks hanging on either side.

"I could cover this sucker with orchids, ferns, stuff like that," Bill offered.

"The Japs are supposed to have been the last tenants, not Trader Vic."

"Well, kid, it's sorta Trader Vic now, sure, but I was thinkin' more of Clifton's Cafeteria."

"No, I want something with the cyc behind, maybe a beautiful sunset."

"Stop thinkin' Technicolor, kid."

"You're right. Paradise in grey."

"Back to Clifton's. I could put a little waterfall down that thing. Angle your stage over there, and what? Quonset hut, a piece of it anyways. Doughboys hunker down in between, nice massed feel, good long shot."

"Why not?"

"Bless your heart, kid. I'll draw it up. Now what about the lagoon scene. You're not thinkin' of Catalina, say it isn't so."

"On my budget? What have you got?"

"I got no lagoons, kid. A romantic tropical pool I got. *Valley of the Jaguar?*"

"Didn't see it."

"Yeah, well, you're over twelve. Not much over, but enough. Pool's around here."

We circled behind the plaster wall and through a forest of giant houseplants, each in a gallon can. This part of the lot backed up against the Rose-Holly Cemetery, eternal resting place of many of the industry's founding talents. A ten-foot fence and some huge eucalyptus trees separated the dead from the quick. A few yards away, a wooden superstructure punctuated by an irregular opening lay in front of us. Bill led the way through the hole, which proved to be a simulated cave entrance.

"We just come from the Elephants' Graveyard in more ways than one. Pool's down here."

An arm of the small lake backed into a permanent set that looked exactly like a jungle glade. Rocks to dive from, even a spot for underwater filming and enough space to provide for the equipment needed for a high crane shot. Paranoid used it fairly often. I had been locked out of it for *Pardon My Sarong* because it was dressed for an A feature called *Women of the Bounty*.

"Great! Judy catches Eddy without his dungarees on, washing up, borrows his pants to pull the wool over the C.O.'s eyes and steal a generator she needs for the show. She gets back and he's wrapped up in a bush. They've got a number called 'How Do I Know It's You?' But this island has been through the War, for God's sake, so it has to be, you know, junked up somehow."

"Plane crash. Jap, natch. Big Zero wing, burned out cockpit, like it's hit a cliff up there and just missed screwin' up the best make-out spot in the South Pacific. It's a cinch."

Bill sketched it for me and it was pleasantly surreal. He was off for his next conference, so I walked alone out of the jungle and onto the Western Street. I was imagining my spurs jingling as I strode fearlessly down the middle of the dusty street toward the bad guy who had shot my hat off. My fingers twitched. That reminded me. I was going to borrow some sort of weapon from props. Short cut through the Silver Slipper Saloon would bring me over to that part of the lot.

As I walked up the steps and pushed open the swinging doors, a voice called my name. Turning, I looked back at the street. It was no cowboy, but he was dressed in black, and he did have a gun in his hand.

"Tirebiter?"

"T-t-that's me."

"Thought you could use one a these."

"Huh?"

"Gun. Nice clean one, .38 caliber, fits under yer coat. Loaded."

The guy in black held out the automatic toward me, grip first. How did he know?

"You aren't from Props by any chance, are you? Psychic?"

"Nope. Max Morgan. Called you this a.m., didn't hear diddly, talked my way through the gate—told the old geek I was yer bodyguard, which I am in a manner of speakin'—cute receptionist said you was somewhere between the jungle and the OK Corral, I said, Who ain't, honey? Rest was easy."

We met in the lonely, sunlit street and shook hands. He transferred the gun from his right to his left hand to do it, then gave the gun to me. I dropped it into my sport coat pocket, where it hung heavily. It made me feel foolish, so I took it out again and handed it back to him. He shrugged and returned it to his pocket. It didn't seem to make him feel foolish.

He was medium tall, and the shiny black suit was tight across his upper body. He had a dark mustache with some grey in it, and he would have a heavy beard in about half an hour if he didn't find someplace to shave.

"Sorry I didn't get back to you, Mr. Morgan. You were next on the list."

"People who put me next on the list sometimes end up on a slab with a ticket on their toe." He took off his hat and wiped his forehead. "There any beer in that saloon?"

"Only whiskey, and it's iced tea. Maybe you could tell me what your business is."

"Investigations." He pushed his hat back on, plucked a card from his vest pocket and handed it over. It read MAXWELL MORGAN, 9400 Culver Blvd., Suite 205, INVESTIGATIONS.

"These are private investigations?"

"Not while we're standin' out here in friggin' Arizona, waitin' for the Gila Monsters to bite, it ain't. There's a place across the Avenue from here called The Cutting Room. Bet they have beer."

Morgan was right, The Cutting Room did have beer. They had Acme on tap, and they claimed it was Ice Cold. He had a schooner. I had the same. He lit a Philip Morris. I didn't smoke. The ball was in his court. I waited. The juke box gave out with 'Laura.'

"Person comes to me with a story about a murder. Happened twenty-five years ago. Never solved. Seems some money and some other things changed hands. Person wants me to trace the things. Movies is what they were."

I drank some Acme. It was awful, maybe a byproduct of Glamorama Soap's manufacture.

"Seems these movies went to somebody for safe-keeping. People died, they disappeared. I traced a dame that had a daughter. Father's a rich old geezer, but he's in a home. Daughter's got control of the family lettuce, safe deposits, all that stuff. May or may not know about these movies. Anything in that for ya?"

"Not a thing."

"Lillie LaMonte, born Lillian Marie Ames, married to one George LeRoy Tirebiter?"

Two studio carpenters came in out of the bright afternoon. They nodded at me and went past, into the back to play a game of snooker. I used the interruption to figure out what to say next.

"You think Lillie is in possession of what? some old movies your client's looking for? And if so, why not talk to her?"

"I did. She said she didn't know what I was gassin' about, so I called you."

"What was that business about giving me a gun because I might be in danger?"

"Got your attention. For all I know, you might be in danger. Probably are, the way you grabbed for it."

He finished his beer. "Laura" segued into Sinatra's latest, "Nancy." I remembered Phil Silvers telling me how he wrote the lyric because Johnny Burke wasn't in the mood. "It oughta keep me in spaghetti for a while," Phil cracked. It probably kept him in Rolex watches and gave Bilko that toothy grin.

"Whaddya say, George?"

"Well, Mr. Morgan, if Lillie hasn't anything to say to you about it, I certainly don't. And, by the way, so far as I know, my mother-in-law was never involved in a murder."

"That's so far as you know, George. Name Taylor D'Arcy King mean anything to you?"

More than I'm going to admit to you, Max Morgan, Investigations.

I shrugged. "Too young. Ancient Hollywood history. This is the Forties, a new generation. Look, Mr. Morgan, I'd like to say I'd like to help you, but I have no reason to, even if I could. And I can't."

I started to slip out of the booth. Morgan put a heavy hand on my arm.

"It means a bunch to my client to get that lost property back. In the very near future. I'll keep in touch."

"There's a barber shop two doors down, Morgan. I suggest you go get a shave and a shoeshine."

He reached up and stroked his jaw. It made a rasp I could hear over the juke box.

"Maybe you're right, George. Stockholders at Gillette depend on me to keep 'em in business." He gave me a big, friendly smile. "Be sure and say hello to the wife for me."

CHAPTER 9

MELODY FOR THREE

I telephoned Lillie after my script conference to meet me for dinner at Musso's. Over a couple of Martinis I sorted through the events of the past three days. I'd always felt myself to have, well, not a charmed life, but a lucky one. Learning to read, effortlessly, at four had been my gateway to the kind of fantasy life that an only child needed. It also meant I could read scripts. That led me to playing a stuttering Lost Boy, a premature Puck, and a bloody corpse in Eva Le Gallienne's "Medea" before my big break—a long run as Tommy Edison at the Chicago World's Fair, back in 1933.

Here I was now, twenty-five, an age at which kids used to think Life would simply go on, for better or worse. (They probably still think that, only cynically.) Suddenly, my predictable future was clouded with inexplicable threats and sudden violence. I drifted toward self-pity, and would have beached myself there, had my attention not snagged on a near-by discussion between two agency-looking men—some kind of deal to write radio dramas.

"Bottom line is no goddamn Corwin poetry, okay, Rich? Thrills an' chills! Thrills an' chills," the younger one was urging.

"Tony, Tony, you want chills, how about Lucille Fletcher?"

"Sorry, Rich, wrong number. I'm talkin' 'Mr. District Attorney' here."

"You want a lawyer? I gotta line on Perry Mason."

"Could be somthin' in that. Yeah, could be."

"I see you got started without me."

Lillie stood by the booth and cocked her head at the leftover booze carafes. "I'll have what he's having. All six of them," she told the hovering waiter.

"Dialogue by Dash Hammett, Mrs. Thin Man."

"The Thin Man," she said, slipping in across from me, "was not Nick Charles."

"Nope. The Thin Man was Clyde Wynant, played by Edward Ellis, who hasn't made a picture in years."

"So much for cinney-mah history."

"Not quite enough history, Lillie. Even the Thin Man goes home. Let's flash back to 1920. I think the picture was *Passion For Two*? Mary Maple Murray,

Basil Brewster, and Monte Burke, last credit for Taylor D'Arcy King? I did some research in the Academy files."

"You talked to Basil today? Did you give him that part?"

"Sure I talked to him. He called me, thanks to you. So did one Max Morgan, also thanks to you."

Lillie tapped out one of her red-tipped Marlboros and I lit it with a Musso's book match.

"Private Investigations?"

"So his card said. Lillie, when you and a complete stranger bring up the King murder and you ask me to give one of the suspects a job, all within a day or two, not to mention nearly getting shot—well, you see what I'm getting at."

"Not exactly, George. Seeing Basil stirred up some old memories, that's all. Morgan went on about some reels of film. I'm sure I know nothing at all about them."

The waiter returned with drinks and took our dinner order. There was a little stir in the restaurant and we poked our heads out to see Joan Crawford being seated next to a balding gent who looked like a wealthy surgeon.

"The guy, Morgan, put the arm on me at the studio today, honey. He's a shark."

"He knows nothing, can prove nothing, and you know nothing either, George. He'll go away."

"What do you know, Lillie?"

She looked at me long and hard. "D'Arcy King died falling off the deck of a yacht moored in Avalon Harbor. They said he hit his head on something, maybe the prow of a launch tied up along side. Nobody could prove it was murder, but it wrecked some lives. It was twenty-five years ago, almost exactly, and it gets dragged out in some dime movie magazine every year or two so they can publish that same old bosomy snapshot of Mary Murray. How would I know any more than that?"

"How would you?"

"Eat your spaghetti, George. Private investigators are leading men in the movies and shabby crumbs in real life. He won't be back."

I hoped not. We finished eating, had coffee, talked about the "Madhouse" script and laughed together about the Bulgarian Gypsies who would kidnap Lillie in order to install her as a mentalist and crystal ball reader in their circus act.

"So you'll be telling fortunes at the Shriners' carnival on next week's show, completely in disguise. Oh, and word came back from the executive suite— Ronnie Reagan's doing that broadcast for sure—a comedy sketch with me and a patriotic pageant with chorus and orchestra."

"How were the ratings last week?"

"We're holding our time. After all, 'The Lone Ranger' doesn't match our audience contour."

Lillie laughed at the double-talk we'd become accustomed to from the CBS research department. Actually, CBS had a solid line-up on Friday nights, beginning with a wild comic named Jack Kirkwood at seven, and continuing after "Madhouse," with "The Aldrich Family," "The Thin Man," "It Pays To Be Ignorant," and Jimmy Durante.

"The Hoopers are due out next week, and I expect we'll land somewhere between Hildegard and Eddie Cantor."

"Just so the sponsor's happy," said Lillie, looking at her watch. A quarter of ten. I always knew what time it was without reference to a clock. Years of radio. She looked back at me with a sigh.

"George. Write me out of next week's show. I'm going back to visit Dad. The nursing home called and Mrs. Pratt said he's been talking about me quite a lot. She thought a visit would do him good."

"Sudden."

"Yes."

"Well, the boys can work around you, I suppose. The weather's lousy in Chicago in January."

"I'll wear my mink." She swallowed the rest of her martini. "I arranged dinner with Ron and Jane for this Thursday. And Joy and Derrick are coming too."

Joy Darling was the star of the CBS soap opera "Tomorrow Is Another Day," and her husband a producer at Monotone.

She stood up and smiled her sexy smile. "See you at home, Georgie Porgie."

"I have an errand to take care of on the way."

"Don't be late, Champ, or you'll miss the preliminaries. I'll be the one in the black satin trunks." She tossed a hip, feinted with her right and touched my lips with her left.

It had turned cold. Nights are always cold in Southern California, but I could feel in this one the end of a week's fine weather and a turn toward overcast and rain. The wind gusted up and blew the eucalyptus branches around, and the boulevard was littered with their leaves, and the occasional palm frond, dry and sharp as a stiletto. I veered around one that skittered across Highland.

Melody had wanted me to meet her at a convenient transfer point in the efficient Los Angeles transportation system where the Pacific Electric lines routed the big Red Cars out toward various points in the Valley. The P. E. rails ran down the center of the Cahuenga Parkway and there was a bus stop in front of the Hollywood Bowl. I parked across the way from it and waited for Melody to get off her bus from work and give me the name and address of a man who had rented a duck costume. What in hell was I doing? Did I want to know? Did I care?

A bus pulled in, its brakes wheezing, and pulled out again, accelerating slowly. A couple of people had gotten off. One of them looked like Melody, a dark coat clutched tight around her with one hand, her hat held on with the other. The street-lamps cast as much shadow as illumination. I gave my old Dodge's horn a honk. The girl looked toward me, ran my way across the street and disappeared into the shadows by the Bowl's entrance, where an arty marble fountain had been put up a few years before with WPA money.

"Swell," I thought. "The kid likes Hitchcock movies."

I got out and trotted up the sidewalk.

"Melody?"

I thought I could hear her heels tapping up the steep walkway.

"Dare I say, linger on . . . ?"

It was quiet, except for the buffeting of the long, dangling branches of the eucalyptus and the dry swirling of the pepper trees. "Swell," I thought again, out loud.

The first entrance into the Bowl itself was a couple of hundred feet away. I walked inside, out of the wind. The little four-seat boxes, where notables could picnic before performances, made a series of arcs in front of the vast white half-clam shell that protected the stage. I could see Melody, or her shadow, half-way across the boxes, running down toward the front of the stage.

"Melody! Hold up! It's me, George Tirebiter! Don't be afraid! I'll walk you back to the P.E. station!"

"Siddown, Firebiter."

The voice from behind reminded me of a frog. No, a toad with a frog in its . . . Wait a minute! I spun around. It *was* a toad, puffy lips, staring eyes. I backed into a knee-high enclosure and lost my balance, flailing into a pile of folding chairs. The clatter echoed like gunfire around the Bowl, ricocheting off the shell, doubling back and then fading into the wind.

"What the hell, Frostbiter? If I wanted the goddamn 1812 Overchur, I woulda come here when the band was playin'." The toad stuck out its hand. "Wild Bull Casey, U. S. Office a Secret Facts. Get up and siddown."

"Where's Melody?"

"Protective custody. Gotta nice little tour set up for her an' her girl friend. They'll be tappin' down the Rude Lapay with General Ike. Fergetin' all about guys in duck suits, 'cause they'll be duckin' G. I.s."

Casey laughed like a bullfrog in heat.

"Yer wanted, Fireliter. Donno why yer wanted. Maybe both sides wantcha, maybe all three sides, but we wantcha first, then you can infiltrate them and work for us. It's wild, Firebiter."

"Tirebiter. Who's them?"

"Them! The Big Set-Up! Doncha know the Commies are eatin' yer picture business from the inside? It's you naive bastards can't see it. The Set-Up! The Take-Over. Red muscle!"

"What about the Nazis?"

"Oh, sure, Talegater. Right now it's Nazis. Then whaddya think? Uncle Sam is gonna stand down? Uncle Joe's not gonna let that happen. It's gonna stay wild, and it starts right here."

"Look, Mr. Casey. I make patriotic pictures. Lt. Reagan is on my radio program next week. Hooray for the red, white and blue!"

"It's Reagan tapped ya. We'll be in touch. Keep yer nose clean, look under the bed. We gotta list. Names, Tirelighter. Yer not on our list, yer on theirs. Wild!"

Casey looked at me with his pop-eyes for a moment, then turned and walked heavily away, toward the stage. He did not hop, as I had half expected. A few yards away he turned back.

"Every goddamn thing you think you know is dead goddamn wrong, Tirehiter. Remember that."

He disappeared around the back of the stage. A few random raindrops blew across the empty seats. A heavy mist was falling, and I was damp as a toad when I got back to the car.

Muriel Albers, *Movie Stories Magazine*

CHAPTER 10

ON THE STRIP

Movie Story Magazine was located in a small corner building about half-way along the Sunset Strip. I drove there late Tuesday morning to raid its files, and those of sister journals *Movie Secrets* and *Screen Star*, for everything on the King murder.

Not long before, I had been interviewed for *Movie Story*. The result was a small but accurate sidebar buried on page 62 inside a re-telling in beauty-parlor prose of *Pardon My Sarong*. A young staffer named Muriel Albers had done the piece, and I particularly remembered her generous and genuine laughter. She would be happy to help me, she said, when I called her the morning after Max Morgan's privately investigative snoop.

The Strip, as most picture fans know, is a sinuous couple of miles of Sunset Boulevard, home to Ciro's, Mocombo, The Trocadero and other hot spots. The Boulevard passed through L. A. County between West Hollywood and Beverly Hills, and certain kinds of vice found a happy home there, thanks to the County's pliable Sheriff and its convenient tax laws. Besides nightclubs and agents, the area attracted small-time producers and the fringier entertainment industry types.

The Strip surges west from Crescent Heights, a intersection which used to harbor Schwab's Drugstore and its celebrated lunch counter and The Garden of Allah, a notorious enclave of Mediterranean villas just a gin bottle's throw from the exclusive Chateau Marmont. All were convenient hideaways for burned-out members of various Lost Generations. The Strip is a place where "seedy" can also be a state of mind.

The magazines' offices were cramped and filled with the clacking of elderly typewriters—stories destined for the next editions of the popular monthlies whose framed color covers decorated the tiny reception area. When she met me, Muriel had several manila folders she'd pulled from the over-stuffed files.

"Well, Mr. T., I wish I could ask you into my private office, but I even share my desk, so, maybe you'd like to buy me a sandwich and I'll show you this stuff." She had a New Jersey-ish edge to her voice, wide brown eyes, and wavy hair piled on top of her forehead.

"It's a date, Muriel. I can even do better than a sandwich."

"Gee. I'm a sucker for lunch with the stars. That place across the street has booths, I know. It'd be quiet anyway."

We walked across the boulevard and east a few doors. The place was a half-timbered roadhouse with dancing after dark, but it hedged its bets by serving up an inexpensive lunch menu. Years later Dean Martin owned it, and it was known as "77 Sunset Strip" on TV.

Once we were seated, Muriel produced a copy of *Movie Secrets* from February 1940, which had a twentieth anniversary layout on the case, including, as Lillie had remembered, a photo of Mary Maple Murray in a low-cut black bathing suit, posed stepping off the end of a pier. She had widely spaced eyes and a nose that seemed too large, but her open-mouthed smile promised as much sex as could be publicly suggested in 1918.

"The suit's retouched." Muriel pointed at the scoop of the neck, attached to thin shoulder-straps. "And so is she. Otherwise there'd be cleavage out to here." She laughed. "I'll bet the suit was itchy, too."

"She looks completely different in this one."

On the facing page, Mary was fetchingly posed in an oval frame, her eyes glancing sideways over her bare shoulder. Her left hand was elegantly curved up, covering her breast. It was more Ziegfeld than Keystone. An inscription read: "Mother. I love you. Just you. Mary."

"She's wearing some kind of satin dressing gown, I think, pulled halfway off," Muriel observed.

"Odd sort of snap to give to Mum," I said, doing my best Noel Coward impression.

Muriel pointed with a french fry to another picture. "I think this guy probably had a copy of it."

Taylor D'Arcy King looked a little like Clark Kent—square-jawed, clean-shaven. He wore rimless pince-nez glasses and a handsome pale felt hat, which probably matched the chalk stripe in his suit. His tie might have had flowers or starfish on it.

"When they did this story back in '40, they tried to bring events up to date—you know, a where-are-they-now? hook. All the correspondence and interview transcripts are in this file," Muriel passed a thick envelope across the table, "and I found a bunch of stuff that must have been swiped from the coroner's office—death certificate, depositions. You know, it happened over at Catalina, so some one-horse local deputy in Avalon probably made the file available for a contribution to the Policeman's Fund. Ain't that Hollywood?"

She grinned at me and passed over another large envelope.

"Luella Parsons better watch her step if you decide to stay in the gossip business."

"I doubt it. I'd really like to write for radio. Original short stories. *The New Yorker* maybe, someday."

"Radio needs good writers. I'll call Bill Keighley at the Lux show, see what he might have available. It's all anonymous, but steady work."

"You'd really do that?"

"Why not? If you've got ambitions in this town you need introductions."

She nodded. "That's the truth. Thanks, Mr. T. You didn't say why you're interested in this ancient history. Writing a movie? Maybe I've got a tip for *Silver Screen*."

"No, no movie. I'm using Basil Brewster in a small part and this murder . . ."

"Possible murder. Unsolved."

"Possible unsolved murder came up, and I thought I should know more about it than I do."

"This is Brewster over here."

She flipped to the next page which featured an elaborate layout with a large photo of Brewster's studio-built, three-masted schooner, "Mystery Girl," surrounded by pictures of those who were on board during the fatal cruise.

"You look, I'll eat. I've got to go see Ray Milland this afternoon."

"In person?"

"At his tailor's. It's a picture shoot and Twenty Questions. 'Gee, Mr. Milland, can playing a hopeless drunk actually help your career?' That kind of thing."

In faded brown rotogravure, the other stars of *Passion For Two* looked up at me. There was a studio still of Brewster made up as The Christ, from a silent called *The Fisherman*. The angular profile and carefully coifed wavy hair had not changed.

Across from him, one of the rare Asian faces in Hollywood's segregated history—"Tommy" Takasago, a cinematographer who, the article explained, had worked on some well-known sound films after breaking in with American Film, Lasky and Majestic. He was a stern-faced fellow with his soft cap turned backwards and his arm around a hand-cranked camera, just so we'd be sure he wasn't a grounds-keeper.

Takasago had been the cameraman on *Passion*. The Boy to Mary's Girl in that film was Monte Burke, best remembered as a minor comic who had retired in the mid-Thirties, probably due to lack of work. He was shown full-length in a summer suit with open-collared shirt and white bucks. His face was bland under curly hair roughly parted in the middle.

A series of three photos showed Mary's sisters, Pegeen and Iris, and Mrs. Wilson Murray, their mother ("I love you. Just you.") Iris had been photographed in a studio with a large white rabbit. She had Sweetheart curls and looked eight or ten. Pegeen, who had been in a few movies at the height of her sister's fame, was shown with her blonde hair bobbed, a single strand of pearls around her long neck, and a come-hither lift to the corner of her mouth. The mother had been lit and posed to give more character to a round Irish face. A single strand of pearls and a hint of something with feathers below her shoulders completed the image. I would have cast her as Tugboat Annie.

The last picture was of a face I knew well enough to have had bad dreams about. F. Oliver Tulley. His 1919 photo showed a slender, weak-chinned face, decorated with a waxed mustache and topped with a receding hairline. When I worked with him in 1942 the hair was gone, but the mustache was still in place, its thick ends twisted but frayed, like broken ropes.

While we were putting together the script for my first feature, *Babes in Khaki*, he regaled me with jokes about the old days at studios both famous and long-gone, where he'd been writing "nothing but shit," he said, since 1911. I remembered him telling me, "I went back to Majestic for a Hoot Gibson. And a lot more Gibsons after that, until I didn't give a hoot."

Ollie had recently appeared to me in a vivid Dickensian nightmare as the Hack of Christmas Past, accusing me of stealing the writing credit on *Babes*. Actually, an unpleasant Guild arbitration had given me a "story by" card. Ollie took it badly and we had seldom crossed paths since. His appearance in the commissary a week before had undoubtedly cued the sour memory.

"I know Ollie!" I said. "He's on a picture at Paranoid right now."

"Say, maybe I should suggest we run a new 'where are they?' in *Secrets*. It is the twenty-fifth anniversary coming up. You can help me with the research."

"Wait a minute! I thought you were helping me."

Muriel chewed on the last of her egg salad and sipped her soda.

"Your company is nice," she said. "And I don't have a car."

"I used to have a car, but it drowned."

"So I read. We're running that shot of you standing next to it in the 'Faces and Foibles' column this month."

"I'll think about it, Muriel. I really don't know if I want to get, ah—deeply into all this just so's to chat up an old character actor."

She shrugged and pursed up her mouth. "Where are they now? Somebody must want to know."

"That's true," I nodded. Truer than you imagine.

"If I sell the story to my editor, I'll call you at the studio, Mr. T. And I'll need the files back before the end of the week, OK?"

"Day after tomorrow."

"Duty calls. Thanks for the grub." She slipped out of the booth and smoothed the wrinkles out of her slacks. She wasn't Kate Hepburn, but she did look great in slacks.

"Ray Milland, watch your step. The lady wants to be a writer."

She laughed. We walked out onto the Strip, where it had begun raining. A familiar Hudson Terraplane was parked in front of the restaurant. The license plate was 1W5049.

CHAPTER 11

CROSSROADS

The Hudson stayed where it was, and I cruised back on Sunset into Hollywood. I kept a small writer's room hidden away up a flight of curving steps at Crossroads of the World, an eccentrically designed shopping and office center complete with cruise ship, lighthouse and European Village. My place had a window overlooking the Directors' Guild, and I could watch Huston, Milestone, Capra, Ford and Vidor come and go.

I laid the two thick folders on the desk. I still didn't know how much I wanted to know, so I decided to read the *Secrets* article first. The prose was breathless:

Was it murder? Moving picture fans couldn't believe the headlines: CELEBRATED DIRECTOR DEAD! WAS YACHT FATAL LOVE NEST? STAR IN SECLUSION! Twenty years ago this month, Taylor D'Arcy King, at 43 reaching the heights of his directing career, was found face down in the gelid waters of Avalon Harbor, a hideous bruise marking the spot on his forehead where he had been struck unconscious. King was widely known to be a "fool for love," with a string of filmdom's beauties pining for his affections. Insiders suspected that he had succumbed to the charms of Mary Maple Murray, the 22-year-old star of his final motion picture, "Passion For Two," whose well publicized escapades had included trysts with Charlie Chaplin, Doug Fairbanks and Francis X. Bushman before handsome leading man Basil Brewster won her hand.

The fatal yachting party was intended as a celebration for the completion of filming on "Passion," whose storyline found Mary married to mogul Brewster while pining for boyish socialite Monte Burke. Could real life be stranger, and more dangerous than fiction? Burke himself was aboard the pleasure craft, named after Brewster's 1916 hit, "Mystery Girl," along with cameraman Takago "Tommy" Takasago, screenwriter Oliver Tulley and his wife, and as chaperone Mary's mother, Mrs. Wilson Murray of Chicago, with her traveling companion, whose name was never revealed. Also partaking of the ocean air were Mary's sisters, Iris, 13, and Pegeen, who, at 17, had just made her first feature, "Spell of the South."

It was widely supposed that Mary and King were romantically involved. Suspicion fell on Brewster, but police investigators could find no evidence of his involvement in foul play. Each of the party-goers supported one another's alibis, but in the mad world of the Silver Screen, any of them could have wanted King out of the way.

Los Angeles Police Captain Syd O'Morrison was quoted as saying, "We know something was going on out there that was against the law, but we can't prove it as yet. The books will stay open on this case, and if there was murder committed, the perpetrator will be brought to justice."

Iris Murray—She married a gangster when she grew up

Mary Maple Murray—Was she also a star of silent porn? (1917)

Mary Maple Murray—Star of "Passion For Two" (1919)

Elmer "Lonesome" Todd—Basil Brewster's pony wrangler (1921)

Taylor Desmond King—The Murder Victim (1919)

F. Oliver Tulley—B-Movie re-write man since the silents (1919)

Pegeen Murray—The Victim's secret lover? (1919)

Monte Burke—Now he runs a Nudist Camp! (1919)

Basil Brewster—A Profile in Purple Passion (1919)

Mrs. Wilson Murray—"I would have cast her as Tugboat Annie."

The article continued in this over-ripe fashion for another couple of columns, concluding with an up-date on the "party-goers." Mary Murray had died back in 1931, probably of drugs and drink. Monte Burke had "dropped out of sight" after producing a film famous with adolescents of my day—the first nudist feature, *Elysia*. Pegeen Murray had divorced an actor named Dickey Muldoon and was, in 1940, anyway, married to W. S. Gilbert, an oil man and rancher. Iris had "wedded" a well-known restaurateur with a somewhat shady reputation, Rickey Villandros, whose Shaynu Grill was still in operation on La Cienega.

Max Morgan had claimed to be interested in retrieving some "movies." Of the available cast, the most logical movie-maker seemed to be Takasago. I decided to start with him. I walked down, and through a light sprinkle, to the courtyard and called the American Society of Cinematographers on the Crossroads payphone.

"We have no current information on Mr. Takasago, sir. His last picture was *Texas Bride* in 1942. He was relocated to Utah in September of that year and hasn't re-registered with the ASC."

"You don't have any forwarding address for him?"

"Sir, I can only suggest the War Relocation Board. They're probably in the Federal Building downtown."

The guy had been born in Oakland in the 1890s. That made him an enemy alien? The government had been re-relocating Japanese internees for the past year, however, and I knew they made sure that the people they let back into "normal life" had jobs. Possibly, with his specialized talents, Takasago had been routed toward the Signal Corps or Army Intelligence, now that an invasion of Japan seemed likely. Maybe Reagan had heard of him. I'd make sure and ask.

Ollie Tulley was the next best bet on my list. I called the studio and asked to be connected to the Writers' Building. One of the girls tracked him down to Soundstage 7, where they were shooting interiors for a cornball Western featuring a comedy team named Olsen and Louis. An assistant director found Ollie for me.

"Georgie, Georgie! Long time!"

"Well, Ollie, I saw you were here, but you had your soup-strainer too full of Lemming's Chicken Noodle to notice me. I know you're busy, but . . ."

Tell me you'll buy me a drink, Georgie. I've been standing around for three hours waiting to put some zing in this crap. So far they've spent the day rigging a goddamn table to toss a couple of stuntmen into a pile of horseshit. Is that movies or is that horseshit? Say, maybe you need me on this WAC picture, right?"

"I wish, Ollie. Sorry. But I will buy you a drink if you'll entertain me with one of your great Tales of Hollywood."

"I got a book of 'em."

"I need the chapter about Taylor D'Arcy King and a yacht party in 1920."

The line buzzed for a few seconds.

"Ollie?"

"That's a good one all right, Georgie. It'll be in the deluxe edition. Woops! Sorry, chum. They need me on the set now. Goddamn horse probably needs a rewrite on his punchline. Be seein' ya around the store."

Click. Buzz.

Two strikes.

Of course, there was Basil Brewster himself. He had been the principal suspect in 1920. If anyone knew all the details he did. But something told me he wouldn't be talking to me either. Not in return for two days at scale anyway. The *Screen Secrets* files beckoned. I called Buzz at CBS to let him know I wouldn't be in for the music rehearsals and went back upstairs to dig in.

It was a dark and stormy night. At least according to the police report. "The Mystery Girl" had made a day-trip from San Pedro to Avalon Harbor. Although the island had been a resort destination for thirty years or so, it was just beginning to develop its tasteful California-Spanish appearance and cultivated style since being purchased by chewing gum and baseball king William Wrigley.

When the January weather turned rotten it was decided that Mrs. Murray, her young daughters, and the Tulleys would spend the night on shore at an Avalon hotel, the brand-new Atwater, leaving Brewster and his wife Mary, director King, cameraman Takasago and actor Burke aboard the yacht. Mrs. Murray had traveled from Chicago with a woman friend, whose name had been kept out of the papers, possibly by way of Wrigley influence. She, too, may have been at the hotel, occupying one of the three rooms reserved for the "Murray party."

Early in the morning, a crewman discovered King floating in the water, lodged between the yacht and a small motor-driven shuttle craft. Police, searching King's shipboard quarters, found a monogrammed cigarette case belonging to Mary Murray in a crack between the bunk and the cabin wall. Speculation about a revenge slaying by Brewster started with this discovery. Murray's man-eating reputation added fuel to the theory. It was also suspected around police headquarters that Brewster was not entirely the ladies'-man he played on screen, although such things could hardly be spoken of at the time.

The coroner's investigation suggested that King had been struck unconscious before hitting the water. It was certain he had been drinking. Brewster admitted that a bottle or two of contraband champagne had been consumed before he and Mary retired. Takasago, queasy from the rough water inside the harbor, claimed to have gone to his cabin before anyone else. Burke said that he and King had stayed up talking over plans for a new film together. Burke nodded off, he claimed, after King went on deck to have a smoke and "contemplate the lights of Avalon."

Those who had spent the night on shore were hardly questioned. The researcher who had traced their whereabouts in 1940 was treated to a variety of "no comments." Mrs. Wilson Murray's "traveling companion" could not be identified. She had left the island by aircraft before the morning steamship arrived carrying the police and a clutch of studio public relations people. Clearly, or should I say obscurely, a veil of some kind had been drawn over the events, and an agreement had been made to avoid discussion of them.

I closed the last folder and tucked it back into its envelope. I was absolutely no closer to solving my own mystery—who had hired Morgan and why was he interested in Lillie and me?

I went back downstairs to the payphone and called a fellow I knew in the 16mm film distribution business.

"Dick, Happy New Year! It's George Tirebiter."

"Georgie! What can I do ya for? How's tricks?"

"Tricks are good. I've got a question about an old nudie movie."

"Nudie? You? Ain'tcha still married to that gor-gee-us blond?"

"Lillie, sure. No, I'm trying to trace an actor. You remember *Elysia?*"

"I opened that flicker in 20 houses in the Northeast back in '39. Producer was four-wallin' it. Second or third time around. Grossed a potfull. You'd think nobody in Massachusetts had ever seen pew-blic hair. Christ! Maybe they don't look in a mirror back there!"

"The producer was a guy named Monte Burke, I understand."

"Monte, yeah. Did time in the silents, but he wasn't much of a thesp. *Elysia* made a mint for him. Probably still out there, playin' little hick burgs in the Midwest, South, wherever. Monte did another one about the same time. *Marijuana Maniac.* Usta get booked with 'Nurse In Attendance.' Loada crap, but a bread-and-butter flicker. You lookin' for Monte?"

"That's the guy."

"Talk to Max at Eagle Rock Releasing. He's yer exploitation man. GLadstone 7102. Say, I'll be listening Friday night, Georgie. Good luck!"

Dick rang off and I dialed the number for Eagle Rock. Max van Os had a pleasant Dutch accent, offered to send me the current catalogue, said he could make a terrific package deal on *Elysia, The Anatomy Lesson* and *Sex Madness,* and gave me Monte Burke's address—a post office box in Topanga Canyon. The county operator—why didn't I think of her sooner?—gave me M. Burke's number.

The phone rang five times before a woman answered, out of breath.

"Hello, hello. This is the Burke's. Did you ring before? I was outside."

"Is Mr. Burke around?"

"Mr. Burke is always around. Mostly under-foot. Who wants him?"

"George Tirebiter. I'm from Paranoid Pictures."

"Monte don't work in pictures anymore. Monte don't work, period."

"It's a personal call."

There was no reply. I heard the phone clunk down on a table and the lady's voice calling, "Monte! Monte! Telephone!" After a longish pause, he picked up.

"Hi, there."

"Mr. Burke, my name is George Tirebiter. I do a radio show . . ."

"Tirebiter on the radio talks like Frank Morgan."

"So he does," I said, like Frank Morgan.

"That's him. That you?"

"That's me."

"How can I help you, son?"

"I'm interested in silent comedy, Mr. Burke. I'm a director at Paranoid, mostly musicals, but the old slapstick style interests me. I thought maybe you'd chat with me about your work."

"That was a hundred years ago. Hardly remember a thing. You wanta come out here to the Camp one day, sit by the pool, though, I'll talk your ear off!"

"That'd be swell, Mr. Burke. I'll do that. I've got a free day tomorrow."

"I've got a free day every day. Come along."

"You said 'the Camp'?"

"Elysian Fields Nudist Camp. Second right-hand dirt road on the Old Canyon Road as you come up from Malibu. Look for the big yellow mailbox. Drive on in, open the gate. Can't miss it. Don't mind a few nekkid bodies, do ya? Always some folks up here, even on weekdays."

"Do I have to . . . ?"

"Take yer pants off? Damn straight! No prudes allowed!"

The line clicked dead. On my way home I stopped by the Owl Rexall at Hollywood and Vine and got a large tube of Hawaiian Tanning Liquor.

CHAPTER 12

FANNIES BY GASLIGHT

Lillie and I took in *Wilson* at the Carthay Circle. It was a Big Picture, with vast crowd scenes and vivid recreations of the trivia of American history. *Variety* had reported it cost Fox over three million to make, and I watched it hungry for Technicolor, extras and a big budget.

Once at home and in bed, I had a chance to return to "Nightmare in Black Glass." I'd spilled coffee on the first page two days before and hadn't had an opportunity to continue reading until now. If I was going to meet the mysterious Stella Sue at the Chinese the next afternoon, I thought I'd better be able to compliment her on the book, as well as her perfume.

The novel continued, in suitably hard-boiled style, the story of the nameless hero, an immaculately dressed private eye who bore no resemblance to the actual item, (assuming Max Morgan *was* the actual item), and his assignment to body-guard L. A. newspaper publisher Wallace Colby. It was a quick read until I arrived at page 18:

The "Mysterious Lady" was a swell yacht, all right, if you care for pirate movies. It had a busty broad with a black mask for a figurehead, sails the color of sunset in Acapulco, and portholes with phony cannons poking out. Colby liked to think of himself as Captain Blood anyway, only without the red satin sash and gold hoop in his ear. I followed him on board, wondering if anyone was going to have to walk the plank into Mexique Bay.

"It's a murder boat, you know," said Colby, grinning.

"Oh, yeah?" I said. The deck was polished teak. The brass was polished too, probably by the little guy in the white outfit who took Colby's bag and scuttled off crabwise.

"Hollywood director. I got it from the guy they said did the deed, but he was nothing but a joy-boy actor got caught with his pants down. Guilty party got away cool as

ice. I got a good idea who she was, though. Come on, we can use some Scotch before the wops get here."

Murder boat. Sure, that's Colby's style. Probably had a few mounted heads on the galley walls. Former business associates.

The "Mysterious Lady" was a dead-ringer for Brewster's "Mystery Girl." Another coincidence? I dreamt about pirates and gangsters that night, cutlasses and tommy guns locked in battle like a projection room collision between *Treasure Island* and *Public Enemy.*

The sky was denim blue the next morning, and I headed out Ventura Blvd. to Topanga, which was a fair jaunt on the two-lane state highway, followed by a winding drive to the crest of the Santa Monica Mountains. The hills were beginning to green up, and it was warm in the Canyon as I dropped south on the Old Highway. The big yellow mailbox was easy to spot, and after about a half mile of dirt road that wound down among sycamores, I came to a closed gate with the sign "Enter at Your Own Risk" mounted on it. I got out, pushed the gate open, drove through and closed it again. Another sign hung on the back—"Come Back Soon & Bring A Friend."

Monte Burke's nudist camp was rustic, but appeared to have all the conveniences. A sprawling stucco ranch house occupied the high spot of a two- or three-acre glen. There was a good-sized swimming pool with diving board, south-facing lawn with a few cabanas and picnic tables, tennis and volley ball courts, and next to a dusty parking lot occupied by three cars and an old Ford truck, a one-room shack with a big Coca-Cola cooler outside. A radio inside the shack was tuned to Oxydol's own "Ma Perkins."

A highlight of Burke's nudist movie, at least for a teen-aged boy in the 1930s, was the sight of a dozen bouncy-breasted girls playing volley ball, screaming with delight and crashing into one another with riveting abandon. As I pulled into the lot and the old Dodge creaked to a halt I could see that four men were using the court, and that they weren't bouncy at all—at least in places I considered interesting.

A tubby fellow, coconut-brown, lifted himself from a green-and-white striped deck chair next to the Coke machine and waved in my direction. He was white-haired and looked a boyish fifty. Monte ("not much of a thesp") Burke.

"Hi, there, first-timer!" He waved at me and strolled over, clad only in worn sandals.

"Hi, there," I replied, looking him square in the eye. "I'm George Tirebiter. I called you yesterday?"

"Lemme hear that Frank Morgan voice."

"Pleased to meet you, Monte. Lillie and I would love to have you visit our Hollywood Madhouse some Friday night. Come as you are!"

"That's him! Why the hell you use that voice, George, young guy like you?"

"The illusion of experience is a big part of success in Hollywood, Monte."

"Damn right!" He stuck out his stubby-fingered paw and we shook hands. "Well, thank the Good Lord it's a beautiful day. Take your clothes off and stay awhile. Mamie! Come on out and meet Mr. Tirebiter. This is the office here. We take your dollar, rent you a locker, sell you a Coke and let you be."

Mrs. Burke came out of the shack, a small key attached to a large chunk of wood in her hand. She was the same color as Monte, with her grey hair worn in a bun. I had never seen a woman twice my age with her clothes off. She looked as ordinary as if she'd been fully dressed.

"Glad you could come, Mr. Tirebiter. Except, for heavens sake! I thought you were our age and you're nothing but a pup!"

"It's something, ain't it, Mamie? Total fraud."

Mamie Burke gave me her hand to shake, and it was a firm one. "I'm only a fraud on the radio, Mrs. Burke. The rest of the time, I'm as real as . . ." I looked around at the naked bodies. "Anybody else."

"Well, that's fine. You have a good time, now. Don't let Monte talk your ear off. Here's your locker key."

Monte pointed up to the ranch house. "We live in the old place up there, but I built on that addition with showers and lockers for the guests. You just go on up, get your clothes off, and we'll settle down in a quiet place and chit-chat." He bent his head closer. "I'll put a dash of Old Faithful in your Coke, to make you feel at home."

I walked as casually as possible up to the house, past the pool. A Teutonic-looking couple lay side-by-side. Smooth-bodied, blonde, in their forties, they looked like an advertisement for the nudist monthly, *Sunshine and Health*, except without the blur of pubic airbrushing which allowed that journal access to the U. S. Mail. An older woman in a white swim-cap was doing lengths in the pool. I hurried into the house, found my locker and stripped. I regarded the contrast between my Toluca Lake backyard pool tan and the pale white area previously covered by swim trunks. I could feel the newly exposed parts of my body shriveling in a vain attempt at invisibility. That was certainly better than the alternative. I hung up my clothes in locker No. 12, gathered up a clean towel, draped it casually over my arm, and strolled out into the sunlight, key in hand. I immediately collided with the soft flesh of a tall red-head.

"Oh, excuse me! Don't I know you?"

I established that she was a genuine red-head before locking my eyes back on hers.

"Ah, do you?"

"Well, you sure do look familiar. You come here a lot?"

"Never. I mean, this is my first time. Here. At, ah, this camp. Heard about it, you know. My—ah—wife couldn't manage to come along today. Nice to have met you, Miss . . ."

"Missis. Ruth Talmadge."

"George, er, Typewriter."

"George Tirebiter! I've seen you at Paranoid! I'm in the studio orchestra. I didn't know you were a nudist!"

"Well, sure. Like to try everything."

"Me, too."

She held out a beautiful hand with rose-colored nails. I took it and shook it vigorously.

"See you around the pool?"

"After a shower. I'm just running sweat." She wiped her fingers across her stomach, flicked them at me and giggled. I lowered my towel six inches and strolled quickly away.

Monte Burke was standing at the end of the porch, two ice-filled glasses of Coke-and-whatever in his hand.

"Come on down by the crick-side. We'll relive the old days."

Monte and I stretched out on a couple of redwood lounges, strategically located where he could keep an eye on the entrance road, the pool and the front of the ranch-house. A winter-rains-fed stream burbled among boulders in a shady arroyo. I began to get an idea of what retirement might be all about.

"This was the Barnaby Ranch in the Twenties. Believe it or not, I was a bad hombre in a Tom Mix flicker shot right here in '28. Love at first sight. Come back in '34 for *Elysia*, place was all but abandoned. Just Mrs. Barnaby left. When the movie hit, I bought the property and started the Camp. Life imitatin' Art."

He took a swig of the icy Coke and winked. "Art movie is what I called *Elysia*. You ever see it?"

"What kid didn't, if they could?"

He chuckled. "That's what I figgered at the time. Good, clean nekkid fun. I had a buddy into blue reels, but they was strictly under-the-counter stuff. Made the rounds at Legion conventions. I figgered, keep 'em outta bed, out in the open, no harm done, dollar a head." He gestured around. "And here I am. Now, Mr. Tirebiter, what do you want to know?"

"Well, I know I told you I was interested in comedy technique . . ."

"I never had no technique. So I knew you was butterin' me up. So what else might be on your mind?"

I took a deep breath. "I'm interested in the King murder. If that's what it was."

"No surprise. Private dick in a shiny suit drove up here uninvited a couple of days ago. Some people I haven't talked to in a quarter-century sendin' me letters and phonin' me up."

He sipped his drink. I sipped mine. It was about half bourbon. The woman climbed out of the pool and stripped off her bathing cap. A short crop of grey hair fell around her head. The blond sat up and tossed her a towel, which she wrapped around herself. Monte nodded toward them.

"Frau Altehertz. Met those folks on a trip to Austria in '35. Younger woman's her daughter. Wrote a couple of movies for UFA. Wife and I brought the whole family over in '40. Husband was a drama coach over there, but he's Jewish, you see. We struck up a friendship, kept in touch. They skipped out to Sweden with the little girl, left a whole house full of books and stuff behind. I sent 'em boatfare, put 'em up here. Wife is Elsa Schriber. Done some work for Warners last couple a years. Nice people. Probably be dead by now, at least him."

As we admired the family scene, a young girl came out of the women's locker room with a beach towel wrapped around her.

"She's a looker, all right," said Burke. "Anna, the daughter. Fifteen, about."

The girl dropped the towel and dived quickly into the pool, a flash of tawny skin.

"Mr. Burke, why would a detective be poking around in the King case? My wife and I had visits from a fellow called Max Morgan. He wanted some information about lost or stolen movies from us. How would we know anything?"

"Morgan. The guy in the shiny suit, yeah. How would you know anything?"

"That's what I'm asking you."

"How old're you, Tirebiter?"

"Twenty-five."

"I was about the same age as you when I did *Passion For Two*. It was a good break for me. Mary Murray was gettin' to be a big star. King was a classy director. It was a change of pace from third banana with Sennett. It was a change of pace, period. I swear to God, Mary didn't have a sober minute the five weeks we were shootin'. Her mother kept an eye on her, kept her from overdoin' it when she had to work, but she was a gin-soaked sugar-plum. Everybody knew she was supposed to be King's sweetie, but that didn't keep her from puttin' the eye on every man on the set. King must've hated her for it, but maybe it gave him a rise, too."

"What about Brewster?"

"He kept his business to himself. Gave me that look, you know, when we met. Knew I wasn't his type. He helped keep Mary out of trouble, I will say that. Stayed with her in the dressing room between takes, along with Mrs. Murray."

"Do you think he killed King?"

"Not a chance. Why would he? He wasn't jealous. He was Mary's cover. Not that Taylor King was a nice man. He wasn't."

"You were the last person to see King alive?"

"Except who killed him, I guess. I was pitchin' him an idea over drinks that night, but he wasn't really listening. I nodded off, woke up later. Damn boat was gettin' slapped around by the tide. I went to my cabin, fell back to sleep and first thing I knew there was a knock at the door. King was dead in the water and the boat was in an uproar. How's about a refill?"

Monte Burke drained his glass, took mine and walked off toward the house. The four volley ball players had finished their game, showered off and dived in the pool. The red-head, Ruth Talmage, was obviously with one of them, an athletic-looking man in his forties. I could hear laughter, splashing and a mourning dove, cooing in the stillness of the oaks. A Ford convertible drove up and parked. Two women in dark glasses and sun-dresses got out and Monte met them as they neared the house. Two of the volley ball players splashed out of the pool to greet them, and then they disappeared into the dressing rooms. Monte returned to the house and re-emerged with fresh drinks.

"Busy day," he remarked as he sat down, handed me my glass and drank half of his. "Hot for January. Won't last long."

"More regulars?"

"That's right. Talmages—he's a mathematician at Cal Tech, she's a 'cello player at one of the studios."

"Paranoid, she said."

"That's your lot, right?"

"Right."

"Other folks are their friends. Been here a few times."

He paused, stirred the drink with his finger and rattled the ice. The girl was standing by the pool now, her thin arms wrapped under her breasts, staring toward the chaparral-covered hills.

"Here's the fact a the matter. I may have been on that damn boat, but I was on the outside of whatever was goin' on. You know, Mary's sisters were on that cruise, and another little girl. At the time, I thought King was hot for Pegeen Murray, who was even better lookin' than Mary. It was close quarters, and I was just waitin' for a time to pitch King with a new flicker. You know. Christ, it's all the same in Hollywood. Name of the game is look out for Number One. I got drunk enough to make my play and then I was out of it. I don't know about cans of film, or blackmail, or who was on that plane out of Avalon. My name in the papers got me exactly one more feature, and then I had to fight for every bitty part I got for the next dozen years. So I got out, Mr. Tirebiter. I got out, took my goddamn clothes off, married a nice woman and made my wad. I told the same thing to that damn dick."

Burke drained his glass and set it down on the little redwood table.

"Enjoy the view. Come back anytime."

He rose and walked unsteadily away.

Chapter 13

Destiny Rides Again

It was a long drive back to Hollywood, especially without a car radio. I contemplated the growing number of "mysterious ladies" involved in the King affair: The yacht itself, with its masked figurehead, and on board, according to Monte Burke, not only the unnamed companion to Mrs. Murray, but a third girl-child, probably a playmate of the younger Murray sisters.

Another mystery woman, masquerading as "S. S. Van Dyke," ("nice looking, if you like the Sonny Tufts type") might or might not be revealed to me at the Chinese Theatre's five p.m. show. I checked my watch as I negotiated the curves of Sunset Boulevard as it passed north of the UCLA campus in Westwood. Three-twenty. Plenty of time.

There was a "Final" script of Friday's "Madhouse" waiting for me at CBS, a second copy for Lillie and a rehearsal schedule with a note in Buzz Melnik's prescription-form penmanship which I worked out to read "Geo. Missed you but all silk for tomorrow. Rita & Red hate each/o guts. Write in? BDM."

I flipped the script open to the segment in question. The "Two Sleepy People" duet was still in, and to make it fit, the sketch had been written around the fact that the Hollywood Ranch Market stayed open all night. Like Anaheim, Azusa, Cucamonga and Palm Springs, the Ranch Market was a favorite of radio writers in those innocent days.

My old loaner was running on fumes when I pulled it into the parking lot next to the Chinese. I had used up the week's "A" allotment of four gallons of gas on the round-trip to Topanga. A few servicemen were buying tickets to the show, *Winged Victory*, Moss Hart's "right stuff" saga of the Air Corps. It had opened before Christmas and was still doing pretty good business. The house lights were fading as I pushed through the red velvet curtains at the top of the aisle.

"Plenty of seats, sir," whispered the usher. Dexter D. Duck was cavorting on screen as I made my way down to the fifth row, pushed past a pair of sailors and on to the center of the row, which appeared to be otherwise empty. I watched the cartoon, in which Dexter, joined by Murph The Mouse, was captured by a platoon of grotesque uniformed bats with huge front teeth—"Bat-Nips"—and imprisoned in a cave. Hanging upside down, wrapped in chains, Dexter had just quacked, "Now, here's my plan . . ." when the syrupy essence of gardenia wrapped around me, and Stella Sue, in almost perfect unison, whispered:

"Here's my plan, George. You know where the Courtyard Apartments are? On Formosa?"

She was sitting in the row behind me, her lips next to my left ear.

Gulp. "Yes, I think so."

"They look like the Seven Dwarves built them in their spare time. Wait ten minutes, then meet me in the third cottage on the left. Knock twice."

The lips touched my ear like white petals caressing a pool of still water. I turned to see a slim figure slip away and disappear up the aisle. Loony duck laughter and the Marine Hymn blared from the screen. The Emperor of the Bats crashed in flames. The Cartoon War was over. The real War went on via Movietone News. I waited until the feature titles came on screen, then left the theatre and walked across the Boulevard and south on Orange Street, where I followed the scent of tropical flowers into the gathering desert night.

I stood for a moment in the dark tangles of foliage that half concealed a small cottage with a fairy-tale roof-line.

Somewhere a fountain was burbling. A heavy curtain was pulled across the single front window. A yellow light glowed in a pierced-work lantern next to the entrance. I knocked twice.

A little window opened behind a grill in the door.

"George!" she whispered.

The window closed and the door opened. I could see into a room that, contrary to my Bros. Grimm expectations, was furnished in chromium Moderne. I stepped in and Stella Sue shut the door behind me. Her face was so familiar I was sure I'd met her before. Her black hair was bright with reflected lights. She wore a black silk dress with a scatter of flowers printed across the bodice. Gardenias. She reached out her hand. Short cut nails with no color. I'm afraid I grabbed it.

"I feel I already know you, George."

"That's how I feel . . ."

"I'm Stella King."

"You certainly are! "

"Please sit down. You'll have a cocktail?"

Stella gestured toward a comfortable-looking sofa, the fabric covered with geometric plant shapes. Nowadays, that roomful of furniture and the back-lit bar with its handsome glassware would fetch many thousands of Melrose Avenue dollars. In 1945, it seemed slightly foreign, and years out-of-date.

I sat, she poured two large martinis. I suppose I had expected a wildly mysterious Mata Hari, but Stella actually appeared to be about my age and, although very attractive, not the least bit exotic. She handed me my glass, sat at the other end of the couch and crossed her legs.

"Here's to crime," she said, holding out her glass to touch mine, "And to detection."

"What kind of crime did you have in mind?"

"Murder."

"How did I know that already?"

"You're in it up to your attractive chin, George."

"I don't know what I'm into, or why I'm here, or who you are."

She laughed just like the girl next door. "I have laid it on thick, haven't I?"

"Indeed you have," I chuckled in my Old George voice.

"I love it when you talk like that."

"Thank you. I've been enjoying your novel, Stella. It's terrific for someone so . . ."

"Young? You seem awfully young to be a network radio star and movie director, George."

"It's the manpower shortage. Sorry. No reason why you couldn't have written a couple of novels."

"They're pulp. 'Nightmare' took me exactly six weeks. I wrote the first one when I was twenty-three and sent it to an agent friend of my mother's. Under a male alias, naturally. There's a market for tough-guy stuff and it was fun to get up in the morning and pretend I'm hung-over, need a shave and have to put a Band-aid on my knuckles where I'd skinned 'em punching some bum in the teeth the night before. It puts me in the mood to go upstairs and write. Besides, I had murder on my mind."

"Whose?"

"My father's."

I had two twos now, but I still hadn't put them together to get four.

"God, I'm sorry. Who was he?"

"Taylor D'Arcy King."

King? Stella King? Bingo! I was in so deep now the carpet closed over my head.

"He was your father?"

"That's what Mother told me when I turned twenty-one. I'm Pegeen Murray's daughter. She was pregnant by King when he was killed. I'm pretty sure she knows who killed him, but she's buried it in the debris of her messy, messy life. I want to find out. I think somebody else does too."

"I'm sure of it. I've had a private detective brace me at the studio and pester Lillie. She's supposed to know about something—some movies—that I guess he's been hired to recover."

"That's what he said to Mother. Accused her of concealing evidence."

"Look, Stella, you told me I was in danger, being followed. I think maybe I am, and not by the detective. What do you know? Where do I come in?"

She sipped her martini and looked at me. Big dark eyes, perhaps a little too far apart. The Murray face under King's black hair.

"Well, George, at first I was just a fan. You make me laugh on the radio, and when I realized you were my age, it made me laugh even more—that silly old man's voice. I kind of fell for you. I wanted to meet you, but I thought, well, you're a star, married to a star. I know what stars are like from being around Aunt Mary and her friends before she kicked off. And then, my Mother always acted like a star, even though she'd only made a couple of movies, and before she married Bill Gilbert and moved out to the Antelope Valley, we had some of her has-been pals hanging around the house. I thought you'd just treat me like a fan, and I'd hate that. Then, when I found out Lillie was mixed up in my Father's murder . . ."

"Wait a minute! How mixed up?"

"Her mother was on the yacht when my Father died."

Finally, two-and-two-plus-two clicked. "Mrs. Ames was the traveling companion."

"Mother remembered her name and said she had a daughter who went on to star in Dillingman's *Vandals of 1927*. I checked the newspaper files at the Main Library, found out it was Lillie LaMont. I couldn't believe it! I was seven years old when she was a Broadway star!"

"So was I."

"Well, I figured that out, and so I decided I'd try and meet you after all. I called your office, put the note in my novel, tucked in the page that mentions 'The Mysterious Lady,' and here you are."

"Two birds," I said in my elderly radio voice, "with one stone, so to speak."

"Hmmm . . ." she said, getting up and setting her glass down on the glittering bar. "I hope so."

Her double strand of jet beads had been the first thing to go. They rolled and drifted around and under our bodies for an hour or so, facets like brilliant little mirrors. The jet-and-ivory color scheme, the faint touch of gardenia in Stella's hair, the pearly glow from the Lalique lamp by the bedside, all combined into the most erotic experience I'd ever known—at least since Lillie had first Black-Bottomed into my life, wearing nothing but a white feather boa.

When the phone rang, as it always does at the wrong moment, Stella slipped out of bed and into the other room to answer it.

"Mother . . ." I heard her say. "Please don't cry . . ."

She protested a couple of times, then gave herself over to listening and whispering, "Yes, Momma."

Left alone, I tried mightily to collect myself. It was nearly nine o'clock. My car was several blocks away and out-of-gas. In spite of the syrupy Hawaiian stuff, I had an all-over sunburn which had gotten painfully chafed during the successful completion of recent illicit, but most pleasurable acts. My wife, who would probably be curled up right now, smoking her red-tipped Marlboros, reading in bed, had apparently lied to me about what she knew of the King murder. I tried to visualize a list of "suspects," but the names and relationships kept disintegrating and re-forming, like the patterns of sharp little jet beads I found myself sitting on.

"Ouch!"

I got up, brushed myself off, picked out a couple of beads that had embedded themselves in me, and got dressed. Saved by Ma Bell from too much romance and not enough answers. I was slipping into my shoes when I heard Stella say good-bye to her Mother and hang up the phone. She came back into the bedroom with a sort of Cubist afghan wrapped around her.

"I'm sorry, George. I couldn't not listen to her. She always threatens to kill herself if I don't listen. Do you have to go?"

"I think I do. But, look, if, ah . . . you need some help on this murder thing, well, we could get together again, maybe in a couple of days. I have my show to do, and Lillie's leaving town on Saturday . . ."

Stella's eyebrows rose. "Is she?"

"Yes. To visit her father. He's in a sanitarium near Chicago."

"Well, then. I'll be home. My number's GRanite 5525."

"I'll call."

"Good." She put her arms around my neck and planted a kiss on my lips. In the process the afghan fell to the floor. She didn't pick it up again, but stood like one of the naked silhouettes in the crystal bed-lamp and watched me go out the front door.

I walked up to Hollywood Boulevard and the cab stand in front of the Roosevelt Hotel and got driven home by a muscular woman in her fifties. She rattled on about that night's wrestling bout at the Legion Stadium and I pondered what I was going to say to Lillie. "Nothing" seemed to be the obvious choice, at least for the moment. As it turned out, the house was dark and Lillie was, according to a note I found on the breakfast nook table, "at Tail o' the Cock with a couple of pals."

CHAPTER 14

DRESS TO KILL

"Rose Garage, Dave speakin'."

"Dave, this is George Tirebiter . . . The blue Mercury coupe . . . ?"

"The wet one."

"I'm afraid so."

"Well, sir, it's spotless now, inside and out. 'Cept the headliner's never gonna be quite the same. And the seats aren't quite dry yet. But, shoot—I gotta let you know we're havin' some trouble with the wiring. We thought it was just them paper separators in the generator, but it looks like it may be the whole cockamamie system, so we're gonna have to keep it—Let's figger—this is Thursday—two or three more days."

"Waiting for the electrical, eh?" I said.

"Or somepin' like it," said Dave.

I called the Studio to send a car for me. When the driver arrived, he had a message. I was to go straight to Western Costume and approve Basil Brewster's "banker, small town type" outfit. From Western, I was to go to a studio screening room for a playback of Judy Shay's song numbers, then on to CBS for two "Madhouse" runthroughs. I felt a long way from George Tirebiter, the Old Guy. How did I make my voice do that? I could hardly remember.

"What did you say, sir?"

"What?"

"I thought you mumbled something, Mr. Tirebiter."

"Just running my lines."

Stormy, Pacific Ocean weather had blown up during the night, and hard drops spattered on the roof of the Chrysler. I rubbed the moisture off a side window and watched the Cahuenga Pass go by. Hollywood Bowl. Hollywood Hotel. Hollywood High. Oh, Little Town of Hollywood. It had the look of wet cardboard packing boxes left scattered in the rain.

We turned East on Melrose and pulled in at Western's building. I told the driver to go back to his warm, dry studio cubbyhole. Paranoid's East Gate was only half a block away, and I was wearing a dark felt hat and my Chicago topcoat. Western's lobby was overheated under the circumstances.

"Mr. Brewster's waiting on the second floor, sir. Ask for Lois."

Lois Olafson was a woman of both extraordinary size and considerable platinum-blonde beauty. She'd been pinning up cuffs and padding shoulders here since 1932 and was always assembling clothes for a half-dozen films at the same time, including all of mine so far.

Brewster was sitting on a worn horse-hair couch, dressed in a too-tight double-breasted pinstripe and a wing-collared dress shirt, reading the morning *Times*.

"Mr. Brewster?"

He folded his paper carefully, stood and shook my hand.

"Thank you for this opportunity, Mr. Tirebiter."

"I've been wanting to meet you, Mr. Brewster. You're a Hollywood legend, as they say."

"There were legends in my time—Swanson, Valentino, Griffith. Retired. Or just gone. Legendary status does not guarantee Guild employment."

"In your case, it certainly does, Mr. Brewster. At least for two days. This is not your personal wardrobe?"

"I should hope not."

"It's being too tight is Lois's comic touch?"

"I thought I might give him a nervous gesture . . . always tugging his cuffs down, smoothing his coat-front. Very appearance conscious."

"I'll buy that. Do you mind if I ask you a personal question?"

He lowered his eye-lids to half-mast. "Many have."

"Who do you think killed Taylor D'Arcy King?"

He looked at me that way for a few seconds, then gave a theatrical snort of laughter.

"How many times do you suppose I've been asked that question since January 26th, 1920? By policemen, studio executives, two-bit magazine writers, casting agents, flacks . . ." His eyes narrowed again. "Lovers. Strangers."

"And now by me. And I wouldn't ask except my wife's been accused of having something to do with it, and I've been threatened, followed and, ah . . . harassed." Thinking of Stella, I finished clumsily.

"I see."

Lois suddenly filled the dressing room with her own Nordic bulk and a wheeled rack of clothing—military uniforms and a short, dark blue striped farm-girl dress that Judy Shay was to wear while singing "Animals."

"It's a rainy day, isn't Mr. Tirebiter? You know Mr. Brewster? I dressed him back in 1936 or 37—a comedy. You were royalty in some little country, weren't you, Mr. Brewster?"

"Transylvania." He pronounced it "Trahn-seel-wain-ee-ahhh."

"Fangs are on the fourth floor, Count. Is he okay, Mr. Tirebiter? I thought maybe a button-ear rose, and a straw boater in the train station."

"He's fine, Lois, thank you."

"You're through! Leave the suit in the booth. Write your name on the tag."

She threaded the rack through the far door.

"'Scuse me."

Basil Brewster nodded to me and disappeared behind a curtain into the changing booth. I waited for him to say something. He didn't. I heard change jingling in his pocket as he got back into his own clothes. I walked over and spoke softly through the velours.

"You'd be helping Lillie out. I know you're old friends."

"Since she was a little girl. Why do you suspect King was killed? The Coroner's jury found it to be an accident."

"He was killed, wasn't he?"

Brewster reappeared through the curtain, wearing his own well-cut suit, with a light violet silk shirt and blue silk tie.

"Mary told me she did it."

"The police suspected her."

"The County prosecutor wanted a front page murder trial. It would have caused a great deal of public attention to fall upon his head, as it had upon fortunate prosecutors in Beverly Hills and Downtown. Naturally, he suspected everyone. There was, however, no real evidence against anyone. Nothing enough to bring a case to trial, at any rate. Mary confessed to me several days after the jury finding."

"Why did she do it?"

"I don't believe she did do it."

"But she told you she did?"

"King had been sleeping with her sister. She said she did it to protect Pegeen. Revenge. But Mary wouldn't have had the strength or the will to kill him. She was alcoholic, Mr. Tirebiter, and what we would nowadays call a psychiatric case. Mary was a gorgeous image on the screen, but rather a difficult mess off stage. If King did not simply slip on the deck and fall over the side, striking his head on the motor dingy, if instead someone cracked his skull and sent him flying, I don't know who it was. Nor will I speculate. I'll see you on the set, Mr. Tirebiter."

We shook hands again and Brewster slid from the room like a silent spectre. His face had been almost supernaturally expressive. It had vividly illustrated every emotion behind a fairly long, full close-up speech. His words, however, had felt more like printed silent film titles: "Revenge." "Nor will I speculate." "Comes the Dawn."

Marry Murray the murderess. That's what the tabloids and movie pulps had speculated for a quarter-century.

I followed Lois into the next room and asked her about Irv.

"He works renting retail to the public. Downstairs. Mr. Laughton's scheduled to come in for his fit at two. Will you want to see him? He's got a hook, a peg-leg, and pink egret-feathers in his hat."

"Too good to miss."

Irv Pendleton's recollection of costume minutiae was apparently bottomless. Crater Lake would not contain it. Lake Michigan would overflow.

"Sure, sure," he said. "I rent, on the average, maybe eleven Dexter's a week, mostly size 5, 6, 7, little quackers, then some Saturday matinee adult regulars, a 46 Stout, that's Jerry Patton, does a different cartoon animal every week out at the Alex in Glendale, masquerade party or two a month, always 38 cadet to 40 long. Suits always come back. Cost seven dollars and change to make, plus the celuloid duckbill useta come from a little plant in El Segundo, went into ball-bearings or some damn thing. Can't import 'em, but we bought out a Jap curio store the owner had to sell down to the floorboards in '42. Last duck bills from Imperial Japan. Six gross and change. Charge a customer twenty bucks if they wanta steal it. It's all real feathers, red, yellow and blue."

"This would have been a week ago."

"Sure, sure. Had a fella come in to say the dog ate it. I said, bring the goddamn thing back however it is and we'll fix it. He says he had ta vacuum it up all over his house. Twenty bucks. He gave me cash."

"His name on file?"

"Renter or dog owner?"

"Somebody else rented it?"

"Sure. Said it was for a surprise party. Name was Reburn or Rayborn or some damn thing. Fella with the dog was military and younger than you. Crew cut. Civvies didn't fit so good. Didn't have a house to vacuum was my guess, but who am I to figure? It's only a job. I been here nearly eighteen years. Sure, it was a size 40. Practically new. All real feathers."

Rainwater was raging down the street, pooling at the corner drain. I stood in the doorway for a moment, contemplating my run up the block. An older limousine pulled up outside of Western's brick facade. I recognized Turhan Bey getting out of it and sloshing across the sidewalk, a briar pipe clamped between his teeth.

"Terribly suave," the movie magazines called him. Frankly, he looked better in Technicolor.

CHAPTER 15

HOME OF THE STARS

The "Madhouse" rehearsal had been exhausting. Rita would not speak to Red except on mike, and their love duet could as well have been about linoleum. Lillie was so distant that I was sure she'd found out about me and Stella, and Ben Bland seemed unable to keep from spoonerizing one of his lines, reducing the cast and especially the band to tears of laughter.

The laughter helped, however, and by the time we had driven home, Lillie seemed herself. Ricarda, our cook, and Benito, her brother and our occasional bartender, had made sure the place was full of lights and flowers and that the gin was ice cold.

Lillie had a way with ration points, or maybe with the chef at Tail o' the Cock. In spite of the meat shortage, half-a-dozen thick steaks lay marinating in Petri sherry and Worcester sauce next to the brick barbecue in our patio. Bing Crosby was on the big Philco for Kraft cottage cheese, singing "Ac-cen-tchu-ate The Positive." Everyone seemed to be doing their best.

Joy and Derrick Darling were first to arrive, a few minutes before eight.

"Old boy!" Derrick, who was Canadian, played cricket with the expatriate British community, and had learned to splutter like Nigel Bruce. "Bloody good of you to have us!" He shook my hand vigorously. Joy offered her cheek, which I pecked. She was awash in a mink wrap, her hair swept up to the top of her head, topped by a hat that imitated a fresh cabbage leaf.

"Can I help?" she cooed, in a voice known to millions of women who followed her harrowing romantic adventures every day on the radio.

"Only with the martinis, dear," said Lillie.

Under the mink wrap, Joy was wearing a simple, but dramatically low-cut dark green dress. A few years younger than Lillie, Joy had gone to New York City from a small town in Colorado and played a few ingenue parts on Broadway before landing the lead in what had become one of CBS's most popular morning soap-operas.

"What do you think, Lillie? I'm going to spend a month in the hospital!"

"My God! What's wrong?"

"They haven't decided. It'll take a specialist to figure it out, and we'll meet and I'll fall in love with his bedside manner. They've signed Ed Begley to a six-month contract."

"In role of doctor comes healthy change of pace from Charlie Chan," I noted.

The ladies ignored me and went to "freshen up." I freshened up Derrick's martini, and my own.

"I hear Lemming has you doing another musical."

"I hope it's my last. I'd like to do a straight comedy. Lillie and I have been talking about something set backstage on Broadway. Bitchy and sophisticated, she calls it."

"Ha!" He gestured inclusively to his elegant pin-striped suit, silk tie and pencil mustache. "Only our outward appearance is sophisticated, my boy. We are well-dressed garbage collectors. I myself am producing the first Monotone feature to star an actual Queen of Burley-que—*The Pasha's Daughter*, with Dixie Cupps, the Red-Headed Hurricane."

The doorbell rang. I excused myself to answer it. Standing on our porch were Ron Reagan in his khaki uniform with shiny new Captain's bars, hair tousled across his forehead, and Jane Wyman, her hair hidden under a black satin turban, cheekbones poised high over a full-lipped smile. They were a star turn, no doubt about it.

After the customary greetings and introductions we settled down to munch canapés. The discussion centered on *The Lost Weekend*.

"Ray will win for Best Actor, I have no doubt," said Jane. "And I've played my last empty-headed cutie."

"I thought you were wonderful in *Doughgirls*," said Joy.

"Did you see the ad they're running? Ann and Alexis and I bent over backwards, with our tits pushed up in a row, like the Grand Tetons, for God sake! No more! I was thirty-one last week. It's time to do some real work."

"Speaking of Tetons," put in Derrick. The wives glared at him. "My star boasts 36 double-D's, and she can revolve them contrariwise independently at moderately high speeds without injury to herself or others. 'Hot as a Robot Bomb!' At least that's what they say down at the Burbank Burlesque."

"She won't be revolving them in your movie, will she?" asked Ron.

"No, unfortunately, our designer seems to have captured them in huge things that look like the front end of a B-29, but with ruby sequins."

Joy looked at her husband with what I took to be pity. "Derrick really hates these pictures he's assigned to, but he has a plan."

"Yes. I'm going to own Monotone Pictures. And then I'm going to star Joy in glamorous features tailored expressly for her."

"Thank you, dear. How about you, Ron? Back to Warners?"

"In about six months, yes. First thing I'm going to do, though is spend a month at Lake Arrowhead with Jane, doing absolutely nothing."

Jane looked a little sour.

"If she's not making a serious grown-up movie, that is."

Joy ended the awkward pause which followed that exchange by bringing up Bogie's new co-star, a nineteen-year-old peach named Betty or "Slim," or something, who was about to burn down the neighborhood screens with a line about just putting your lips together and blowing.

"They let her get away with that?" Jane wondered.

"Big as life! Just whistle, she says!"

We all whistled a wolfish two-tone blast.

I drifted away to the patio to check on the steaks, which Benito had put on the grill, and which smelled delicious. It was hard to concentrate on the show-business chatter. Bing was outside, still singing on the portable—"It's Easy To Remember." My mind, which had been full of questions for Ron about dead doubles and my apparent election into the secret society of American spies, continually drifted to visions of Stella, doubts about Lillie's truthfulness, and the search for connections between an old murder and my happy home.

"Join the party, George!" Ron came up behind me. "And turn those steaks."

"Let me show you around the garden, Ron. I know you're a farmer at heart."

"A country boy, George. Tom Sawyer, that's me."

We walked a couple of yards beyond the French doors and admired a grove of bamboo and banana trees that continually threatened to take over the neighborhood. They were still dripping from the day's rain.

"I met your Colonel Casey on Monday," I began.

"He's quite a fellow."

"He said something about you recommending me for—well, I don't know what he meant. He said I could work for them—us—and infiltrate them—er, them—the Communists. What the hell was he talking about, Ron? I don't know any Communists."

"Yes you do, George. Look, I'm as big a bleeding-heart as anybody, but I do know Commies are behind what's going on with the Hollywood unions. Casey thinks the industry is ripe for a takeover, first behind the scenes—the carpenters and cartoonists and set decorators—then right up to the top. Script writers, directors. He says Hollywood's going to turn into a left-wing propaganda machine. He wants me to run for president of the Screen Actors. I suggested you might be interested in getting inside the Writers Guild. Keep an eye on guys like Ring Lardner and Budd Schulberg."

I didn't know what to say. I was only old enough to have voted for President once—for Roosevelt the previous November. Union politics interfered with my funny bone.

"Ron, what about the body on the beach?"

He chuckled. "Good, wasn't it?"

"Wasn't it what? I mean, what was it?"

"Complete fake. A prop. People down at Fort Whacky can duplicate anybody. You ought to know that."

"What was it doing on the beach? What were you doing?"

"Wellp, George," and Ron lowered his voice confidentially, "It kind of got away." A shiver ran up my spine.

"Oh, George! Ronnie! Dinner is served!" Lillie's voice called from the house. Ron gave me one of those cocked-head smiles and put his finger to his lips.

"But, Ron . . ."

"Think about getting involved with the SWG, George. They could use some young blood." He ruffled his hand through his hair. "Come on, I'm starved, let's eat!"

Dinner wound down to Ricarda's brandied *flan* and coffee. There was laughter throughout the meal, but it seemed to me that a shadow groped after each of us. Jane's decade as a dazzling featured player in her twenties had come to an end with *Lost Weekend*, she was poised in pursuit of an Oscar nomination, and I felt that her relationship with Reagan had cooled. Ron, in his turn, had been suspended by his military service from stardom, and like most of the town's military men, was unsure of his reception after three or four years away from the screen. Hollywood itself, according to him, was in for a radical change, and we'd all better watch our step, whom we were seen with and what causes we supported.

Derrick, who had as little interest in politics as I did, enlightened us with backstage stories from the Burbank Burlesque, where his star did her famous bathtub strip between baggy-pants comedy turns. Pasties were put on with toupee tape, he informed us. Who put the "G" in G-string? Nobody seemed to know.

Lillie, who was preoccupied with her trip to Chicago, discussed cold-weather wardrobe with Joy. She explained how concerned she was for her father's health, which had been none too good since Mrs. Ames had died late in 1943, leaving a large estate and a Frank Lloyd Wright home in the suburbs, which had been closed up and presumably deteriorating ever since.

At last we said our good-byes and sat in the living room, listening to the sounds of dish-washing from the kitchen.

"You were very funny at rehearsal today, George."

"Thank you, Lillie. It'll be a good show. Next week, when Reagan flies in to save you from the Bulgarian acrobats, that'll wow 'em in Waukegan."

She lit a cigarette and stared out the window. We listened as Gabriel Heater told us the night's good news—the Red Army had taken Warsaw in the fourth day of their Winter offensive.

"There's a car parked in front of the house, George."

I looked past her, out to the street, where mist gathered in a filmy cloud around the streetlight. It was a Hudson Terraplane. As we watched, it pulled away from the curb, headlights still off.

CHAPTER 16

THE BIG BROADCAST

"Stay tuned everybody, for HOLLYWOOD MADHOUSE!"

Ray Knight cued the band and the "Madhouse" theme, an old toe-tapper called Temptation Rag, featuring xylophonist Presty Roberts, filled Studio A with happy music.

The APPLAUSE sign flashed red and our studio audience broke into applause and cheers.

"Brought to you each and every Friday night at this time by Glamorama Soap, the soap with no foreign oils whatever. Germ-free Glamorama—it's double-purified to protect your whole family's delicate skin! Look for the beauty-conscious Hollywood Starlet on every bar! And now, let's drop off at Hollywood's most famous address—just around the corner from Sunset and Vine—the madcap mansion of . . ."

Ben Bland gestured with his script-filled hand toward Lillie and me, waiting in the wings. The script flew from his fingers and scattered like a flock of pigeons across the stage. The audience thought it had witnessed a hysterical *gaffe* and fell out of its collective seat with a roar.

" . . . the Tirebiters, George and Lillie!" Feigning embarrassment, Ben slunk to his seat at the rear of the stage, collecting pages on the way. Lillie, as gorgeous as Max Factor could make her, swept on to a wave of applause. I followed, dressed as always in a well-cut tuxedo.

We were off and running, the clock stepping through the seconds from four-thirty p.m. Pacific War Time. It was the first of our two live Friday performances.

"Lillie!"

"I'm in the breakfast room, George."

"Lillie, for heaven's sake!" I moved in on the microphone, spluttering. "There's a human skull in the bathroom! What is this, a medical school?"

"Really, George. Sir Lionell thought you'd like a new shaving mug."

"Shaving mug!"

"Certainly. Flip the top open. It's full of soap."

"What's the matter with my tube of Acme brushless lather?"

"Sir Lionell used that skull in his London production of *Hamlet*, dear. You always turn down his quaint little gifts."

"The last thing he offered me was a drinking cup from *Romeo and Juliet*. I think it still had poison in it!"

"Hail, sweet spirits of the morn!" Phil Baines plummy voice rang out and he made his usual sweeping entrance onto the mike, shaking his mane of white hair. "Thy fair musick falls upon my ears like petals from the dewy rose."

"Good morning, Sir Lionell."

The APPLAUSE light blinked again, although the audience hardly needed its prompting. Our regulars were popular in their own right, and Phil's eccentrically comic talents had been on display in a couple of dozen movies, including most of Fred Astaire's musicals.

"Madame . . . ah, George! I hope you found Yorick's toothy grin soothing as ruby-fingered dawn."

"If you mean that hideous object next to my sink, I think the most charitable thing you could do is give it a decent burial."

"Alas, poor old Yorick. You had to know him!"

"George," prompted Lillie, "don't you think it's time to offer Sir Lionell a part on one of your Immortal Theatre broadcasts? It's simply a crime that his great talents have been hidden from a legion of admirers for so long."

"Yes. Ever since he fell off the wagon in the third act of *Macbeth*."

"Please! We theater folk refer to Shakespeare's masterpiece as The Scottish Play."

"The Scotch-and-water play is more like it!"

"Avast, charlatan! It was slanderous Rumor—a dab-fac'd dame, all triple-tongued and dithyrambic—that did bring myself asunder. Fie upon such miscreants! Fie! What's for breakfast?"

"Breakfast! What about three weeks of room and board? You've been sleeping in the den since New Years."

"Some people would be proud to have an *artiste* of Sir Lionell's stature as a guest in their humble home!"

"Not to mention in dair humble re-frigerator!"

The APPLAUSE sign went off again as Mattie Daniels swaggered on stage. Unlike one of our radio comedy competitors, which featured a white male in the role of the Negro housekeeper, "Madhouse" had a genuine Black woman, albeit in a stereotypically subservient role. During the rest of the week Mattie cracked jokes and played the piano at her own Club Malabar in South L. A.

"Ah, Porcelain!" rhapsodized Sir Lionell. "Thy sweet words tinkle on the wind like little bells. Like little, little bells . . ."

"Dis little Tinkerbelle got yo' two three-minute eggs on white toast, Mr. T. I'd put 'em on the table, but I 'spect you want 'em wit'out *ham*."

Sir Lionell harrumphed. I said my next line from memory while silently turning to the next page of my script.

"Thank you, Porcelain. I'll read them while I eat my script . . ."

There was a moment of stunned silence. Lillie clapped her hand over her mouth and turned away from the mike. Mattie's eyes and grin widened. Phil looked at me sympathetically.

"I told you you'd eat your words someday, George," he ad libbed, pointed to the script, and then cackled.

I had somehow turned my line around. As the audience realized I had made a mistake, laughter spread. Rita, waiting for her cue, hesitated. In the control room, Buzz gestured frantically for her to "enter." If the laughs died down we'd be in danger of dead air, the radio director's worst nightmare.

"I'm sure your *eggs* would taste much better, dear," Lillie said, turning back on mike, suppressing a giggle and attempting a rescue. "Why, good morning, Rita. Do come in."

Rita had to jump a line in order to find her cue. In the instant of silence, Phil couldn't resist another ad lib.

"You're just in time for an unusual gustatory performance, Rita."

"Good morning, Mrs. Typewriter."

"It's Tirebiter, dear."

"What?"

"Never mind, dear. Are you ready for your audition?"

The audience could see we were back to the script now and, after applauding Rita, quieted down. How had I blown that line? My concentration was off.

"Oh, yes, Mrs. T. I've been practicing the Vandals Girl walk you showed me. Look, I can balance a book on my head and everything."

"That's my script!"

"I can even balance a plate. Watch!"

"Those are my eggs!"

"George hasn't finished reading those eggs, Rita," put in Phil, who was unwilling to give up a good thing.

"Now cut that out!" I mimic'd Jack Benny and punched Phil on the shoulder, hard.

"Be careful, Rita!"

Our chief soundman, Fred Earle, ever ready to take the spotlight, dropped a large hammer and smashed a pane of glass.

"I guess I need more practice, Mrs. T."

"That's all right, dear. I'll help you work on your song instead."

The soundman made our doorbell ring "Roll Out The Barrel," a running gag that had been making the audiences laugh ever since the bells had been "given" to us by Ben Bland several weeks earlier.

"I'll see to the portal gate," proclaimed Phil, back into character. "Knock, knock, knock! I come upon the nonce! Anon! Anon!"

"An' on an' on an' on. Ah'm 'fraid yo' eggs is scrambled now, Mr. T. Ah'll make a new set."

"Thank you, Porcelain. Maybe I'll just have some Melba toast on my way to the studio."

"You leavin', Georgie? What'ssa matter? Forget I was gonna drop by and practice my guest spot?"

"Well, for mercy sake—it's Red Bunyon!"

The APPLAUSE sign went off again, and the crowd broke into cheers and whistles. Bunyons' first movie, *That's My Hat!*, titled after his now familiar comic punchline, had been a gigantic hit. There had been some management talk about breaking him into radio as the summer replacement for "Madhouse," thus his appearance.

"Say, Georgie, I been up all night on the Superchief, writin' my bit. Ya wanna hear a joke about a crockagater?"

"No, I don't think I do, no . . ."

"OK, Georgie. One cat says to another cat, 'I just crossed a alligator with a crocodile, and boy, is he mean!'"

"What's the difference?"

"It's got the head of a . . . Whaddaya mean, 'what's the difference?' I'm tellin' ya a joke, that's what's the difference!"

"Calm yourself, Red. I meant, what's the difference between an alligator and a crocodile?"

"That's easy. One of 'em's got a head at one end . . . Wait a second, Georgie! Are you tryin' to confuse me?"

"I'm just trying to find out if you're erudite."

"I never been air-u-dite in my life."

"It means smart, Red. Well-read."

"Well, Red, what?"

"No, no, no. Well-read. You do read, don't you?"

"Sure! I read everything I can get my hands on. This box a cereal, for instance! 'Boys and girls. Getcher great new 1945 Young Tom Edison secret decoder ring today!' Wow! Say, Georgie—you need this boxtop?"

"Red, I don't think you have any linguistic ability whatsoever."

"Are you tellin' me I can't eat Italian food?"

"Not linguini. Linguistic! The gift of tongues. Do you know any Latin?"

"Only the Rumba."

"Latin! What does 'Novus Ordo Seclorum' mean?"

"Don't say that again, Georgie! Those are fightin' words where I come from!"

"Don't be silly. Those words are printed on every dollar bill."

"Bill who?"

"Bill! Bill! It's got a picture of Washington."

"George Washington?

"Yes! Yes! Finally you understand."

"Not Bill Washington."

"There was no Bill Washington."

"What about the bill Washington threw across the Potomac River?"

"That was no bill, that was silver."

"Heave ho, Silver, away!"

"Now stop that! Get out of here! And take this with you!"

"That's my hat!"

The audience chorused Red's tag line, the band came in fast with a burst of theme music, and Ben Bland stepped back to the mike.

"Here's Ray Knight and the Glamorama Goodtimers with their rendition of an old favorite, 'Darktown Strutters Ball.'"

Red looked pleased with himself, gave me a thumb's up and went back to sit next to Rita, who promptly moved away to whisper to Lillie. I looked up at Buzz in the booth and he gave me the sign language for "speed it up just a bit." We were running a few seconds late.

I was distracted. Sometimes a thing gets to be so much fun to do you begin to think that it's easy. A slip of the tongue live on the network was a dangerous thing. My mind had wandered for an instant.

Friday had begun with a threat, a love-letter and some interesting information. The information came from Muriel at *Movie Story*. I had been trying to read the re-writes and mark the cuts in my pencil-corrected script after our morning run-through when she called.

"Mr. T? It's a Hollywood madhouse *here* today too! B-i-i-i-g discussion about whether **Secrets** should have Van Johnson or Errol Flynn on the cover next month."

"Bobbysoxers will swoon which ever way it goes, Muriel."

"Hang on." There was a pause in which the background voices diminished in volume. Just like a good radio sound effect, I thought.

"I tracked down the crewman on Basil Brewster's yacht."

"Who?"

"Don't you remember? The man who found King's body?"

"Er—Tod somebody?"

"Somebody Todd. Two D's. Also known as "Lonesome" Todd. He was a wrangler on the old Mixville lot when he wasn't being a sailor. He made a few pictures in the Twenties. After that, he really *was* a sailor. He was stationed at Pearl Harbor and got wounded in the attack. Now he's at the Military Hospital on Sawtelle. Apparently, no one here ever thought of interviewing him, if they even knew he existed."

"The job is obviously yours."

"I'm going out Saturday. Tomorrow. I hope the weather's better. Do you want to come with me?"

"Give you a lift is more like it."

"I can take the streetcar . . ."

"Of course not. I'll be glad to drive. It's my day off. But I have to take Lillie to Union Station first. She's going to Chicago."

"Great! You can pick me up at my office. It's on the way. Now here's a rumor you can chase down on your own. Not for publication. Obviously. Did you ever hear that Mary Maple Murray made a stag movie?"

"She seems to have done everything else."

"Well, one of our photogs, a guy named Whizzer, says he saw it in 1919, on his 19th birthday. Swears it was her. Being a gentleman, he wouldn't discuss it further. But he hasn't forgotten it."

"Being a man of the world, I know who to call," I said.

There was a distant cheer on the other end of the line.

"And the winner is . . ." Muriel listened. "Van Johnson. I'm supposed to be at the Hospital at 1:45."

"Thirty seconds over Hollywood."

"Over and out."

The boys in Ray Knight's band enjoyed getting the chance to play what Ray called "Hot Licks." His upper-crust Mayfair accent gave a comic twist to the Hep Cat expressions he affected, so we frequently wrote him into the show. I found myself hardly listening as the music ended.

"We-ee-l-l . . ." I ad-libbed, hunting for my place in the script. "That's a great old number, Ray."

"So are you, Georgie old pip! So are you! Vooot! Rooty!"

"Well, thank you. I think."

The rest of the company was poised in front of me, sound effects men at the ready. Their image wobbled for an instant, then went steady as Phil Baines swept on mike, gave me a piercing look, followed by a silly smile.

"Ah, Red! Red!" he exclaimed as Sir Lionell. "A fellow of indefinite jest. I shall give him a starring role in my Hollywood Bowl production of Shakespeare's "Midsummer Nightmare."

"I thought it was "Midsummer Night's Eve.""

"It would be a nightmare if it starred Red Bunyons!"

"You'd star Red in Shakespeare?"

"Yes, George, I would. As Bottom, the . . ." Phil snickered, but swallowed it with an discreet cough.

The line had come from my writers as "Bottom, the ass who loved a Fairy Queen." Phil had played it brilliantly in rehearsal, capturing every nuance of double-entendre. Mort Skully, the agency censor, naturally demanded that it be changed. I was half-afraid Phil would ad lib it back in.

" . . . donkey-headed buffoon."

We both had to turn away from the mike and cover our snorts of laughter as the sound-effects doorbell rang again.

"I'll get it, George," Lillie trilled her line standing off by her folding chair.

Buzz had engaged three AFRA union regulars as the Gypsy circus act. They could ad lib furiously with one another in mittel-European gibberish, puff and pant in unison while miming a strenuous juggling act, and work for scale. They stood, script pages in hand, all eyes on Buzz up behind the glass windows of the booth, waiting for a cue, poised for their entrance. Manny, Moski and Yackov.

The love letter, if that's what it was, came completely from left field. I had picked up my mail from Paranoid Studios on the way to CBS. Slipped into my In box was a pale rose envelope with a handwritten note:

"Dear George,

"It was such a pleasure running into you—literally—at the Camp on Wednesday. It's so unusual that a well-known person like yourself would risk being seen the way God made us. I know that it must be hard when you do it for the first time. I'm sure you know what I mean.

"Anyway, I hope we can have a much longer chat the next time. I'll be in the scoring room all next week long doing *The Harry James Story.*

"Ruth T."

Acute embarrassment flushed my toes and rose upward in my body like a fever thermometer. *Did* I know what she meant? It hadn't worried me at the time, but what if people around the Studio found out I had spent the afternoon at a nudist camp? There was no where to safely put the letter in my CBS cubby-hole, so I tucked it in my inside coat pocket.

The coat was in my off-stage dressing room. A picture of it hanging open on the pipe rack flashed before my eyes, momentarily fading the words on my mimeographed script page.

"Halloo, Mrs. Tirrebotter!"

"Halloo, Comrade Madam!"

"Goot morneeng, Beautiful Ladyee!"

Lillie giggled girlishly. "Oh, George! It's the Balancing Borodins!"

"Oh, Lillie! What have you done now?"

Gleefully grunting and miming, the actors simulated acrobats doing stunts, while the sound men pummeled tables, pillows and themselves, along with a comic "sprooing!" machine that Fred Earl had constructed out of a long fat spring, a saw blade and a Chinese gong.

"Aren't they just marvelous, George? Look at that! Manny can hold Moski over his head with one hand."

Sound effects tore a piece of bedsheet, smashed two wooden strawberry boxes and dropped a double-handful of broken plaster.

"The kitchen isn't tall enough!"

The AFRAns danced around me, jabbering.

"They want you to help them, dear. Just stand right on that."

"Here?"

"Dot's right, Meestir Toebobber!"

SPROOINGG!

"Ahhhhhh-oooooo . . ." I flew straight up ten feet, vocally.

The gong reverberated in an echo chamber built somewhere under a back staircase. Fred and the boys executed a whizzing sound with a piece of garden hose, smashed another couple of strawberry boxes and hurled a variety of thumping, crumbling and bouncing objects to the floor. I groaned pitifully while limping off mike.

"That's just where I've been *wanting* a skylight, George, dear!"

The Band broke into a few bars of our theme as a transition. Ben Bland stepped to the mike.

"The Noblemen join Mattie Daniels in a honkey-tonk take on "Way Down Yonder in New Orleans."

I stepped across the stage, bowed and held my arms out for Lillie. It was a weekly tradition for us to do a little dancing to one of the musical numbers. We never rehearsed where it would come, and the studio audience seemed to really enjoy the suggestion of wedded intimacy it gave. She smiled and floated glamorously into my arms.

The threat that had begun my day had come from my wife.

I heard the phone ringing far away in the breakfast nook. It woke me out of a vivid dream in which everyone at the previous night's dinner party had been cast in Derrick's *The Pasha's Daughter*, along with Dixie Cupps. Joy Darling was modeling a transparent green harem-girl outfit from *Sequel to Sinbad*, and Jane Wyman had added a black veil to her satin turban and was billed as "Button-Nosed Queen of the Tassels." It was pouring prop rain on the oasis and Turhan Bey was following me through the palm trees, in a double-breasted white suit, his pipe upside down in his teeth to keep the water out. I was running through a street of twisting shadows which opened on top of a sand dune and there were Ron Reagan and Lillie, like Cooper and Detrich in *Morocco*, passionately kissing.

The phone rang again and then stopped. I looked over to Lillie's side of the bed. She was gone. She was up. It was 8:30 am. The picture of Lillie in Ron's arms stuck in my hung-over brain. She's probably talking to him right now, I thought. He couldn't wait to call! She's not going to Chicago, she's going to be with him! . . . At Fort Whacky in Culver City?

"George . . ."

When Lillie said my name like that, I couldn't distinguish between her real self and her radio personality. Were my writers writing my wife? I hauled myself up on an elbow.

"Yes, Lillie?"

She entered the bedroom, wrapped in a negligee of a wan pink color that has never seemed "nude" to me.

"George, that was Basil Brewster on the phone."

"Funny time to call."

"George, do you love me?"

"Well, naturally. Of course I love you."

"Then stay out of the King business. Basil doesn't need to be reminded of a tragedy that happened twenty-five years ago."

"Your mother was on the yacht."

Lillie stiffened and took a deep breath. She sat down on the flowered chintz chair by the French doors to the garden and gave me her profile.

"You're doing a Grand Duchess out of some old Lehar operetta, Lillie. Why didn't you tell me your Mother was on the boat, for heaven's sake? She couldn't have been a suspect."

"Leave it alone, George. Leave it alone or you'll be sorry."

"I suppose you're also going to deny that you and Reagan are lovers!"

"What?" She got out of the chair and stood over me. "Have you lost your mind?"

"It came to me in a dream . . . a Technicolor nightmare, Lillie. Starring Turhan Bey."

"Well, there's your problem right there," said Lillie, laughing. She walked toward her bathroom and stopped at the door. "Leave the King murder alone. You know what curiosity did, right, pussycat?"

"Very well danced, George dear, for an up-tempo number," Lillie whispered in my ear as the music ended. We sat down next to each other and listened to the Farmers' Market scene play out, followed by Rita and Red's chilly duet. Buzz and I had moved some elements around at the end of the program in order to warm things up. The winter rain outside had subdued our studio audience, and I could hear radios all over America tuning over to our competition—"Hi yo, Silver, away!"—if we didn't pick up a few laughs.

"Let's follow George as he's about to cross Hollywood and Vine on his way to the broadcast . . ." narrated Ben Bland as Presty Roberts played a cascade of transitional xylophone notes.

"Getcha af-ternoon pay-pah! Read all about it! Tye-ya-byduh Drops In Un-Announced at Star's Pool Pah-ty!" The squawk of the irritating Dead End Kid newsboy was, naturally, played by Lillie in one of those vocal double roles the listener is never told about. The studio audience always gasped a little and applauded in surprise. It was one of Lillie's favorite moments in the show.

"Are you still here?"

"Every day from six-thoity in the a-yem to seven-thoity in the pee-em. It's dis er reform school."

"Reform school! Are you a juvenile delinquent?"

"Let's put it this way, Mac. Alcatraz promised me a football scholarship."

"Well, what made you give up a life of crime for selling papers thirteen hours a day out here on the most famous corner in America?"

"Take a look at dis newspaper story, Mac."

"Er . . . 'Radio star George Tirebiter dunks his auto in Linda Darnell's swimming pool! Too cheap to use a car wash!' Why, those are miserable lies!"

"Yeah—It's a *crime* what dese papers print, Mac. So I feel right at home."

"Oh, for heaven's sake! Just sell me what you've got there. I'm going to be late to the studio."

"I got ten papers here, Mac."

"Well, here's fifty cents."

"Read all about it! Cheap-skate radio actor won't help strugglin' newsie leave life of crime!"

"Here's a dollar! Keep the . . ."

I couldn't read the next word. I stared at my script page through pitch blackness. I had gone suddenly blind. Then a match dimly lit up the engineer's booth. I could see Buzz staring down at the silent mixing console in horror. The audience began a loud murmur with an edge of panic. Our ushers took charge with flashlights and soothing "Keep your seats, please. Nothing to worry about. We'll have the lights back on right away."

Exactly two minutes and forty-eight seconds before we were scheduled to sign off and cue the network and the eight o'clock program, we had lost all power and went off the air. Buzz's match went out. I could hear the telephone begin ringing up in the booth.

One of the union actors, Yackov, I believe, broke the silence. "I ain't done a job in three months, an' the minute I land a good bit, the Japs drop a damn bomb on it!"

The studio audience thought that was the funniest line in the show. Fortunately, it gave me a punchline I've used many times in later years, when telling this otherwise calamitous story to adoring audiences at Old Time Radio conventions.

CHAPTER 17

REMEMBER PEARL?

To arrive by train at the Union Station in Downtown Los Angeles in the Forties was to burst into Southern California complete with lofty palm trees, acres of Spanish tile, delicately wrought iron and banks of flowers, no matter the season. Consider the alternative—days of desert driving, a burlap covered canteen sweating on the fender of your Model T, a succession of sand-blasted gas-'n'-grub stops along Route 66, and the ultimate entrance into a city that looked more like Des Moines than El Dorado.

To depart the City of the Angels, as Lillie was doing at 8:24 via the Southern Pacific, was equally dramatic. Red-caps politely hustled your luggage away, you made your path among smartly-dressed travelers (and what appeared to be several battalions of young soldiers), through the vast, echoing waiting room to the platform along side Track 12, approached by way of a long tunnel. There you were directed to a comfortable seat (in Lillie's case, a tastefully appointed compartment) inside a freshly washed coach.

The chill rain took the edge off of the usual excitement of travel. Southern California was never prepared for the cold, and the enormous open spaces of the Station had grown frigid during a week of wintertime. I had made a thermos of black coffee and cognac which we both sipped on the drive over, and finished in the few minutes before departure.

The disaster of last night's broadcast hung over us like an additional burden of grey cloud. Even if lightning hadn't struck the CBS transmission tower, knocking us off the air, my lapses of concentration had affected the overall timing. Buzz had patted me on the shoulder as we left the studio.

"Tee many martoonies, Georgie?" he needled. "Or did we miss a few rehearsals?" The electricians got the power back on in time for the West Coast broadcast at seven-thirty, which boasted of good laughs and came out to the second, giving way to the network ID and the familiar cry of "Henry! Henry Aldrich!"

The train whistle sounded and the conductor looked in at the compartment door.

"I'm sorry, sir, but you'll have to say good-bye now."

I capped the thermos and got up to go.

"Well, Lillie . . . give my best to your Father, if—if he remembers me."

"I will, George. Don't worry about the show. I'm sure you and the boys will outdo yourselves for next week. And you've got Ronnie."

"Too bad we couldn't let our New York listeners in on that appealing fact."

"See you a week from Monday."

We kissed quickly and I hurried down the corridor and out to the platform. Bells clanged and steam blew into tatters. We waved at each other as the train began to move. I watched it pull away and then walked back into the station to a bank of phone booths.

I had five days to follow through on what I was now thinking of as "my investigation" of the King case. What would Phil Marlowe do? Press on, knight-errantly. I dialed Eagle Rock Releasing.

The phone rang six times before Max van Os picked it up.

"Hallow?"

"Max, it's George Tirebiter. Sorry to call so early. I need to tap your brain again."

"I haf no brain before ten a.m."

"That's fine. How about coffee at ten? You say where."

"Is a Van de Kamps on Orange Grove. You know it?"

"I can find it."

"I will meet you there."

He rang off. I put up the collar on my overcoat and trudged across the Union Station parking lot to Olvera Street, still shuttered, except for La Golondrina, a cafe specializing in Mexican grub, where I brooded over an order of *huevos rancheros.*

From ersatz Mexico to phony Holland was a quick trip via the Arroyo Seco Parkway—the first link in L.A.'s future freeway system. The Van de Kamp bakeries were shingle-sided wind-mill affairs, featuring waitresses in Dutch-girl outfits. Van Os recognized me as I entered and gestured me over to his table. He was, as the song hit had it, "Mr. Five-by-Five," short and broad, with a gleaming bald dome and billy-goat chin whiskers. I introduced myself.

"Monte Burke you found? He is a nice fellow. We play cards sometimes."

"I found him, thank you. Now I need to find something else in your specialty."

Max spread his chubby palms out. "How may I serve you?"

"I'm writing a screen story based on an old Hollywood murder. You ever hear of Taylor D'Arcy King?"

He shook his head.

"How about Mary Maple Murray?"

He grinned. "Yah. Silent sex queen."

"I'm told she made a blue movie around 1919. You ever hear of such a thing?"

"Yah. Collector's item. Is called 'A Union Job.'"

"You have a copy?"

He pursed his lips and drank of slug of milky coffee.

"Unfortunately not."

"Oh."

"I said collector's item. Collectors are known to me. Are you a collector, Mr. Tirebiter?"

"Not of stag films, Mr. van Os. But it would be helpful to me on this project to have a look at it."

"Can be done, possibly. Excuse me."

He got up and did a penguin waddle between tables to the back of the shop where he squeezed himself into a phone booth. I ordered a coffee and butterhorn from the waitress. It was half eaten before van Os returned and dropped into his chair.

"Mr. Tirebiter, I haf arranged you a screening. Can you be in Santa Monica tomorrow efening?"

"Sure."

"Goot. Is a client of mine who admires the unusual."

He pulled his wallet from his coat pocket and extracted a card. With a gold pen he wrote a name and address across the back.

"After eight p.m. He will be expecting you."

Rain continued unabated and I was glad to be driving Lillie's Continental with its effective heater. I cruised back down the Arroyo Seco and picked up Sunset Boulevard where it began at Broadway. Traffic was light, the radio dished out an absorbing episode of "Grand Central Station" ("crossroads of a million private lives" was a good line, but who could forget "dives with a roar beneath the glitter and swank of Park Avenue?"), and I motored half the distance across the vast city to the Strip, where I picked up Muriel, and continued on toward the Pacific, dropping South to Wilshire, past Westwood, and finally through the gates of the Sawtelle Soldier's Home.

Elmer "Lonesome" Todd sat in a wheelchair on a colonnaded sun-porch staring at the rain beating down on the hydrangeas. Muriel and I pulled up chairs.

"Hi, Lonesome," said Muriel.

"Howdy," he replied in a soft voice. Lonesome was missing his left leg and a scar ran up the left side of his face from throat to scalp line. Aside from that, he was almost girlishly attractive for a man in his late forties.

"This is George Tirebiter. You ever listen to 'Hollywood Madhouse' on Friday nights?"

"Nope."

"Well, George is the star. He's very interested in the old King murder case, just like me."

Van de Kamp's restaurant

"Howdy."

"Howdy," I said.

Muriel flipped open a steno book in a very professional way, uncapped her pen and smiled.

"*Movie Story* is prepared to pay you fifty dollars for this interview, Lonesome."

"You told me, otherwise we wouldn't be talkin'."

"Right. Well, then. You were on the crew of Basil Brewster's yacht back in 1920."

"I was the crew. Tub didn't take much crewin'. Had a big diesel engine. Sails was mostly for show. Steered like a movin' van. Horses were my thing then, not boats."

"You were working for Tom Mix?"

"Sure. He come up to Montana for **Big Sky** in '18. I did some wranglin', we got along and he offered me a job at the studio. I was a kid, it seemed like a break. Hell, it *was* a break!"

"How did you meet Brewster?" I asked.

Lonesome looked me up and down. It was an uncomfortably intimate appraisal.

"You seem like a sophisticated fella. You know what Hollywood's all about. Brewster was playin' a Roman general for de Mille and I was wranglin' his pony. One thing led to another and . . ." he shrugged. "He ended up wranglin' *my* pony. Moved me into that chat-toe of his, an' put me to work on the boat. You ain't gonna write about any of that, are ya, miss?"

"Ah . . . well, Lonesome, movie magazines sort of gloss over relationships of an unorthodox kind."

Lonesome snorted, coughed and blew his nose loudly into a checkered handkerchief.

"Yeah."

"So, one way or another, you were aboard the "Mystery Girl" on January 25th of 1920."

"Yep. We picked up the passengers in Long Beach and cruised over to Catalina."

"Who else was aboard?"

"Brewster. King. The three Murray girls. Actor named Monte Burke. Screenwriter named Tulley and his wife. Tommy, the Jap cameraman. Old Mrs. Murray, the girls' mother, and another society-type dame . . ."

"Mrs. Ames?"

"That's right. Ames. And she had her daughter with her, about ten, I guess."

"Her daughter?" My voice cracked. Muriel shot me a look.

"What do you remember about her?"

"Nothin' much. Blondie. Her and Iris Murray kinda floated around in play get-up. Pretendin' to be fairies, you should pardon the word, Miss Albers."

"What can you tell us about that night, Mr. Todd?"

"Well, it was kickin' up. Folks went over to the island for dinner and most of 'em stayed there, in the hotel. I stuck aboard and had me a sandwich. 'Bout ten o'clock, the launch comes back and King and Murray climb up, drunk as a couple a skunks. They was a number then, you know. Both of 'em was snow-birds, and 'd jump on it if it moved, you see what I mean. She give me the eye, but Basil told her the score and she laid off. Offa me, that is. Monte and the Jap were hustlin' King for somethin'—you know Hollywood. I could hear 'em arguin', then the Jap gets sick and goes on deck to toss his cookies, as we say in the Navy."

"Where was Brewster?"

Lonesome gave me another look and batted his lashes. "In our bunk, Mr. Tirebiter. Swell double bunk. Only he was sleepin' and I wasn't. I heard Burke go off to his cabin, then the Jap come back down and the door closes on his cabin. I heard a lot of doors openin' and closin' before I drifted off."

"And Mary Murray?"

"After I helped 'em aboard, she went down to her cabin while the fellas sat in the mess and put away a couple a bottles a bootleg."

"You found King's body in the morning?"

"Sure. I was up with the dawn, brewed a pot a java, drank a cup. Boat was dead quiet. I went up on deck to look around and heard the launch bangin' against the hull, like a line had come loose, so I went to tie her up again. Looked down and there was King, face down between the launch and the hull. I yelled 'man overboard!' threw down a life preserver, tried to get King in it. He was dead weight and soakin' wet. Basil was on deck by that time, and Monte Burke, and they come down and we hauled the body into the launch. Basil and me took it ashore, woke up a doc and the sheriff, and Basil made a couple a phone calls. That was it. I took the sheriff and his deputy back to the yacht. Of course, by that time everybody aboard was awake. Sheriff, he yelled, 'Yer all suspects!' He saw his name in the headlines, that's fer sure."

Lonesome laughed and lit a cigarette. Muriel made a few more shorthand notes and we looked at each other.

"So," I said, "who done it?"

"Coulda been a accident."

"Is that what you think?"

"No more 'n losin' this peg was an accident."

"How did that happen, Lonesome?" asked Muriel.

"December 7th I was aboard the Oklahoma. Outta the war the day it started." He smoked a minute, then squinted at us. "Burke, the Jap, they both had bad dealin's with King that night. Mary, she was out cold, King was in his cabin an' Basil was with me. The Jap was pro'lly too seasick to cold-cock him. My money's always been on Burke. Just a hunch."

"Did you tell the police what you suspected?"

"Hell, no! Everybody was lying through their teeth, me included. Then the studio fixit men came over on the morning steamer and smoothed the whole thing out. The papers made a big play of it, but the cops was paid off. Hell! Hollywood!" He snorted and crushed his smoke out under his right slipper.

Muriel gave him a company check for fifty dollars and we left the Home. The rain was steadily falling.

CHAPTER 18

NOT SO GRAND HOTEL

Lillie had been aboard the "Mysterious Lady." Maybe not on the night of the murder, but that day. Now that her secret had been dis-interred, it lay there, a heap of old bones. Muriel avoided the subject on the drive back to her office, but it was all I could think about. Lillie must be protecting someone. Basil? The late Mrs. Ames? Hardly. One of the Murray sisters?

I was idling the engine in front of Screen Secrets, mesmerized by the windshield wipers.

"Mr. T?"

I looked blankly at Muriel, who had her hand on the door to open it.

"I said, Do you think Monte Burke could do it? Kill King?"

"Not by how he looks now. Santa Claus with a tan. Right naked old elf. He claimed to know nothing about anything. Which, now that we've talked to Lonesome, seems harder to believe."

"Right. Well, I think we could have a story here. Even keeping, ah, certain things to ourselves."

"At this rate, I don't know what's left for publication. Which reminds me, that stag movie of Mary's does seem to exist. I'm supposed to take a look at it tomorrow night."

"Woo-woo!"

"Your magazines are for teenage girls, right?"

"Women in general, Mr. T. Movie fans. They could be 15 or 50."

"Your editor is not going to go for a story that opens up the kind of—well, perversions we're finding here. I think it's a wrap, Muriel. I'm sorry to say."

"Maybe. But maybe I can find another way to write it. Anyhow, I'm going to try and set up interviews with the Murray sisters."

"Good luck."

"Thanks. Did you know Pegeen Murray had a kid? That's why she got out of the business. Must be around my age. Maybe if I could track her down there'd be an angle."

I checked my watch, needlessly. "Er, I have a . . ."

"Oh, gosh! I'm real sorry, Mr. T."

"George."

"I keep thinking you're just a regular guy, but I know you're busy as all heck." She opened the door and plunged out into the drizzle. "Bye, George. Thanks for the ride."

I watched her dash into her building. There's just something about New Jersey girls . . .

Max Morgan's card, which I had slipped into my billfold, listed his office as 9400 Culver Blvd. Culver City, home of the giant Metro lot, was a few miles south of the Strip. I turned left on La Cienega and took it down to Washington Boulevard and then West, past Fort Roach, where Ron Reagan was no doubt exercising his tonsils on behalf of the Air Corps, past the Tara-esque entrance to the old Selznick studio and pulled up in front of the Culver City Hotel. A six-story brick pile with limestone trim, it sat on a triangular lot and towered over most of the other drab buildings making up the "downtown" of yet another drab L. A. suburb.

I remembered that Noel Langley, one of a dozen writers on *The Wizard of Oz*, had once told me that Metro had found lodgings at the Hotel for a couple of dozen German Munchkins during the filming. Their exuberant sexual exploits had been the talk of the town.

Morgan Investigations occupied a second floor office, which was dark. I knocked. The knocks rattled around inside and fell dead. It being a Saturday, I'd hoped the private eye was closed. I looked up and down the dim hallway. A chiropractor named Steal. Jaime Munoz, a Mexican *abogado*. Dr. A. Fish, advertising "high colonics." A dental technician. All dark. What sort of desperate impulse had drawn me to this orphanage of the helping professions?

I borrowed the bit from *The Falcon Goes West*. The celluloid cover from the ID window, under which you keep your driver's license, slipped out and pushed into the door jamb and then up, past the spring-lock. It didn't work. I tried it again. The lock gave a quiet squawk and the door wheezed open. I swallowed hard to keep from throwing up and stepped inside, shutting the door with both hands. It wheezed again. I leaned against it and breathed deeply. My hands were cold and sweaty.

The air in Morgan's office had been pickled in cigarette smoke. The only other odor was Ivory Soap, and that oozed from a yard-square bathroom with a dirty sink full of grey water. A heavy, old-fashioned Gillette razor sat on the edge, next to a frayed shaving brush. Morgan had five o'clock shadow at the hours usually reserved for another refreshing dose of Dr Pepper.

A wooden filing cabinet stenciled Prop. U. S. Gov't lurked in the corner behind Morgan's glass-topped desk. A through J occupied the top drawer. I looked unsuccessfully for "King" at the front of the second drawer. I tried "Murray" and then pulled out the bottom drawer for "Tulley." No luck. As I worked my way back, my fingers paused over a name that, at first glance, meant nothing. "Villandros." Then it rang a dinner bell. Rickey Villandros, Beverly Hills restaurant owner, married to Iris Murray. I pulled the manila folder out and took it to the window, as if the wet grey twilight would help me read the penciled notes.

A sheet of lined foolscap and a receipt for $200 were the total contents. The receipt acknowledged that R. Villandros had paid a retainer to M. Morgan for "confidential work." The yellow sheet had a penciled list of familiar names: Tommy Takasago, Oliver Tulley, Monte Burke, Basil Brewster, Lillie Ames Tirebiter. Next to each was a brief note. Lillie's said, "may have inherited it." Tulley and Burke were bracketed "in it together." Brewster's said, "M. sure he knew." Takasago was followed by a question mark and the word "probably." Scrawled in later was "Johnnie's Groc, 12th & Union."

I slipped the file back into the cabinet and slid the drawer closed. Now at least I knew who was behind the muscle. Iris Villandros. Stella's Aunt Iris. I picked up Morgan's phone and dialed Stella's number.

"Hello," she said.

"It's George."

"I didn't think you'd call. I'm glad you did."

"How about a quiet dinner tonight?"

"Oh, gosh! Sure!"

"Let's make it early. I'll pick you up at 6:30."

"I'll be ready, George."

"I think I have some information about your father's murder. Anyway, let's push a couple of buttons and see what happens. Bye."

I clicked off, put the phone down and left the office. The lock snapped closed with a resigned thud of false security. I went downstairs to the hotel lobby and looked up the number for the Shaynu Restaurant. Yes sir, they would be happy to reserve a table for Mr. Tirebiter, near the dance floor but out of the spotlight.

I caught the radio news on the way to Stellas. General MacArthur, having promised he would return, had, on the beach at Luzon. From Germany, an angry transcription of Nazi-speak, as the short-wave said "Nein!" at some length to an offer of surrender. In Washington, where it was snowing, preparations were complete for FDR's fourth inauguration ceremony, to take place the next day. His doctors had certified his good health.

CHAPTER 19

DINNER I'LL EAT

From the outside, in keeping with "The Southland's" lust for buildings which mimic ducks or bowls of chili or zeppelins, the Shaynu looked like half-a-block of New York tenement brownstones, complete with stoops and fire-escapes. This exterior was supposed to stir nostalgia for the days of Prohibition. The bar was a few steps down, behind a yellow door with a small, grilled window where it was no longer necessary to say "Joe sent me." Dining was upstairs, on small tables with red-checked tablecloths. A piano-bass-and-guitar combo was working out on "I'll Build A Stairway to Paradise" when Stella and I were ushered through the velvet rope into the half-filled room.

"Shoes!" we sang simultaneously. "You're gonna carry me there!"

After that, martinis and antipasto was easy.

Stella had starlight in her eyes. But an edge to her voice. I could feel her two-fisted private dick step out of fiction and join us at the table.

"You know who owns this corner of the Roaring Twenties, don't you, George?"

I nodded. "Uncle Rickey."

"He practically lives here. I'll introduce you."

"That was the idea."

A small candle in a dark red glass separated us.

"What have you found out? About my father."

"Why do you think he was murdered, Stella?"

"Why? Mother thinks so. I told you, I think she knows the murderer. She says things like, 'Baby, he gave me you before they took him away." And 'He was no good, but they didn't have to do that to him.'"

"She says 'they.'"

"Yes, 'they.' I thought at first she was just blaming the universe for the accident that happened to him."

"This afternoon I talked to someone who was there. He didn't think it was an accident. The other two witnesses I've managed to contact claim to be completely in the dark. But I think your Aunt Iris must know better, because she had Uncle Rickey sic a private eye on Lillie and me. Not only was Lillie's mother on the yacht, Stella. Lillie herself was aboard. She and Iris were childhood playmates. She obviously didn't want me to find that out. Why? Because she knows something too?"

"Maybe everybody on the boat was in it together."

"Maybe. And kept it quiet. The police and the papers suggested as much back in 1920. Who's gone and stirred things up again?"

"The detective?"

"Somebody else. That's what Rickey hired the detective to find out."

"Let's ask him." She pointed her chin across the room.

Rickey Villandros had slipped through a velvet curtain and stood, looking around. I had expected to see someone darkly matching the standard movie gangster. A Sheldon Leonard kind of guy. Instead, he had curly blond hair blending to grey, a grey double-breasted suit and a warm smile when he spotted Stella. She smiled back and he was beside our table in a few steps. A Ralph Bellamy look-alike.

"Stella! Why didn't you call? Tell me you were coming tonight?"

"I didn't know. George brought me. Rickey, this is George Tirebiter, the radio star."

He shook my hand warmly. "Sure you aren't his son? Tirebiter must be twice your age." If he was surprised to see me, he gave no hint of it.

"It's all in the voice, Mr. Villandros. Won't you join us?"

"Sorry, gotta look after things. Tell you what. You have a quiet dinner, and after, I'll give you a personal tour of the place—antiques, paintings. Regular shrine to Great Gatsby. Swell to meet you, Tirebiter. You like Chianti? Pre-war. I'll send a bottle over. Drop by and say hello to Iris sometime, Stella. She misses the poker games."

Rickey patted me on the shoulder and tacked away between tables, giving the evening's patrons the owner's best.

"Poker games?"

"She taught me to play poker when I was a little girl—Iris was in her twenties then, living in Pasadena with Grandmother Murray. She was laid up with some sort of nervous condition." Stella lowered her voice. "Iris loves poker. That's how she met Rickey. In a poker parlor in Gardena. He won. She lost."

The wine came with the antipasto. The band segued through "It's Only Make-Believe" and "The Best Things in Life Are Free." A girl singer sat on the top of the piano and did a Helen Morgan medley. "Bill," "Body and Soul" and "Why Was I Born?" Songs which faded in through the ether over earphones hooked up to my 1927 Audiola Super-Het. I was not trying very hard not to fall in love with Stella, who eyed me meltingly over her zitti.

Then the pulp fiction gumshoe squinted out from behind her eyes again. "How long have you been on this case, George?"

"On and off, all week. It's a daisy chain. Lillie must think Basil Brewster killed King. Brewster told me Mary Murray confessed to him, but he didn't believe her.

First Matey Todd intuits it was Monte Burke. Burke claims complete ignorance. Takasago, the cameraman, is in a detention camp in some god-forsaken desert someplace. Maybe he did it."

"Can you trace him?"

"Maybe. I came across a clue today."

"Are we in this together?"

That was a tough one. I finished my Chianti. It was Early Il Duce. "I'm in the middle of a three-way stretch, Stella. I'm starting a picture in a week. I've got a show Friday with Ron Reagan that could put a rocket under our ratings. Whatever I do after we brace Villandros is a solo."

Her black eyes went from melting to hard boiled.

"I understand, George."

"I wish I did. Let's go talk to Uncle Rickey."

There was a private staircase behind the velvet drapes. Stella led the way. The top floor of the restaurant was given over to a large room in the center of which loomed a bright yellow Chrysler Roadster.

"Come on in, folks," called Villandros. His office had been decorated to give the impression of a prosperous banker's library before The Crash. "Take a seat. You might be interested, that's the car that broke the cross-country speed record back in '27. Imperial 80. Seven days flat coast-to-coast and back again."

We sat in front of the fireplace. Rickey turned up the gas so the logs glowed and sank into an armchair.

"So?"

"I'd like to know why you had a detective threaten me."

"It's a family matter."

"I'm not in your family."

"She is. You know what's going on, Stella. What the hell you drag him in this for?"

"I was trying to help."

"Only way to help this family is to keep things inside the circle. This guy's not even a candidate."

"It's blackmail, George. Mom's being blackmailed, so's Iris."

"About the King murder?"

"They had nothing to do with it. Mom was madly in love with him."

"Look, Tirebiter. Please, your meal was on the house. My apologies for any inconvenience you got in being leaned on. Stell, why don't you stick around, I'll run you out to the ranch. Iris is staying with your Mother while Bill's in Denver. You know how she likes to have us all there for Sunday dinner."

Stella looked from Villandros' face to mine and back.

"I think I'd better, George, if you don't mind. I know you've got a busy week . . ."

"I'll take your word for it you're out of the way, Tirebiter. Thing's 'll get taken care of without you." He got up smoothly and stuck out his hand. "Glad you stopped by, we could talk. Tell your wife to give Iris a call, yak over old times."

I shook his hand briefly. Stella held hers up and I took it.

"I'll give you a call when I finish your book. Reads like there's a picture in it so far. Count on me to see what I can do. Goodnight, Stella. Uncle Rickey."

I saluted the yellow Chrysler on my way out. Everybody loves a winner.

Cahuenga Pass, Gateway to Hollywood, California

CHAPTER 20

THAT'S ENTERTAINMENT!

My blue Mercury was in the driveway, and there were two yellow envelopes from Western Union stuck in the door jamb when I got back home. One was from Lillie, sent from Albuquerque: "Sun shining here. Hope you are same. Love, Lil." The second, from my producer, gave me just the excuse I needed: "Geo. Corwin out. Replacement writer? Call. Buzz."

I poured a double cognac, got out my Writers Guild directory, looked up Oliver Tulley and dialed.

"Georgie! Caught me on the way out the door."

"It's work, Ollie."

"The door is locked from the outside, George. I got nothin' but time."

"How would you like to do a six or seven minute patriotic drop-in for my radio show, Ollie?" Nothing like an offer of employment to heal old wounds. "I'll give you Ronnie Reagan and a ten-voice chorus."

"Work! Well, sure, Georgie. Patriotic pap, huh?"

"Something like the stuff you wrote for Pat O'Hara in *Babes In Khaki*."

"What is an American?" declaimed Ollie in a faint brogue. "He's a Broadway zip with a flask on his hip, he's a bum from Baltimore! We shudda got an Oscar nod."

"I wish you'd gotten more credit for it back in '42, Ollie. I was pretty green back then. Is it a deal? I'll meet you at Musso's tomorrow after my regular writers' meeting. Say two o'clock?"

"It'll be like old times, Georgie! We'll win the war!" He clicked off.

Ollie wasn't Corwin, but Ronnie wasn't Welles. The fish was, however, on the line. I planned to pour Gibsons down Tulley's gullet until he came clean about the King murder.

The L.A. phone book yielded a number for Johnnie's Grocery. DRexel 9255. I dialed it. After several rings the other end picked up.

"Good evening," a mature female voice said.

"'Scuse me, how late are you open?"

"I close at seven and open at eight tomorrow."

"Is Tommy Takasago in?"

She hung up immediately and the dial tone buzzed at me for a few moments. I cut the sound off with a finger.

The Rose Garage had left my car damp around the gills, smelling sharply of cleaning fluid and full of Ethyl. When I started it up early Sunday morning the motor coughed once, then settled into a familiar, if phlegmy hum. I pushed buttons on the radio. Uncle Don. E. Power Biggs. FDR. I settled on the President's voice, which sounded frail but determined. Listening to the brief speech, and then to Martin Agronsky's description of the cold wind whipping flags up Pennsylvania Avenue, I drove south and east on streets running deep with rainwater to the corner of Pico and Alvarado.

Johnnie's Grocery, a couple of blocks away, turned out to be a small clapboard structure tacked onto a turreted turn-of-the-century duplex, holding down the space previously held by two fifty-foot Washington palms. It was the corner market for a neighborhood otherwise occupied by modest bungalows which sagged with damp and neglect. Johnnie's was in fact Closed Sundays.

I rolled around the corner and turned down the alley. It was lined with garages, doors swung shut and locked. People who lived around here took the streetcar wherever they needed to go. I slowed to check the rear of the house behind the grocery. The extra-wide lot had a driveway beside the alley garage. Parked in the driveway was a Hudson Terraplane. The license was 1W5049.

Elated, I pulled out the other end of the alley and took Pico to Vermont Avenue where I headed north. Vermont is the longest straight street in urban America. At its north end it corkscrews into Griffith Park and up to the Planetarium. From the Moderne ramparts of the Planetarium you can gaze back down twenty miles south along Vermont all the way to the docks of San Pedro.

I contemplated a drizzly portion of this view through one of the rotunda windows and listened to the world turn under the Foucault pendulum that swung to and fro under the dome. The world seemed to be turning faster than usual, and I was having to hold on.

Pete Potash fingered a curl at the back of his mostly bald head. Florrie Murphy drummed his large hands on the round table, making everyone's cocktail shudder. Dave Marmelstein pushed his hair out of his eyes and sorted mimeographed script pages. Mel Gibson was in the bathroom.

"I got eleven pages here," said Dave. "Draft of the breakfast scene up to Reagan's drop-in. Also the acrobats kidnap Lillie . . ."

"She's not doing the show this week, Dave. We'll have to write her out."

"It happens at the front door, so all you get is a muffled scream, which you can do, George."

"Still screaming for Lillie after all these years," Pete said.

"I thought we could economize by having Rita audition for Sir Lionell this week—a casting call. Maybe put Reagan in it for a fast one-liner," I said.

Mel opened the door, letting the Sunday lunch clatter in for a moment.

"Afternoon, George."

"Welcome back, Mel."

"George wants a scene for Rita and Lionell," said Florrie. "Then we might as well knock off, 'cause it's-never-to-late-to-be-an-Oscar nominee Oliver Q. Tulley is writin' the second half of the show."

"We could use that *Harvey* gag, George," said Mel. "He has the title role in his own production at the Pasadena Playhouse . . ."

"She's auditioning for the Nurse." said Dave.

"For the carrot," offered Florrie.

"She's got an arrangement worked out with the Knightengales for 'Don't Fence Me In.'"

"How the hell are we supposed to put this all together?" grumbled Florrie.

The idea had come to me at the Planetarium. A Tesla size spark.

"Here's the gimmick, boys."

"Speak up, George."

"Ronnie was a radio announcer, right? A sportscaster. He used to fake play-by-plays as if he were at the stadium, instead of in a studio, scanning the ticker."

My writers nodded.

"Let's use that for the breakfast spot. He comes by the Madhouse to discuss our "Radio Salute to Victory" but we end up doing a Army-Navy game."

"Rose Bowl Game."

"Correct! That could be funny, even with the All-American straightman."

"Then what, George?"

"Here's the running gimmick, fellas. The Human Radio. The Human Radio just tunes away from our play-by-play. He comes back a couple of times more and tunes through the dial."

There was a brief pause while the writers considered the possibilities.

Amos Pitz was an odd little man professionally known as "The Human Radio." He had been around since the late Twenties, doing essentially the same act in vaudeville, on the Broadway stage, internationally and, occasionally, on the radio. His act was simply this: Amos tuned across the radio dial and reproduced the sounds and voices coming out of the speaker. It was an amazing simulation. He could do CBS, NBC Red and Blue, Shortwave and the BBC. But that wasn't all he did. His ad libs in the mouths of famous radio personalities had what his agent called "wit tinged with madness." Rudy Vallee had booked him occasionally in the 30s, before his personality had fully developed. He worked in nightclubs, toured with Spike Jones. Lillie and I had seen him work at a New Years Eve performance of Ken Murray's "Blackouts of 1945."

"Pretty damn surreal," said Mel.

"Don't want it to get scary," added Dave quickly.

"Folks at home'll never get it, George." Pete re-lit his cigar.

"I like it," said Florrie. "The guy's a scream. Does a perfect Winchell, Bergan and McCarthy, Eleanor Roosevelt. Hell, he does Amos *and* Andy. So what if it's not a familiar schtick?"

"He's working at the El Capitan in the ***Blackouts***. Mad, but controlled. Funny. He's unpredictable, and it's a risk, but radio is more than singing canaries."

"What you're saying is use him to tune away from Breakfast and across the dial to, say, the music cue?"

"Or the commercial?"

"Personally, I like the singing canaries."

"Into the All-American Pageant."

"Back home to the Madhouse at the end. Transitions."

"E for Effort, fellas. Now, Dave, pass out the pages and let's make radio history!"

My writers excused themselves long before Tulley was due to arrive. Buzz checked in and I told him what we planned to do. He shrugged.

"Nobody ona East Coast is gonna have the faintest idea of where this comes in, George. Remember, same but different, same but different, every week."

"Time for a surprise, Buzz. A few surprises. Look what a hit that Benny thing about 'Anaheim, Azusa and-beat-beat Cucamonga' is. My writers already think they wrote it."

"Network Standards has gotta pass on the script, George. What are you gonna put in for the Radio guy's lines?"

"His act is written down. Or we'll get somebody to write down the funny parts of it. It'll be in the script. Most of it."

"I'll book him. Scale. We gotta budget extra time for band rehearsals, and that's with Captain Reagan. Thursday. Whole cast stays late." He opened the door to leave, first colliding with, and then exchanging hearty Hollywood handshakes with Oliver Tulley.

"Certainly good to work with you again, Buzz," said Tulley. "Well, Georgie, here's just what we need." He dropped a dog-eared script on the table and sank into a chair.

"Take a look at the end of *It Happened at the World's Fair*, Georgie. A regular, W.P.A. Post Office mural come to life at the Aquacade. Sound of bombers, chorus and orchestra. It's all right there! Reagan'll love it!"

I remembered the movie. It had opened big but too late in 1940 to cash in on the Fair publicity.

"But this was written before the War, Ollie. For Bing Crosby."

"Bing-Schming. We'll just have to up-date it a little. Sit down. Order another drink. Order a drink for me. Old Fashioned."

CHAPTER 21

ONCE IN A BLUE MOVIE

Oskar Bachmann opened the door to the stucco house overhung by a grove of drooping jacarandas. He was in his fifties, small, with large teeth, a high forehead, and he spoke with a decided accent.

"Mister Tirebiter? Welcome, please."

It was an unusual interior, with complicated plaster ornamentation painted in dark colors and gold highlights. The wall sconces were hammered copper and the walls themselves hung with oil paintings of European countrysides, and a double portrait of Bachmann himself and a young blonde woman above the sofa.

"Please." He guided me with a small soft hand toward the back of the house. "Van Os told me you are a radio clown, yes? I was myself a circus clown. Then cinema. In Budapest, before the War. You have seen *Hortobagy*?"

"No," I said.

"I worked with Hoellering in '36. Then with Bela Gaal. In, you would say, *Honeymoon at Half Price*. Do you know our cinema from Europe?"

"Hardly," I said. We walked through a door and down some stairs to a lower storey which had been invisible from the street.

"So. I have put up Carné's *Le Quai des Brumes* to begin. An essential film, Mr. Tirebiter. I brought the print across with me. Through bloody fire."

We stepped into a small but opulent screening room. Half-a-dozen rows of reclining loge seats, a plaster relief of dragons on either side of a screen not much smaller than one you'd find in a neighborhood movie house.

"Wow!"

"Yes. This was the—ah, do I say 'party house?' of Elton Thomas. A great star of the silent screen. Take a seat, Mr. Tirebiter."

Bachmann bowed slightly and disappeared through a curtained archway. The lights began to fade and a clattering projector started up, throwing a brilliant arc on the screen. The picture began. It starred a sort of French Bogart named Gabin, and was unlike anything I had ever seen, with its suggestive shadows and poetic pessimism. Throughout it, Bachmann guided my eyes to the images, commenting in a soft voice about the size of lens, placement of lights, cutting.

"There is no real cinema in America as yet, Mr. Tirebiter. Not possible in the studio system."

At last it ended and Bachmann said, "Now, sir, what you thought you came for."

He changed projectors and lowered the lights. A title card popped on the screen: A Union Job.

The first scene flickers up. Mary Murray in a wig of Pickford ringlets awakes and gets out of bed in her chemise. Title: Her First Movie Job Today—For Cecil B. Hardon. Mary does some impassioned miming, then in a giggling fit, throws her chemise over her head. She takes it off and struts naked in front of a standing mirror. Title: Pretty Swell Stuff.

Medium Closeup. Her breasts. Experimentally, she pulls at one nipple, then cups both breasts in her hands and massages them around. Medium Shot. Her eyes look glazed to me, but she might just be enjoying herself. There follows a surprising montage of her hands at play.

Abruptly we cut to an Exterior. A streetcar comes down Santa Monica Boulevard toward the camera. Ready For Work. Mary gets off the streetcar, dressed in high-topped boots, a belted coat and soft hat with a peaked brim. She looks very smart, even with the phony blond ringlets.

Cecil B. Hardon Auditions an "Actress." Another cut, this time to an office set. A couple is vigorously engaged on the couch. Both faces are turned away but nothing else is.

Closeup: Telephone. It shakes as it silently rings. Funny. Back to the couch. The man hears the phone and tears himself away from the girl. He had been wearing a jacket, vest and riding breeches before all the buttons were undone. He hops to the desk where the ringing phone is still shaking.

"My God! It's Oliver Tulley!"

"You recognize the man, Mr. Tirebiter? In spite of the mask?"

"Well, he's wearing a mustache over his own mustache, but that's the guy! I was with him this afternoon!"

Title: Saved by the Bell. The "Actress" does a take at the camera, then gets up from the couch, smoothes down her skirt and struts toward the door. Tulley looks up from the phone and says:

You're Hired!

Tulley may have a black mask and villainous mustache, but the disguise wouldn't fool anyone who knew him.

Cut to the outer office. The "Actress" is coming out of a door marked "Director." Mary is sitting in a straight chair, waiting. The "Actress" says:

Good Luck, Honey. He's a Mouthful.

"From the Indian on the nickel to the Indiana Hoo-sier,
    And don't forget the Sioux

And the Sooners who
Would sooner get to bust some Indian Territory sod
Thank God!
Than work a rail-splitting crew.
They knew America! And how they knew!"

"That's a mouthful, Ollie," I said. "But Ronnie can say anything and make people believe it."

"I'll polish it off at home tonight. Georgie. Getcha a copy by messenger after lunch tomorrow."

"Let's have a nightcap, Ollie."

"Nightcap? It's 5:30. But sure, Georgie, sure. It's all on the show. I owe ya one, old pal."

"You can pay up right now, Ollie. Talk to me about Taylor King."

"Look, Georgie, I was hoping you wouldn't be bringing up the past like this. That was a long time ago. Over and forgotten. I don't remember and I wasn't there, Georgie. Where's my damn coat?"

"Has a private detective named Max Morgan been to see you?"

"Aw, shit, Georgie!" He sank into a chair across from me.

"Me too."

He squirmed and shook his head. "I can't figure it out."

"Neither could I."

"It was a deal, Georgie. Only a deal, that's all. We had a deal going. Almost going. Me and Monte Burke. We were trying to get King to invest. That's all. Mrs. Tulley was getting seasick on that damn pirate tub, and I took her to the hotel on the island. Next thing I hear, the cops are in the lobby and would I give a statement. Knocked me over. The whole deal went dead after that. I haven't seen Burke twice from that day to this. I called him up after the dick dropped by. I got the brush-off from him, I'll tell you."

"Who do you think killed King, Ollie."

"Well, I've given a lot of thought to that. It could only have been Tommy Takasago. There was something up between him and King. Tommy could give a person the dirtiest look I ever saw. If looks could kill, right? He was on the boat, and his only alibi was he was sea-sick. Well, hell, he could've come over on the launch and got a room at the hotel, like the rest of us."

"Burke was aboard the yacht and he told me he slept through anything and everything."

"Maybe. Maybe he was part of it. Things went to hell for a lot of people after the murder, Georgie. Papers were full of stuff about drugs and Hollywood decadence. Started the Twenties off with a bang, I'll say! We never have had much of a good reputation out here—you must've known that when you joined up with Paranoid."

"Any idea where Takasago might be now, Ollie?"

"Never heard a word about him since '42. I think he got taken off a Duke

Wayne horse-opera and the Army sent him to one of those camps."

Tulley slipped into his jacket and picked up his scripts.

"Don't take any wooden ration points, Georgie. See ya around!"

DON'T WORRY I'VE BEEN AROUND.

Mary says these words in a closeup, her first.

"Wait a minute, Mr. Bachmann! Can you run that back?"

After a moment, the film runs backward and the closeup goes by, then goes by again as the projector reverses. Mary Murray looked like Stella. It wasn't Mary at all.

"That isn't Mary Murray at all, Mr. Bachmann."

"No. It is evident to a student of cinema it is Pegeen Murray, who was in Tourneur's *Prunella* and starred in *Polly of the Pig-Pen* for Cosmopolitan."

Pegeen said: READY FOR WORK MR. HARDON. And with great enthusiasm, she bent to her task.

Max Sennett Beauties (Can you find Mary Murray?)

CHAPTER 22

4TH AND PARANOID

Monday morning never dawned. Not exactly. It was the fifth straight day of rain and the sky above Toluca Lake faded up from blackout to the color of old concrete. Our pool was spilling over the edge. The morning radio news reported over seven inches had fallen since Wednesday night. I contemplated the downpour through the breakfast nook windows and drank another cup of coffee.

My dreams had been in glorious black-and-white. Jean Gabin and Pegeen Murray making love in the foggy shadows of backlot Paris. Tulley with a Groucho face and riding crop astride a starlet's back. I searched for a clue through the jumble of fleshly delights.

I was pretty sure that Takasago had been the cameraman for *A Union Job*. Bachmann noted the high quality of lighting and montage in an otherwise purely pornographic endeavor. Burke, Tulley and Takasago were in the blue movie business back in 1919, and must have been trying to get King, who was having an affair with both Murray girls, to invest in their illicit scheme.

None of that pointed toward murder. Ricky Villandros had hired Morgan to find out who had "it"—the "it" that Lillie might have inherited. Reels of film. Burke—was it a slip of the tongue?—had mentioned blackmail. The blackmailer must be the one with the film, probably also pornographic. It could only be Takasago. He had been following me, maybe others, in the antique Hudson.

As I pulled the telephone toward me, it rang.

"Mr. T? George?" It was Muriel. "Sorry to call so early, but I just got out of a meeting with my editor, and it's a go on the Murray up-date. He loved the new stuff with Todd, and has a twist to make the homosexual angle work. He said, 'Honey, we just use a few code words and those in the know get the picture, already.' I have to talk with everybody I can find before the end of the week. I just wanted to say thanks for your help, and maybe you could give me a couple of phone numbers?"

"Aren't you worried about stirring up a murderer?"

"Whoever it is, he can't be prosecuted after all this time. Besides, all I'm going to do is chat them up. If I can fit some clues together in the final story, so be it."

I reluctantly gave Muriel the phone numbers she asked for—Monte Burke and Oliver Tulley.

"Oh, by the way, Mr. T.—I traced the daughter. Pegeen had a baby in Santa Barbara eight-and-a-half months after King died. Family let out an adoption story after she married some actor named Muldoon. Named the girl Sue-Ellen. Kid graduated from Antelope Valley Unified High School in 1939. So long."

I hung up the telephone and looked at the rain. There was no where to put all this rain in Southern California. The news had ended, and relentlessly cheerful "Breakfast Clubbers" were marching around singing, "Fourth call to Breakfast," when I snapped the radio off. I poured a second cup of coffee, drank it, and regarded the phone. It finally rang.

"Georgie?"

It was Oliver Tulley.

"Hello, Ollie."

"I got housebroken."

"Come again?"

"Somebody broke in here last night. Quiet at first, then crashing around. Mrs. Tulley wanted me to go downstairs with a golf shoe in my hand, but I said, 'no deal!' Georgie, you have any in with these people, you tell them I was dead to the world in my hotel room."

"Somebody burgled you? Who?"

"How would I know?"

"Ollie, I saw *A Union Job* last night. You're a collector's item."

"Union Job?"

"It was you with the fake mustache and extra-large . . ." I paused for effect . . . "nose."

Ollie breathed deeply for a few seconds.

"You and Pegeen Murray."

"Whatever happened a hundred years ago, Georgie, it's all in your imagination. But somebody was in my house last night. You've been running around stirring things up. Movie magazine called me just a few minutes ago. Mrs. Tulley is laid up with a bad flu, Georgie. I've got blood pressure and ulcers. Private dick strongarms me on the lot. Georgie . . . I made a few investments in my time—Valley real estate did me good—a couple of nudie programmers kept the hicks humpin'. It's the Biz-ness, you know."

"How's the radio script coming, Ollie?"

"A lotta distractions, Georgie. You'll get it OK. Tulley always beats his deadline. You want to nibble your nails off, you shudda hired Corwin. Show goes on, he's still writing. But you haveta help me, Georgie."

"What could I do? Who was in your house? Who are you scared of?"

"I donno. Maybe that dick, whatsisname—Morgan . . ."

"Maybe a cameraman named Tommy Takasago?"

"You know that much, you can do something, Georgie! For Chris'sake!"

He yelped like a kicked puppy and hung up.

I crawled through the rain at 15 miles an hour. I might just as well have still been at the bottom of Linda Darnell's pool for all the good the wipers did. I finally got to Twelfth and Union, parked across from Johnnie's Grocery, pulled my collar up and hat down and ran across the street.

The door closed with a jingle. Inside, the store had a sweetish, burnt smell mixed with those of coffee and bread. The pleasant-looking grey-haired woman behind the cash register glanced up from the latest *Life* and nodded. For a second I thought I was talking to Jane Darwell.

"Excuse me," I said, my heart fluttering. "I'm looking for someone I'm very interested in employing. Maybe you can help. Cameraman named Takasago?"

"My husband bought this store back in '42 from some Japanese by that name." She didn't look up from a map of Poland cris-crossed with the red arrows of armies on the march. "Japanese all went out to the camps. Never seen any of 'em since. Was it you called me last night?"

"That's right. My name is George Tirebiter and I'm at Paranoid Pictures. I'm starting on a movie next week, saw some of Tommy's work and . . ."

"Japanese don't live around here anymore. Army and FBI saw to that. Or have you been asleep since Pearl Harbor?"

I played another card. "Say, one other thing. That's a swell old Hudson out back. It still running?"

The lady put down her magazine and glared at me over her bifocals. "My son goes on errands for me in it, when we can get the gas. Lucky to have it. Now, Mr. Tirebiter, unless you're shopping here, I'd like to say good-bye to you."

"Well, if Tommy drops in, you tell him to get in touch with me over at the studio. Nice chatting with you, ma'am."

Back in my own car, it came to me. The burnt wood smell. It was incense. What do they call it? Joss sticks. Not something little old ladies usually kept burning in the back room. I pulled through the alley behind the store. This time there was no car parked in the driveway—just a spreading rainbow slick as a large oilspot washed away toward Pico Boulevard.

Nick, the gateman at Paranoid's churriguersque main gate gave me a salute as I drove onto the lot. The usually busy "streets" which ran between soundstages were empty of people and full of rainwater searching for a drain.

Monday I'd be doing interiors on *First WAC In Tokyo* until if and when our Tropical Paradise set dried out. Judy Shay, Basil Brewster and a terrific old biddy type named Jane K. Loofbourrow were scheduled to do the family scenes. Judy and her younger sister, played by one Little Patsy Clancy, were recording the music they would later lip-sync, and I needed to drop in and meet the tyke and her mother.

The red wig-wag outside the recording stage halted and I went in. Everyone was perked up for a playback of the "sweet" song, "(You'll Have) Chocolates Tomorrow." I was listening with my eyes closed—an old radio habit—when I felt a warm hand on mine.

"Hello, George Tirebiter," whispered a warm voice. When I opened my eyes I was gazing into a warm pair of baby blues. It was the red-haired cellist from Elysium.

"Oh! Hello, again, Miss . . ."

"Ruth Talmage. Isn't this a surprise!"

She looked terrific with her clothes on—a smart blue suit and honey-gold blouse. I put a finger to my lips and we listened to the rest of the song. The Musical Director, Herbert Dreihertz, gave a thumbs up and everyone politely applauded the two young singers.

I did my duty, patted Little Patsy on the head, shook her mother's hand, hugged Judy, nodded approvingly to the orchestra and signed off on the take. Someone handed me a bottle of Coke and I swigged at it, listening to a run-down of the "hot" number, "Chewing Gum Boogie." Ruth Talmage hovered a few feet away, putting her cello in its case, drinking a glass of water, tapping her foot. I left the stage as the bell rang for Take One. Ruth was right behind me.

"I wish the sun would shine," she said. "I want to take my clothes off. How 'bout you?" With that, she lifted her cello over her head and walked away down 4th St. toward Little Old Chicago.

I jumped puddles on the way to the Writers' Building, went up to Ollie Tulley's office and knocked. Not there. If he was on the lot he'd probably be parked in a space with his name on it somewhere nearby. Parking was on the other side of the old wooden shanty the Boss reserved for His Writers. I made my way around on the run and nearly slammed into the side of an old brown sedan.

"Oh, boy!"

The Hudson Terraplane was pulled up to the shingle that read "O. TULLEY.

One steamy window cranked down a foot and Wild Bull Casey stuck his froggy head out.

"Tailbiter! Good thing you ran into me. Get in."

"Thanks a lot, but no . . ."

Casey cranked the window down some more and showed me a big silver automatic.

" . . . thanks," I said. The door opened, and I slid in.

CHAPTER 23

THE WORLD OF THE FUTURE

Wild Bull Casey was hunched up in a corner of the back seat, dressed in a woman's black-and-white-checked suit, modest heels and a suede Daché hat with a veil, which he pushed back before offering me his hand.

"Casey. You 'member me, Tilebiber. Office a Secret Fax. This is a disguise. Got the idea that night we met in the Bowl. Dress like a woman, get it? Nobody'll suspect. And it's fun! Everybody in the office goes nuts when I walk in wearing these getups. Wife hates it! You know Dutch Reagan?"

The soldier in the driver's seat started the car, put it in reverse, and turned to look back at us. He certainly seemed to be Ron Reagan.

"Hello, George," he said.

We were off the lot in a few minutes, purring west along Santa Monica Boulevard. The early-Depression Hudson was a fake, judging by the deep, muffled sound of the engine and the glossy leather of the seats.

"Howja like to be the President, Georgie Porgie?"

"But I'm an actor . . ."

Casey and Reagan guffawed.

"Hell, kiddo!" He held up his leg, fashionably silk-stockinged. "Who ain't?"

"I told you that things are coming to a head with the Guilds, George," said Reagan. "I can promise you there won't be a single Red working anywhere in Hollywood by 1950. Actors will be the cleanest professionals in the country. Salesmen for America."

"Who's more famous than a movie actor, Timebuyer? Only Generals. FDR won't last forever, Truman's a nobody, so it's MacArthur in '48. Or maybe Patton. Patton made the cover a *Life* last week, smilin' like a cat. We're gonna get a war hero. After that it's up for grabs, and we're gonna grab it by the gonads. By '56 Dutch here could be a Senator. By '64 he could be President. Hughes likes him, but we're lookin' at a lot of guys. You too, Tireflier!"

Reagan turned and smiled like a cat. "You dance, don't you, George?"

"A little."

"What this country needs is a President who can tap-dance."

"Cohan was perfect." Ron laughed. Casey burbed and burbled.

"You an' Dutch've got a hand on the radio stuff. FDR invented those damn Firehouse chats. We need a guy, he'll say anything, the country believes it."

"Don't forget television, Col. Casey. George, can you imagine a day when everyone in the whole world can watch the Rose Bowl Game all at the same time?"

"Day's comin' when you can carry a radio around in yer hand, listen to yer show comin' atcha recorded on a damn piece of wire!"

Talk of television and wire recording made my palms wet.

"Listen, fellas—I'm flattered you think I have something to contribute, but I'm not an under-cover sort of guy."

"You never contributed to some damn Red-Labor-Saves-the-Slavs thing, didja?"

"One of us is going to get in, George. Right to the top. I'm betting on Duke Wayne or Jimmy Stewart. But it could be you. Or me."

"Maybe just Vice-President," I said. "Sounds like high enough for a B-movie man."

The duo guffawed again, and Casey's hat slid sideways across one bug-eye.

We splashed along Santa Monica, sat still for a slow-moving freight train and turned South on La Cienega. I had only had one previous hallucination in my life—a fever dream when I was seven or eight in which I imagined myself floating above my dead body. It was no worse than this. My mind raced through a dozen opening gambits, but my throat was too dry to try them. Finally, I squeezed out:

"Why was he wearing a duck suit?"

"He went mad, George," said Reagan.

"Unstable mind. Gonna wear a disguise, you shouldn't stand out," said Casey, straightening his seams.

"You didn't . . . you didn't . . ."

"He was a mole."

"I thought he was a duck."

"Mole, George. Counter-counter espionage."

"Good boy gone bad, Georgie Porgie," said Casey. "Top secret."

We had turned East along Beverly. Here in the flats of Los Angeles the streets ran deep with water from curb to curb.

"Start big, George. Run for vice-president of AFRA. Help turn the tide."

"Ron, didn't you used to be a liberal?"

Casey snorted. "He was the other one."

I was still trying to figure that one out when the sedan pulled up outside Paranoid's side gate.

"See you on the radio, George," said Reagan. Or was he the other one?

I stood in the rain as the car pulled away. It had a military license plate. OSF✳MAN 1. The chilly water beat on my hat and ran off the brim and down my neck. The hallucination faded off into the late afternoon gloom.

CHAPTER 24

LOVE NEST

By Tuesday, the whole of Southern California was fed up with the rain. According to H. V. Kaltenborn, even the morale of factory workers was being affected by the grey skies and heavy storms. The Los Angeles River was raging between its cement banks. If the city had any basements, they would have been flooded.

I plodded through the day, trying to sort out reality from dreams and visions which, like the clouds, refused to dissipate. The studio production accountants were figuring the moving of arc lamps and camera cranes from one place to another. The routine parts of "Madhouse" had been rehearsed one time too often, and the rest of the script had not arrived by noon, as per Tulley's contract. My writers had "improved" a couple of jokes into insensibility. Our coffee intake was "good to the last jangle."

A note arrived from Lemming's office asking me to come up with a one-pager on an all-girl *Beau Geste*. "Try and work in a couple of musical spots," it ended.

About four, which was indistinguishable from two, or noon, my telephone rang and blew a Tropical Paradise into my ear.

"Sorry our dinner date didn't end with a nightcap at my place," whispered Stella Sue King, her voice soaked in deadly gardenia.

Only Stella's real name was Sue-Ellen Muldoon, after her first step-father, an older Younger Leading Man named Dickie Muldoon, who faded both out of her life and off the screen around 1930.

"So am I, Stella. I tried to get you off the hook with Uncle Rickey with that remark about optioning your novel. Then I figured he probably didn't know you were S. S. Van Dyke anyway. Sorry."

"He thinks because Mickey Cohen and George Raft eat at his place he's some kind of a gangster."

"Gangsters, cops, beautiful dames . . . we're all actors here," I said in my radio voice, full of age, experience and self-pity.

"How about that nightcap tonight? We could have cocktails first, it's almost time."

"It's been about that time all day, Stella. I thought you were with your mother out behind God's back."

"I came in with Rickey this afternoon. Momma was on the phone with someone early this morning and her blue mood lifted right away. Wouldn't say who called, just 'an old friend.' So I thought I could get away, back to my own place. Take a bath, have a drink and see you again."

There were a lot of things I thought I had to tell her, so I began by telling her I'd be right over.

Stella was still in the bath when I arrived. A note pinned to the apartment door said "Open Me." Another on the kitchen door read "Push Me." The Frigidare was hung with "Get Me Out." I got out a frozen bottle of something with a Norwegian label and two small icy glasses. "Please Knock" it said on the bathroom door. I did.

There was a splash and she said, "Come in, George." I did.

Stella Sue was up to her neck in bubble bath. A rose-tinted lamp set in back of an aristocratic pair of ceramic flamingos warmed the light and the small room smelled of lavender.

"Put down the aquavit. It's hot."

"No, it's ice cold."

"No, it's hot. I stole it from Bill, my stepfather." She giggled and the bubbles rippled. Her knees broke the surface and rose like white sand beaches.

I put the glasses down on the edge of the sink, on a border of blue and white tiles, and filled them. The toilet lid was closed, which I took as an open invitation to sit next to the bathtub. She reached an arm up from the suds to take her glass. Most of one breast followed the arm. Pearl of the Antilles.

"Joan Crawford took a bubble bath in *The Women*. I was eighteen when I saw it. Skoal."

The stuff tasted like ninety-proof Russian rye bread. We downed two loaves. I loosened my tie.

"I'm beginning to wrinkle up, George. Hand me that towel."

She rose in an avalanche of sudsy water and stood with her hands on her hips. Birth of Venus. I grabbed the liquor and fled.

We made love without speaking and then slept. When I awoke, the little radium-tipped hands of the bedside clock were as one. I gathered my clothes and dressed. I was trying to decide whether to leave without waking Stella when she spoke, in that hard-boiled-detective voice of hers.

"Do you know yet who killed my father, George?"

"No." I sat back on the edge of the bed. Stella pulled the sheet up around her throat. "I think it was a business deal gone sour, Stella. Tulley says the cameraman did it, but I think he was only a junior partner. I'm having trouble seeing Monte Burke doing it, but he's a good possibility. There were some pornographic movies involved. Burke may have stolen them from King and then blackmailed him with them."

"Aunt Mary's famous fling? I mentioned it to Momma once and she called it 'vile gossip.'"

"No, I think it must have been something else. Your . . ." I gave it some thought . . . She lay there in bed, her black hair loose and her face like a cupid's heart. How could I tell her I'd just seen her Momma in lace knickers with a face full of Ollie Tulley's villainous black mustache? "Your Aunt Mary's flicker is still around, if you have the money and the inclination to see it. These were something else—movies King may have been paying money to suppress."

"And you think Monte Burke killed Daddy and stole these movies?"

"Somebody stole them, and whoever it was, he was probably the killer. That's as far as I can make it go, Stella. I'm not a detective, and anyway, there's a detective already in it, trying to find the missing evidence. And I may have been stupid."

She frowned. "With me, you mean?"

"Are you working on a book, Stella?"

"Yes. They'd like me to do two a year."

"Get back to it. Lay low. Let this business come to a head without you in the middle of it."

"And without you?"

"For a while." That sounded like a lie to me, and I had to make my exit quickly for fear of really acting stupid. "Good bye."

"Thanks for the memories, George," she said, slipping down into her pillows and pulling the white satin spread up and over her head.

CHAPTER 25

THE SCENE OF THE CRIME

The phone rang again. Buzz Melnik at CBS. Tulley's script was now a day and two hours late. Ray Knight was working up from frantic to hysterical about the underscoring. I suggested he rehearse the band and chorus in the Army Air Corps Song and "Battle Hymn of the Republic," and said I'd try to reach Ollie on the lot.

It was Wednesday afternoon and I was fighting off a tendency for the movie and the radio show to merge together into "Hollywood WACHouse" as I sat in my office at Paranoid and went over the pages for the first week's shoot. It was still raining in L. A., and all the exteriors, including three musical routines, had been put off indefinitely. The choreographer was reworking a tap number for the Mess Tent set.

Ollie didn't answer at home. I sent a messenger to his cubby-hole in the Writers Building. Not there.

Of course our WAC wasn't actually going to be the first WAC in Tokyo. She would, in the picture's last line, promise to try and be there when the time came. We were taking that last line first, against a rear projection of the Stars and Stripes, next Tuesday morning. Spunky Judy Shay, who has just been upgraded to corporal and promoted to the General's secretary, would either say "Pretty soon our front line's gonna go right through the Emperor's living room. And when it does, I'll be there!" or "First WAC in Tokyo! Sure! And behind me a whole planeload of the best gals America has to offer!"

I was trying to come up with something better when the phone rang again.

"Mr. T? George? It's Muriel." She paused, caught her breath and gasped "Help!"

"What's up?"

"He's dead! Just a . . ." she covered the mouthpiece and said, "Just a minute! I told you he was. Well, call them! Oh!"

"Muriel?"

"George, I have to call the police. This is the only phone. I'm at the El Patio Motel on Ventura, across from Republic. Please meet me!"

The clouds were low and heavy as I crossed over the Cahuenga Pass and the Valley stretched out ahead, shadowless and dull as chewing gum. Republic Pictures was a couple of miles farther West than Universal—a cluster of stages on the south bank of the L. A River that had once boasted of Mack Sennett and the Little Rascals.

The El Patio was easy to find. Three black-and-white LAPD sedans were parked randomly in front, and the slowly spinning red light of an ambulance flashed periodically down the driveway and turned the street into a sea of blood.

The motel was a modest one-storey adobe square, tiled-roofed and half-covered by a giant, bedraggled bougainvillea. Grey, beefy succulents cascaded out of baskets hanging from the archways. I parked in front of a used-car lot across the street and followed the crimson beacon into the courtyard. I almost got there, too.

"Yeah?" The blue-uniformed officer stopped me with a large red hand on my chest.

"Is there a Miss Albers here?"

"Who's that? Guest, maid, B-girl, what?"

"She called you guys! Is she OK?" I must've pushed back at the Officer's hand, because he shoved me harder than he had to against the picturesquely jagged adobe wall.

"You better have a good reason for being here, pal."

"I'm George Tirebiter!" I said, as loudly as I dared.

"Mr. Tirebiter?!" It was Muriel. She emerged from the "Office" door, with another Officer at her heels. "Gosh! I'm so glad you're here!"

Visions of handcuffs danced in my head . . .

Two uncomfortable hours later we were eating sandwiches at Du-Pars, a few blocks down Ventura at Laurel Canyon. Muriel gave me her side of the story, between bites:

"He told me to meet him there at four, and I didn't give a thought to it, except I was surprised he called because he'd acted before like he really didn't want to talk to me. Anyway, I came out on the bus and it was very foggy and gloomy when I walked up the driveway and came into the patio part—where the cars are parked. There were three cars—a Rolls Royce and a little MG sports car and an old truck. The Rolls was in front of Number 8, that's where he said to meet him, and there was a light on in the window. There was a light on in the Office window, too. I made sure, just in case. And then I thought, Am I taking a big risk here? After all, it was a real murder, not an accident."

"Was it? Are you sure?"

"Of course. My money's on the mother. She must've hated King for . . ." She shook her head. "What he did to those girls."

"There's more about Pegeen," I said, and wished I hadn't.

"Tell me," said Muriel.

"It wasn't Mary Murray in the stag film after all. It was Pegeen. My host is a connoisseur of things like that, and he assures me it's a well-known fact in art film circles."

"Was it horrible?"

"Horrible! You just fell over a dead body lying in a pool of blood! That's more horrible than anything I saw in that movie."

"It wouldn't have been so horrible if I hadn't stepped in the blood. I never saw his face at all. I knocked and the door swung open and I stepped in and there he was. I looked down and it was like a red rug. One of those oval hooked rugs. Only it was blood and I was standing in it."

I put down my chicken salad on rye. "Spare me the coroner's report, Muriel. Go back to your theory. King was undoubtedly sleeping with both sisters and probably got the seventeen-year-old pregnant. You think Mrs. Murray avenged her daughters' honors with a silk blackjack?"

"You have to admit it gives *Screen Secrets* a good reason to feature a 25th Anniversary spread."

"Why didn't you tell Lt. Wassisname what you think?"

"A reporter protects her sources. Including you. Why didn't you mention the missing movie?"

"My wife's involved in this somehow. She could still be in danger, and more than she could know about."

Muriel sighed. "Thanks for coming to my rescue, Mr. T."

"Look, Muriel . . . I haven't been as, ah . . . candid with you about my . . . researches as I should. I believe that there was a—what you might call 'smut ring' aboard the Mystery Girl. Burke, Tulley, King and Takasago were in on it. Even Pegeen. They probably drugged her. There was a falling out among the partners and I think one Little Indian got the drop on King and pushed him overboard."

"There is now one less Little Indian."

"And one of the other Little Indians has what he's wanted since 1920. A couple of thousand feet of 16 millimeter nitrate film, assuming that's what was in those empty Bekins Van and Storage boxes the cops showed you."

"You may be right." She smiled and finished her coffee. "But I may be right too."

"Muriel, I did some poking around and I may have poked Tommy Takasago too hard. If the film was enough to kill for, then maybe he's all through killing. But maybe not. I'm going to drive you home. Close the door and start writing. Don't open the door for strangers."

"Strangers? Somehow when Basil Brewster opened his motel room door, I don't think he saw a stranger standing there at all." Muriel shuddered. "He saw an old pal with a rusty bayonet in his hand."

CHAPTER 26

THE HIDEOUT

The stabbing of Basil Brewster made the Thursday morning papers, and the grisly image of the bayonet and Muriel's bloody footprints on El Patio's patio struck the tabloids as perfect accompaniment to my morning cup of coffee.

I had escaped the reporters who clustered around the "murder scene" by waiting until Brewster's body was being hauled out by the men in white, and then ducking through a laundry-room service entrance to the alley. Muriel hadn't been so fortunate. The *Mirror* photog caught her walking next to a grinning police detective, looking distraught, and then blinded her with his flash.

Film fan magazine writer Muriel Albers, 28, discovered the former actor's body when she arrived to question him about a sensational Hollywood murder case some twenty-five years unsolved by the LAPD.

"Mr. Brewster was there when it happened," said Miss Albers, "I was anxious to see if he could shed any light on the Taylor D'Arcy King mystery for **Screen Secrets**. *We've already uncovered some exciting new facts."*

The quote lay framed in sunshine on the breakfast nook table. It took a second to recognize the bright stuff for what it was—a crack in the overcast and a beam of warmth. A spotlight on Muriel.

That frightened me. I had to call Lt. Wassisname at the Studio City precinct, tell him what I knew about Takasago. A man-hunt, a posse, a mobilization of our forces . . .

The telephone jangled.

"George, dear."

"Lillie, darling! I was just hoping you'd call. How's Dad?"

"He doesn't remember my name. He doesn't seem to know I'm there, except sometimes he'll ask for some water. Once he asked for a toothbrush. He insisted on it, and I got one for him and he was so angry. He said it wasn't a toothbrush, it was too big for a toothbrush. He wanted a match, really, to light his cigar. Of course he didn't have a cigar either."

"I'm sorry."

"George," her voice was shaking with some kine of emotion, "Basil's murder was in the *Tribune* this morning."

"I'm sorry about that too, Lillie."

"It changes everything. I'm coming home. I've got a commercial flight from Chicago tonight, arriving at Burbank Airport in time for me to make the West Coast broadcast. Can you write me back in?"

"You've only got an off-mike scream on page 4, Lillie. We cut the newsboy bit to go out on a big patriotic note with Reagan, but I'll see what I can add. I'll have a studio car pick you up and bring you directly to CBS. Buzz is going to hate us for this, you know."

"The show must etcetera, George."

I took a stab in the dark. "Did you find what you were looking for back there, Lillie?" I heard her breathing.

"I told you not to meddle in this thing." Her voice was chillier than Lake Michigan in January. "I told you it would be dangerous to dig anything up. It's killed one innocent person already."

"Somebody else is stirring things up, Lillie. Now I'm worried for you. You're in danger."

"Not if I do what I need to do. Stay out of it. Please, George, just stay out."

Why was she slamming the door in my face? "I'm too far in," I said.

"See you on the radio, George."

The long distance line went dead. The moment to have called Lt. Wassisname passed with an empty click and the waspish buzzing of a million miles of copper wire.

Boris Karloff was laughing. It was a nice laugh, and not the one he would be using later on "Suspense." We nodded at one another as he left the CBS greenroom with his director, Bill Spier. I was not laughing. Ollie Tulley's script was still among the missing. The housekeeper reported Mrs. Tulley had gone to Palm Springs to nurse the flu. Of Mr. Tulley she hadn't the faintest.

I found my writers in the second-floor conference room trying to justify eight extra string players, two solo singers in addition to the Knightsmen and the Knightengales, and a contract with the U. S. Government for the use of a certain Capt. R. Reagan, USAAC.

Florrie, who was dressed for the occasion in a Royal Hawaiian pink shirt emblazoned with white leis, had come up with a sketch about a bomber pilot getting sent back from Heaven to be a hero, more than a little based on *Here Comes Mr. Jordan*, and he and Mel were vigorously trying to spin it off as a movie vehicle for Reagan and Jack Benny when I sent them all down to Nick's, the office bar on Gower, a block away.

Manny, Moeski and Yackov, the three AFRA dialecticians, had left me a thank-you note and the news that, based on the "boffo laffs" they had received, they were "hashing around" a "Brothers" act, and would I consider using them in my next Paranoid feature? "See you on the radio," they added, and I had a grisly vision of five-dollar extras ad libbing through my carefully scripted lines.

The rain had really finally stopped and Bill Most called from the backlot to let me know "the damn rubber plants look like a real tropical island jungle, but the damn cardboard waterfall looks like a wad of paper-mashay, which is what it was, more or less. How about we build an outdoor shower stall out of bamboo? Judy sings while she soaps."

I thought the Army censors would have a problem with that. Bill did too and we agreed on more potted palms.

Film-moppet Little Kelly Clancy (or whatever her name was)'s schoolteacher called to say "the little bitch has a cold and she deserves it!" The moppet would probably not be "available" for work on Monday and could we shoot around her? We could not, I said, and we would dub her lines in later.

I paged through the Academy directory, looking at Characters & Comedians, trying to find a suitable replacement for Brewster, who would be available for viewing not in my picture, but at Cairn & O'Dell's Funeral Home on Saturday afternoon. I made a few phone calls and settled on Ralph Morgan—a dead ringer for his brother Frank and used to working in programmers. His latest picture was something called **Weird Women** at Universal.

That done, I called Muriel to see if she was okay. She claimed to be hard at work on her story and rather abruptly said "So long, Mr. T!" and hung up.

Lillie called me again, collect, from Chicago where our recent storm system was now dumping an inch or so of rain on their airport. "Just checking in, darling. I'll be there, don't worry," she said.

Oliver Tulley called at three-fifteen. "How come, if I work with you twice in five years, Georgie, the first time I get screwed and the second time somebody wants to kill me?"

"Where are you, Ollie? The band's been on a break so long they won't be sober enough to play the background music! Where's the script?"

"It's finished. I've got it. I had ta hide out, Georgie, after the break-in and then the Basil Brewster thing. I know I'm late, but you can come over and pick it up."

"Where?"

"I got a partnership in this auto court on Glendale Boulevard, 2500 block, near Silver Lake. Go all the way to the back cabin on the left."

On the East side of Hollywood a series of low hills and narrow valleys interrupts the North-South grid of streets, and miles of bungalows line curving streets embellished with parallel stands of tall tropical palm trees. The afternoon sun was

SILVER LAKE AUTO COURT

AUTO COURT

2500 GLENDALE BOULEVARD — LOS ANGELES, CALIFORNIA

Silver Lake Auto Court postcard.

drying the streets and turning the stucco and tile-roofed houses gold. Sunset on Sunset.

I turned north off the Boulevard onto Alvarado and blended into Glendale Boulevard a few blocks later. The auto court was on the right, just past a block of derelict buildings that had once barely contained the Keystone Komedy of Charlie Chaplin, who had made his first one-reelers there in 1915.

I was trying to keep comedy on my mind as I pulled into the driveway and threaded my way past a dozen green cabins which looked exactly the same, like Monopoly houses. The right rear was No. 38. It was distinguished by a vast, spiky pyrocantha, stretching its limbs from porch-pillar half-way around the building, and the front steps were covered with crushed red berries. As I opened the screen door, Ollie Tulley swung the inside one open, pulled me in, latched the screen with a hook-and-eye and shut the inside door firmly, turning a skeleton key in the lock.

We said, "Anybody follow you?" and "Nobody followed me," simultaneously.

"Sit down, George. I'll take the bed. There's only one chair. There's the script, anyway, on the table."

Ollie's portable typewriter was open on the knee-high night-table, a dozen or so white pages stacked on top of it. I sat carefully on the two-dollar chair and picked the script up, weighing it in my hand.

"This better be long enough for the spot, Ollie."

"It is, it is. Use a lotta music, you know, take the swells up for fifteen-twenty seconds on the cross-fades, you'll eat up two minutes if you need it. Look at it. Look at it!"

The script started: MUSIC IN: A FANFARE. SEVEN OR EIGHT RINGING TRUMPET CALLS, ECHOING ANTIPHONALLY.

"Echoing antiphonally, Ollie?"

"Yeah. Good, huh? Go on."

The script continued: JOINED BY STRINGS, ENDING IN A TRIUMPHANT CHORD.

"I knew you had a big band, Georgie, so I used 'em."

The script went on: THEN, WITHOUT TRANSITION, A MOURNFUL MARCH WITH KETTLEDRUMS UNDER.

"I think kettledrums under come extra, Ollie. Look, half the page is gone and you haven't come to the end of the music cue yet."

"Read on."

THE MARCH FADES UNDER THE NARRATOR.

"Finally," I said.

"Reagan's the Narrator."

"That part I got, thanks." I read on. Happily, the Narrator spoke:

'The wind was an ice-covered gauntlet among the gusting clouds,
The moon was a ghostly battleship tossed between purple shrouds,
The road through the night-sky was moonlight over the endless seas,
And the bomber-squad came flying,
Flying, flying,
The bomber-squad came flying, up to the Japanese!'

"Ollie, this is an old poem about the Highwayman."

"I know. Stuck with me all these years. A lot better than that Crosby stuff anyway, which was pretty much Walt Whitman with a New Orleans beat to it. This fits Ronnie Reagan like a new Ike jacket."

"I hope so, or he'll end up dead in the Pacific with Manny, Moeski and Yackov as his guardian angels."

"Basil Brewster sure as hell never had a guardian angel worth the name."

"Who killed him, Ollie? It must've been Takasago, for the reels of film. What were they?"

"What do I know? I only was in on that one, *A Union Job*. I only did that because I had the hots for Pegeen and I put in the most money. Every dime I made from writing a Houdini serial, I put in because Burke convinced me we'd make fifty thousand dollars in six months renting out prints."

"You were on the yacht that night trying to get money out of King?"

"King had something over Pegeen, and she wanted to do more of 'em, but made up to look like Mary. There was a terrible feud between the two girls. Just bare-ass jealousy, I'll bet. Anyway, sure, Burke thought he was onto a money-maker and wanted to make another quickie before the magic wore off, whatever it was. We pitched it, and after Mrs. Tulley and I went back to the hotel, he was gonna pitch it some more."

"What did Mrs. Tulley make of all this?"

"Georgie, that was my only indiscretion in forty years of marriage. I swear to you! Believe me!"

"How was Takasago involved?"

"Well, he was cameraman and editor on *Union Job*, of course. That was after hours. Liked it. 'I have a taste for this,' he told me. He was King's eyes on those last three big flickers of his before the murder. Got a nomination for *Under New Mexico Skies* in '31, so you know he was good. They had something cookin', though, after hours too, King and the Jap. I don't know what, Georgie. Honest."

"Then why are you afraid he's after you, too, Ollie? Don't you think he has what he wanted? The films that Brewster took out of storage?"

"Sure. I guess so. Look, Georgie, I was Monte's partner once or twice over the years, but I'm completely in the dark about any more stag reels back in 1919. And, Georgie," he said, sliding off the bed onto his knees, "Keep it quiet I'm back here. I did your show on Grand National's time. I owe them a Jack Ingram oater. Texas Rangers."

He reached up a hand and I shook it, grabbed the thirteen pages of "The Bomber Squad Came Flying, Flying" and headed back to CBS to have it mimeo'd, distributed and in rehearsal before our budget was blown to the tune of one entire additional program.

CHAPTER 27

DRAWING ROOM COMEDY

Rehearsal ran late. By the time I left the studio, the Moon was up, and its light, spangled by frost in the stratosphere, illuminated the white letters of the HOLLYWOODLAND sign that stretched across the bare flank of Mt. Lee and iced the igloo dome of the distant Observatory. Its phosphorescent reflection on the hood of Lillie's Lincoln blurred in my eyes for a second, as I bent to open the door.

It was hedging down toward a big Southland freeze. I slipped in, sat as lightly as possible on the crackly leather seat, started the car and let it idle, hoping the heater would kick in. I clicked on the radio and picked up the Frost Warnings—a government service to orchardists in the hinterlands of the city who would be firing up the smudge pots to warm their trees tonight.

"Ontario, 29. Pomona, 29. La Verne, 30. Cucamonga, 30. Claremont, 29. Chino, 31. Upland, 28 . . ."

The scorecard of orange blossom communities continued as I pulled out of the parking lot into El Centro, holding the steering wheel with my right hand, the sleeve of my coat protecting me from the frozen plastic.

"Turn left, Tirebiter."

It was Max Morgan. When I felt what I guessed was a gun stuck into my neck, I turned left.

"Where's the little woman?"

"Some detective you are, Morgan."

"I might say the same thing about you, Tirebiter. Go south on Vine. You were telling me where yer wife is. I thought you was all one big radio family."

"She's off this week. What's it all about, Morgan? How long have you been out here?"

"Long enough to freeze my ass off. I saw the Army take yer movie star home a hour ago."

I stopped for a signal and started to turn around. The frozen O of the gun barrel poked at me and I turned back ahead. I kept on driving south on Vine, past the mansions of Rossmore, and was ordered to jog left on Wilshire to

Western. The Frost Warnings were over and the radio had returned to "that Rockin' Chair Lady, Mildred Bailey, already in progress." Mildred was singing "Prisoner of Love."

"Is this a kidnapping, Morgan?"

"It's a surprise party. Right on Western."

A couple of miles further south, Morgan poked me again, and I turned into Barclay Square—an enclave of private streets in the Adams District—a haven for the oldest of Old L. A. money. The gloomy brick houses had been fashionable about the time Irving Berlin revived Ragtime.

"That one at the end. Park around the back."

Now Bailey was singing "I Love To Take Orders From You." Art was aping life at too high a level of coincidence for me. I switched the receiver off and pulled into the carriage-way of a turreted Victorian. Three storeys of stained and faceted glass windows, complete with not one but two iron deer grazing on the moon-lit lawn. The service entrance opened out of a low brick ell to the rear. The door was open and warm yellow light fell on me as I parked.

"Get out. Cocktails and can-a-pees is served inside."

The gun poked me again, but at least the barrel had warmed up on the drive, along with everything but my stomach. It contained a snowball with a rock at its heart.

Morgan walked behind me into the house, through a tastefully modern kitchen and into an oak-paneled hallway. I caught sight of him as we passed a gold-framed mirror. If he'd shaved before dinner, his face gave no evidence of it now. Off the hall to the right a pair of doors opened into a large sitting room decorated in a gaudy stage-set manner. Before I saw them, I knew my hosts must be Rickey and Iris Villandros.

Rickey stood and held out his hand. He looked even more like Ralph Bellamy in a wine-colored velvet smoking jacket and soft grey gabardine slacks.

"Drink, Tirebiter? I don't think you've met Iris, my wife."

Iris was curled up in a wing chair. She wore a shiny white-legged lounging outfit in the Marlene Dietrich vein, and she nodded at me, tall Scotch and soda in her small pink hand.

"What she's having, Uncle Rickey."

"I'll make it." A deeply tanned man in his sixties was standing at the drinks wagon. Cowboy boots, a head full of salt-and-pepper hair, and a Western-cut suit coat gave him a matured Randolph Scott air. I figured I was outclassed three-to-one by the ersatz star-power.

Randolph Scott said, "Bill Gilbert," and handed me a tumbler of Johnny Walker with ice and a splash of soda.

"You're Pegeen Murray's husband."

"Get the dick out of here," said Gilbert, glaring at Max Morgan, who stood by the open doors like a butler from Central Casting, listening to his beard grow.

"Thanks for making the pick-up, Max," said Rickey. "Go have a cup of coffee or something for a few minutes. Shut the doors, okay?"

"Sure, Mr. Villandros. How about I make it a beer?"

"Sure, sure. Just shut the doors."

Morgan went. The doors clicked smoothly behind him. I sat down in a comfy armchair matching Iris's and took a long sip of whiskey. It was warm enough to start my stomach thawing.

"Where's Lillie, Mr. Tirebiter?" Iris had a chirpy little-girl voice that put me in mind of her *Screen Secrets* photo—the one with the white rabbit.

"She's out-of-town, Mrs. Villandros."

"We expected to see both of you after your rehearsal tonight," put in Bill Gilbert in a chummy sort of Will Rogers drawl.

"She had important personal business."

"I'll bet she did. In Chicago," chirped Iris. The three exchanged what I took to be a significant look.

"Is that correct, Mr. Tirebiter?" drawled Gilbert, looking at the pointy toes of his shiny boots.

"I think I know most of what's going on here, folks. Why don't you include me in a little. Then I'll make room for you."

Another exchange of loaded glances.

"My wife has disappeared from our home out in Pearblossom. My step-daughter isn't in her apartment, and we have good reason to think they might be together. Have you heard anything from Stella?"

"Nothing since Tuesday evening."

"Peg seems to have taken one of our cars and driven off early Wednesday. She's a near-invalid, Mr. Tirebiter, and she never drives herself, so her absence came as a surprise and a shock. She spoke to your wife on the telephone Tuesday morning. I thought she might have come in to see her."

"Lillie's been gone since last Saturday. She must have called from Chicago." I shut my mouth hard, but the name had still popped out.

Ralph, Marlene and Randolph exchanged theatrical nods.

"See, Bill?" said Iris. "Lillie called to tell her she'd found it. You said she was happy as a clam afterward."

"You're right, Iris," I said. "At least I'm reasonably sure you are. Whatever it was she went to Chicago to find, she found it. It's coming back with her tomorrow on American Airlines. My bet is that it's some movies no one here wants anybody to see. That would be fine with me if poor old Basil Brewster hadn't been killed for more of the same. That makes me worry about Lillie."

"Poor old Basil Brewster!" Bill Gilbert snorted and refilled his drink. "He was a pervert, Tirebiter. Good riddance!"

"I'll protect your wife," said Villandros. "I'll put two of my boys next to her the minute she sticks her toe off the plane. If she's got what she went for, they'll take it off her hands. No danger in that."

"Not unless she doesn't want to give the film to them."

"Mr. Tirebiter." Iris stretched her glacial legs, toes pointed, to the floor, touched them down and rose. She was barely five feet tall. She walked the few steps to Uncle Rickey and allowed him to fold his arms around her, protectively. She had my attention all the way. "Neither Lillie nor I knew Mrs. Ames had possession of these—films. We thought they had been destroyed in 1920. The first hint they might exist came in a phone call to Pegeen a couple of weeks ago. The caller didn't identify himself, but she recognized his voice."

"Tommy Takasago," I said.

"Yes. He said they still existed, and that if we didn't pay some money to him, he'd make them public. Of course, Pegeen called me immediately and I told Rickey. He put an operative on the job to investigate."

"Max Morgan. Hell of a guy."

"He's not one of my personal hard numbers," put in Uncle Rickey. "But he's done a couple of jobs for me, quick and quiet."

"Both Morgan and Takasago had the same idea, didn't they?" I was putting the twos and twos back together again, same but different. "Scare up some action and find out who really had the film. Surprise! It looks like there was more than one print."

"Apparently." Bill Gilbert took back the floor. "Brewster has been sitting on a copy all these years, assuming the storage boxes they found where he was killed contained what Takasago wanted. I thought that your wife might have them, based on how she treated Morgan."

"And that call to Pegeen seemed to prove it," finished Iris.

"Anybody care to tell me what these movies are of?" I asked.

The three of them posed stiffly, looking like stand-ins for the real stars, patiently waiting out a new camera set-up, exchanging reaction-shot glances. I decided to go for my close-up.

"I've already had a screening of *A Union Job*, Iris. I know King got Pegeen with child before someone pushed him off the 'Mysterious Lady,' and I know the love-child, if I can call her that, is Stella Sue."

"None of that," said Iris, still held in Rickey's clutch, "has anything to do with what Lillie may be bringing back."

"There's the matter of what Takasago will do, now that he has the reels from Brewster. Don't you expect him to really put the blackmail screws to you, if he has the evidence in hand?"

"Perhaps," Gilbert said.

"Morgan knows where he's been hiding out," put in Uncle Rickey.

"Johnnie's Grocery, Twelfth and Union," I said.

"How do you know that, Tirebiter?"

"My mother once told me my real father was Sherlock Holmes. After that I got a magnifying glass, a deer-stalker hat and started to keep bees in the back yard. I was a nosy kid."

"You're still a nosy kid," said Uncle Rickey.

"I was about to admit that," I said. "Never mind how, but I traced an old Hudson that had been trailing me around town back to the alley behind the grocery store. I was going to give the police the information after Brewster was murdered, but Lillie's life means more to me than Brewster's death. I'm surprised you haven't sent in the hard boys, Uncle Rickey."

"Look, Tirebiter. I've been ignoring the Uncle Rickey crap, but I'm runnin' out of good will."

"Just trying for a friendly atmosphere, Mr. Villandros."

"Morgan's had the place staked out for a week. He saw you nose around Sunday, then go inside the store Monday. While he was watching you, the Jap seems to have beat it out the back. No sign of him since."

Iris disengaged herself from her husband's arms and handed him the empty highball glass. He crossed to the drinks wagon. She counter-crossed to the fireplace, faced it and gazed up at what looked like a genuine Old Dutch landscape with lots of haystacks and peaceful cows. Bill Gilbert sat on the divan and stuck out his legs. The cowboy boots were two-toned alligator. I had the feeling I was watching a summer stock company go through the motions of an early Bernard Shaw comedy.

"Curtain going down on act two," I said, getting up. "Intermission. I think I'll take a stroll."

"I'm serious about protectin' your wife, Tirebiter. You tell me when, I'll have the boys at the airport."

"If you should hear anything from Stella, anything about Peg, call me here," said Gilbert in a quiet voice. "I'm extremely worried, as you should be."

Rickey handed Iris her fresh whiskey and went to the door, opened it and yelled for Morgan, who clumped in from the hallway looking more disheveled than usual. He'd had time for a quart or two of Acme's best suds.

"Mr. Tirebiter is leaving, Max. Escort him to his car."

"Sure, Mr. Villandros."

I looked back at the room from the doorway, trying for a little John Barrymore class in my curtain speech.

"You'll be hearing from me," was the best I could manage. I took a couple of steps down the hall after Morgan, then had to go back and ask Uncle Rickey for his phone number.

George B. Shaw it wasn't. George S. Kaufman maybe. I Groucho-walked all the way back to the kitchen, puffing heartily on an invisible cigar.

CHAPTER 28

THE CHASE, PT. 1

The open-all-night Melody Lane coffee shop on Wilshire and Western wasn't crowded. I sat down in a pink-and-green plastic booth and stared out the plate glass at the bank across the street. Security First. Good advice.

A 4-Star Edition of the *Daily News* lay folded into the back of the booth and I snagged it. It was warm inside the diner, and brightly lit. I spread the paper out and ordered an early breakfast.

A long day of rehearsal and two network broadcasts were set to begin in about ten hours. I was wide awake. Keyed up, I thought. Playing a part. The thin line between the parts I found myself playing and whoever the real George Tirebiter is was blurring again. I've had that problem all my life.

My avocado omelet with French fries and hot Java arrived just in time to bring me back to what the newscasters call the "present moment." COPS BASH WEED PARTY! The front-page photo showed a couple of skinny Mexican boys in peg-leg pants between a burly pair of L. A.'s finest. Below that, in much smaller type, MACARTHUR CLOSING ON MANILA! Above the masthead, inside a blood-red box, it read 'MORE CLUES IN SEX SLAYING!" A pair of bloody high-heeled footprints decorated the headline.

Someone dropped a coin in the juke box and "San Fernando Valley" came up. I turned to page 3 and scanned the story. ACTOR'S MURDER LINKED TO HOLLYWOOD SCANDAL." Some ace reporter with a long memory had linked Brewster to his fellow suspects in the King case. The list was not entirely inclusive, I was happy to note.

The police were busy following up leads in L.A.'s "notorious lavender underground." The El Patio was a well-known "trysting place" where Brewster had been a "familiar client." It was assumed "a friend" had stabbed Brewster in a "lover's quarrel." I knew the bloody footprints they'd found were Muriel's and hoped the cops weren't giving her a hard time.

It would cost me a nickel to tip off the Studio City squadroom anonymously that the man they ought to be interested in was almost certainly holed up in the house behind Johnnie's Grocery.

I turned back to the shoe-prints on page one. Muriel had stepped in the pool of Burke's blood and tracked it back out into the courtyard of the motel. Her feet had been made famous before the rest of her. Fame was something you stepped in out here in California, and you could never quite wipe it off your shoe.

I had a refill on the java and put a nickel on top of the paper. Twelfth and Union, boys! Go get him! The cops in the grainy flash picture looked as if they had enjoyed roughing up the two drugged pachucos. Something was out of focus. The nickel would send in Uncle Rickey's bad guys and I could call the PD afterwards. I put another nickel next to the first. Not out of focus. Plain wrong. Muriel didn't wear high heels. She wore penny-loafers.

I added a quarter to the nickels, waved goodnight to the waitress and shivered all the way to my car.

I knew where Stella Sue was, and that meant that I knew where her mother was. I could have called Bill Gilbert, but I was fresh out of nickels. I thought about visiting Stella and Pegeen myself, surprising them in the middle of a cold night. Probably a dangerous idea, seeing as how the Murray sisters and their well-connected husbands could slam their tent flaps shut, hide their peculiar affairs in the folds and slip away to the Antelope Valley.

If Lillie's visit to Chicago threatened the closed circuit of their lives, she might be in danger from the people she probably considered her friends. Brewster, her only other friend from the "Mysterious Lady," had been murdered. Monte Burke seemed all innocence out there in sunny Elysia, but the more I thought about him the chillier my blood ran. Then I thought I would understand everything if only I could talk to Tommy Takasago.

Wilshire came to a dead end at Westlake Park. I skirted around the block, past the Elk's Hall and the Boathouse, and took 4th St. to Union. After the War they would rename the Park for General MacArthur and run Wilshire right on through the middle of the lake, creating two lily ponds separated by auto exhaust. I turned right at the alley between 11th and 12th Streets and parked in the empty driveway behind Johnnie's Grocery. It was 2:30 a. m. on Friday morning.

Since the front of the sad old wooden house was attached to the back of the Grocery, I had no choice but to knock on the rear door. I expected to have to rouse the household, so I jumped back a foot when the door flew open and the Jane Darwell woman took a step out toward me. She had her hat and coat on and car keys in her hand.

She started to slam the door. I stepped in to keep it from closing. She changed her mind and pulled the door back and I blundered across the threshold and we I did a quick tango dip together to keep from sprawling on the floor.

"Get out of here," she said, in that sweet old lady voice.

"We've met," I said, tipping my hat, which had fallen over my eyes. "George Tirebiter."

"I know who you are."

"That's more than I know, m'am."

"What?"

"Who are you?"

She took a deep breath. "I'm in a hurry, Mr. Tirebiter. As you might be able to guess, it's a family emergency. I have nothing more to say to you than when you bothered us the other day. My name is Mrs. Wren, and I'll thank you to get out of my house and my driveway immediately."

"Mrs. Wren, I don't know who Tommy Takasago is to you, but the police are after him for something I don't think he did. If he didn't do it, and you're hiding him, let me talk to him. I don't have very many hours to go before real life takes over."

She sighed and leaned her back against a cabinet filled with dusty quart bottles of preserves. Her pocket book fell from her shoulder to the floor. She closed her eyes and opened them again to glare at me.

"Tommy's my husband, Mr. Tirebiter. "He wasn't my husband when they took him off to the desert. His first wife died in the camp. They were family friends, and I acquired this property after Pearl Harbor to protect it for them until they came back. Tommy hadn't worked in several years—he never could get much work after the silent days—and this place was all they had. Tommy and Toshi. When he came back, Toshi was dead and he was alone and angry at everybody. The President, the Army, the studios, the men he said ruined his life. I tried to keep him from going off into the past, and raking up all the cold ashes."

She bent and picked her bag up and hung it back on her shoulder. "He needs all the help he can get right now, Mr. Tirebiter."

"Is he here?"

"No."

"Are you going to him now?"

She looked at me for a long moment. "Have you got gas in that car?"

"Some."

"You drive me."

She shut the door firmly behind us, locked it, and strode briskly to the Lincoln. "He's at a little place I own in Glendale. Come on, Mr. Tirebiter!"

We sped through the icy night, back up Alvarado to Glendale Blvd., past the Keystone Kops, the Silver Lake Auto Court, under the Red Car railroad bridge, over the L. A. River, past the lighted cross and the Buckingham Palace gates of Forest Lawn Cemetery, the auto dealers on Brand Blvd., the Woolworths, the Alex Theatre, across a humpbacked little iron bridge, and up into the quiet streets that climbed the hills above the City Beautiful.

Chapter 29

Poppy Blossoms

The late Mr. Wren had been the long-time manager of the Brand movie house, and before that an engineer on the Vitaphone lot at Prospect and Talmage. He and Tommy had been poker partners and then, after Toshi came from Japan, the four of them played bridge on Tuesday nights.

That much she told me, at much greater length, on the drive up to Mountain Street. Mrs. Wren's house was a plain one-storey, two-bedroom stucco on a street of somewhat grander homes. She and Mr. Wren had lived there "since Roosevelt's second term." Mr. Wren had passed away in 1943.

There was a separate garage at the back of the tidy lot. My lights struck the closed pull-down door as we turned into the driveway. I supposed there might be an old Hudson locked inside.

We entered through the service porch. Mrs. Wren turned on a single overhead light in the breakfast nook. It was only 40 watts in the shape of a flame, but it was enough to see Tommy Takasago by. He sat at the white-painted table, blinking milky eyes at us.

Mrs. Wren dipped into her pocket book and took out a medicine dropper and a small brown pharmacy bottle. As she put the drops into Tommy's eyes she said, "Mr. Tirebiter came with me."

His was a proud voice, but tired and edged with bitterness. "I saw well enough there were two of you."

Tommy was fifty or so, but sunken and aged twenty years beyond that. He was dressed in a collarless white business shirt buttoned to the neck, shapeless brown pants and Black Watch bedroom slippers.

"He says he can prove you're innocent," Mrs. Wren said.

"I doubt you can see well enough to commit a murder, Mr. Takasago. I'm George Tirebiter. It's . . . interesting to finally meet you."

"They will say she helped me. They will destroy both of us."

"A woman might have killed Brewster, but not your Mrs. Wren here. I could send a lot of angry people here after you, but it makes more sense to find out first why my wife is involved in this business and how I can get her out of whatever danger she's in."

"She was never in danger from me. The only time I saw her was on the yacht over to Catalina when she was ten years old. You came around the grocery Monday and then we figured out who little Lillie Ames had grown up into."

"You've been following me."

"I came to your house one night last week, thinking I might talk to your wife. I saw the place lit up and the big Packard. Parade of stars. Then I thought to come in, but Jack got scared and drove me home."

"Jack is my son," said Mrs. Wren. "He's sixteen and Tommy has always been like an uncle to him."

"I also saw your car on the Strip and took down the license plate."

"I was seeing an eye specialist."

"One who's willing to treat a Japanese," Mrs. Wren put in. "Tommy left the prescription at the grocery when he drove up here after the murder."

"There's a twin to your Hudson that's been on my tail, then," I said. "I guess that must be the Office of Secret Facts."

"The United States Government will not be happy until it has put all of us in camps and given us someone to watch us day and night."

"Mr. Takasago. My wife is bringing some motion pictures here from Chicago tomorrow. Is she in danger?"

Tommy's eyes seemed to be dimmed by the mists of time as much as with disease.

I tried again. "Do you know who killed D'Arcy King?"

"Yes. I thought that day, How delicious!"

"Was it Monte Burke?"

"Perhaps, Mr. Tirebiter. Perhaps it was, but I have lost the evidence and so I called each of them and said, I have the dirty film and it will expose you for what you are! Then, I knew things would happen."

"Something happened to Basil Brewster."

"He knew nearly everything, I think. Smooth. Did you ever see *Poppy Blossoms*, Mr. Tirebiter?"

"No. A famous silent film, right?"

"With Brewster and Dorothy Pickwood. Brewster plays a Japanese man who loves the innocent blond Pickwood and then repents of his un-natural carnality to commit suicide. It was a picture of racial hatred, much like other pictures of that time, where white men coal their faces and dress as murderous Negroes or pinch up their eyes into slants and fondle white women. I have no sympathy for Basil Brewster."

"You didn't kill him."

"I have killed no one. I am not proud of what I was, then, in the time I worked for D'Arcy King. I was an immoral man, Mr. Tirebiter. When Toshi came from Japan, she was so clean, so pure, I had to purify myself before I could marry her. We were unbelievably happy, even going with two suitcases on the trains to the camp in Utah, because we would be together. I told her, I was born here, we are no danger to this country, have no fear. But she was full of fear in that prison. She was afraid the soldiers would send her back to Japan and so she killed herself. One dark day, I saw her body lying in the wind, lying in the cabbage garden she tried to keep growing. She took a poison they use to clean latrines. From that day, I think of all the white people I can hurt to revenge her."

Tears ran out of his pale eyes.

"A detective traced you to the grocery."

"We saw him," said Mrs. Wren. "He spied on us and Tommy was always ready to escape from the house. He did, after you came to ask for him, then we never saw the man again."

"Well, he can trace you there, and so can the two Murray sisters and their husbands, because that's who he works for. It's only a matter of time."

I stood up. "I'm sorry, Mr. Takasago. About your wife. But the *Times* has a page every day devoted to the names of dead Americans, and right now the Japanese Army is responsible for thousands of them and more to come. You'll be packed away for any killing that the cops can accuse you of, and they'll hang you because Japs are the enemy. Keep him here, Mrs. Wren. Wait until you hear someone else has been arrested for Brewster's murder."

The sky was light enough, as I drove back to Hollywood, to make the frosty suburban lawns gleam as if a snowfall had passed over during the night. The radio said it was "a chilly 28 degrees at Columbia Square."

CHAPTER 30

THE CHASE, PT. 2

I called Monte Burke at eight a.m.

"Is the sun shining out there, Mr. Burke? This is George Tirebiter."

"Yes it is, son, and it's colder than the tits of hell besides. You thinkin' of comin' on out here, wait 'til the frost melts."

"Nope. It's a busy day for me. I'm just repeating the invitation I gave you the first time we met. Be my guest at the broadcast this evening. Seven-thirty. There'll be a nice party afterwards with Ron Reagan and the wives. Can you come?"

"Well, I'll tell ya, Tirebiter. It's just we never leave the canyon out here. But thanks . . ."

"Funny, I thought I saw you in North Hollywood on Wednesday afternoon. I recognized that old Ford stake-truck you drive." It was a wild guess, but it was either true or not.

"Yeah, well, I had some business in the Valley."

"It's business I had in mind, Mr. Burke. Same kind of business you were in with Ollie Tulley back in 1920."

"That was then. I'm strictly over-the-counter, like I told ya."

"I think we should talk. About the movies this time. CBS on Sunset. Just give your name to the usher at Studio A. So long, now."

I had half a bottle of orange juice, lay down on the floor of my office and caught forty winks. The outside corridor was beginning to buzz with secretaries and salesmen when I woke up, had the second half of the bottle and called Stella. The phone rang a dozen times and I hung up. Iris Villandros, however, caught my call on the third chime.

"Good morning, Mrs. Villandros. We met last night. My name's Tirebiter."

"Of course. Are you calling with information about my sister?"

"Well, it's the darndest thing, but when I got into my office this morning, there was a note from Stella saying she'd be coming to the show tonight. It's a special broadcast, you see. Ronald Reagan and a cast of thousands. I thought I'd ask you to come along too. My wife and I will be hosting a after show party at the Cock 'n' Bull. Perhaps I can return a little of your hospitality. Lillie's coming back tonight, you know and seemed anxious to see you."

The little girl voice went up a few notes as she caught her breath. "I'll have to speak to Rickey, of course. Perhaps, thank you. Stella didn't say where she was, ah—staying?"

"No, I'm sorry. Until this evening, then." I laughed genially in my Old George voice, "He he he . . . See you on the radio."

I needed to give the pot another stir. The manager at the Silver Lake Auto Court was reluctant to take a message all the way out to Cabin 38, but when I explained it was life and death he relented. I waited on the line, listening faintly to a radio. It was Joy Darling explaining her symptoms to Young Doctor Begley. "Could it be malaria?" she asked, a note of panic in her well-modulated voice. "Could it be fatal?"

"Tirebiter! Goddamn it! It's life and death you want, get somebody who has time for it!"

"I hardly have time for it myself, Ollie. Listen, your script plays like a dream, Ronnie says it's the best thing since Knute Rockne. You've got to come to the broadcast."

"Georgie, you know I can't come out . . ."

"Safe as mother's milk, Ollie. Come for the second broadcast, we'll have all the kinks ironed out. Be a proud poppa! There's a party after."

"I donno about the party, Georgie . . ."

"But you wouldn't miss the show! Great! See you then!"

I hung up, drank a cup of coffee and wrote a short note on CBS stationary and tucked it in an envelope. First dress rehearsal was in less than an hour. I hurried down to the lot, got the car and drove a few blocks to the Courtyard Apartments.

Stella had told me she "went upstairs" to write. Since there was no upstairs to her apartment, her writing place must be nearby. Since the only second floor in the complex was over the five-car garage, that must be it. A wrought-iron spiral staircase went up to the single door. I went up and knocked.

"Stella? It's George." I didn't think she'd answer and she didn't. I slid the envelope under the door, knocked again and sped back to the studio, where I slipped into another skin.

⁕

I found the Old George Tirebiter voice in the voices of several brilliant character actors, Charles Ruggles and Frank Morgan among them, but first and foremost I found it in the voice of Richard Henry Sellwin. Sellwin played Tom Edison's Father—my father—in every performance of "The Pageant of Electricity" from the opening of the Century of Progress Fair in 1933 until it closed in late summer of 1934.

Sam Edison, at least as Sellwin portrayed him, was something of a bumbler, a Port Huron, Michigan entrepreneur who had built a tourist attraction—"the highest tower in America." Young Tom at age eight scampered up the rickety tower stairs after him to stand high above the heads of the audience. Sellwin and I had a scene there, three times a day, in which he would tell me, "I cannot fathom you, boy. You are either stupid or a genius. You will not be disciplined. Your teacher declares that you are addled! You show no aptitude whatsoever for mathematics!" To which I replied, "Father, I can always hire some mathematicians if I should need them."

Sellwin had died suddenly of heart failure, the year after the Fair closed, but his voice never left my mind, and I called on it occasionally as a maturing radio actor. Finally, the voice became my career. On the morning of January 26, it became my disguise. With a little prayer for the soul of Richard Henry Sellwin, I put on Old George and began my broadcast day.

Chapter 31

Radio Daze of 1945

The clock showed four-fifty-eight-and-thirty-seconds. I handed the show over to Ben Bland for a final word.

"Of course, I'll remember, George. We *all* need to remember The March of Dimes, marching to mop up infantile paralysis just like our boys are mopping up the Nazis. A dime, or better yet, a dollar, speaks louder than words in a battle that must be won and won soon against this childhood crippler. Get in step with The March of Dimes!"

Music Up and Out.

At four-fifty-nine the second hand on the studio clock made its last upwards tick and we were off the air. Ray Knight cued the band for another chorus of "The Ballad of the Bombardier," Reagan took a modest bow and brought the entire cast down to receive the cheers of our studio audience.

Buzz came on stage applauding. "Great show, everybody! Now, you have ninety minutes to eat, blow your noses and powder your cheeks before we do it all over again! Six-thirty sharp! Right here!"

He crooked a finger at me, and we met back by the empty band chairs. "I gotta call from Mr. AAAcme right after Reagan got through the part about the 'Boy from Lynn, New Jersey,' he was in tears."

"Joy? Laughter? Hated our guts? What?"

"Great contribution to the war effort on the home front, he said. He's going to award you his own personal 'E for Excellence' flag, given to him personally by the Secretary of Commerce."

"That's a relief."

"Now you're about to screw up my perfect program."

"No, Buzz, just put Lillie back in. Maybe a few little tune-ups here and there. Punch up those dead spots."

"You're sure Lillie is going to make it?"

"She called from Salt Lake at two. The plane was warming up. I've got a car at Lockheed Terminal—driver should have been there four minutes ago. With a makeup girl. Lillie should be landing anytime now."

"I hope so. This whole house a cards could still fall in on us, George, so don't do anything different. Ha ha. Fat chance!" He walked away, shaking his head.

Amos Pitz was standing in the greenroom, looking a little bewildered by the activity. He had performed brilliantly on the program and I told him so.

He gave an Ed Wynn whoop-and-giggle. "T'anks, Mr. Tirebiter. I ain't been onna air since before the War, but I listen good. I 'preciate the opper-toonity."

I got him a Coke and gave him a couple of new lines to replace the ones he'd done in the first show. "We always make a few changes for the West Coast listeners," I told him.

Reagan had the use of Lillie's dressing room, which was next to mine, one floor above Studio A. I knocked on his door.

"Jane?" he said from inside.

"No, it's George."

"Come on in."

He was sitting in Lillie's pale gold armchair, dress uniform coat off and a high-ball in his hand. He stuck the other one out to shake hands with me. I did, heartily, and closed the door.

"Two old radio guys from the Central Time Zone make good on the Coast, eh?"

"It was a lotta fun, George."

"Ron, do you mind if I ask you a question? About the body on the beach . . . You said he was a spy?"

"George," Reagan said, giving me that understanding grin he would become even more famous for, "In order for you to get on the inside, there are, wellp, certain tests. My assignment was to see if you could keep a secret, and then ask you to join us. That was easy—it was just acting, and of course Jack Houseman helped you out my way."

"But I asked him . . ."

"He would have invited you for a stroll anyway. He's still under orders. Once in the service of Secret Facts, it would be a betrayal not to do as you were told."

"But, it looked like a real dead body."

"How many dead bodies have you seen, George?"

"I'll admit, that was the first one."

"Wellp, he came as a surprise to me, too, I'll have to confess. Col. Casey is a terrifically funny guy, George, and we have some pretty smart fellas in the prop department at Fort Roach. For a minute there, I thought they'd actually killed me." He laughed and took a long sip of his drink.

"Sort of an early April Fools?"

"It got your attention."

I felt my teeth clench. "How can I be sure that they didn't kill you?"

"What?" Reagan grinned that wide Irish grin again.

"How can I be sure you aren't the mole?"

"Wellp, George, the mole wasn't human."

I nodded and shrugged. "I rest my case."

He looked startled and then laughed. I laughed with him. "See you on the radio, Captain Reagan."

I left him sitting in Lillie's chair, chuckling to himself.

Our cast was so large we were spilling out of the greenroom into the nearby hallways. The evening's other actors were arriving, and "The Aldrich Family" had a particularly large group, including the ubiquitous Ed Begley and Agnes Moorhead, several teen-aged boys and girls and the amazing Ezra "Henry Aldrich" Stone.

Capt. Stone was thought to be globe-hopping with "This Is The Army" (the stage show, not the movie in which George Murphy over-played Ron Reagan's father). Much to his understudy's annoyance, he had made it home tonight for his broadcast. Stone originated "Henry" in 1938 and went on playing a sixteen-year-old kid on the radio right through the war and after, until he was thirty-five. I found that inspirational, and once told him so. He replied that he was sure I'd be playing a sixty-year old codger until I was seventy-five and so far, he's been correct.

The CBS doors opened at seven and the audience, which had been shivering on line outside, bundled against another thirty-degree evening, hurried in to collect their seats. I always liked music piped in before the warm-up and Sammy Kaye was noodling away on "You Always Hurt The One You Love" from the Flame Room at the Hotel Radisson in Downtown Minneapolis as the seats filled up. An usher let me know that my invited guests had arrived and were seated, not too close together, in the front rows.

At seven-twenty, Ben Bland and Ray Knight went out to tell a few jokes and instruct the audience in radio etiquette.

"You know how to applaud, don't you?" said Ray in a sultry voice.

"Just put your hands together," replied Ben in falsetto, "and please *don't* whistle."

Just as I was about the replace the pink replacement pages with the original white ones, Lillie came bursting through the artist's entrance, the chauffeur behind her with two heavy suitcases, her Max Factor girl bringing up the rear.

"George! My God! The plane I told you was warming up?"

"Yes?"

"It was warming up in Denver, but it never warmed up enough, so it never got to Salt Lake! I'm afraid I had to put my foot down! I told them I had a broadcast to do, and if they didn't put me on an airplane instantly. . ."

"Lillie! You have a broadcast to do instantly!"

Buzz appeared. "Five minutes, Tirebiters!"

"Put the bags in my dressing room," Lillie pointed upstairs.

"No, no! I'm sorry, Lillie. I put Ron in your dressing room. There's a crowd here tonight. All your things are in my room."

"You never thought I was doing to make it, did you, George?" Lillie called back at me as she hurried away.

"Always, Lillie. Always. Your script is on my dressing table marked in red pencil."

I could hear chilly laughter over the backstage speaker as the audience remained un-warmed up half-way through a usually sure-fire routine.

"Let's go, kids!" I said to the empty hallway. "We've got to win their hearts tonight!"

"Stay tuned, everybody, for HOLLYWOOD MADHOUSE!"

MUSIC: TEMPTATION THEME IN

The good-time strains of "Temptation Rag," wise-cracked their way onto the airwaves, Presty Roberts' xylophone and Danny Ward's saxophone dueling the counter-melodies under Ray Knight's energetic direction. Ben Bland put his coffee cup down on a near-by stool and took two steps back and one step forward to the microphone and signaled the music to drop to half volume.

"Brought to you each and every Friday night at this time by Glamorama Soap, the soap with no foreign oils whatever. Double-purified, germ-free Glamorama protects your whole family's delicate skin. Remember to look for the beauty-conscious Hollywood Starlet on every bar! And now, let's drop off at Hollywood's most famous address—just around the corner from Sunset and Vine—the madcap mansion of . . ."

He gestured grandly towards us in the wings, his finger outstretched. At the end of his gesture, one of the sound guys broke a pane of glass, Ben reached back to see if he'd fractured his spine and Lillie and I fox-trotted onto the stage, tripping over one another's feet and nearly falling down in front of our mikes. We had reached the required degree of silliness which allowed the audience to be silly too, and the game was afoot!

Ben whispered conspiratorially, " . . . the Tirebiters, George and Lillie! And you know, this morning there's a real *hush* over the Madhousehold. The Balancing Borodins are still fast asleep in their tent in the backyard . . ."

I leaned forward and stage-whispered, "And they'd better stay that way! Ben, those three lunatic jugglers cracked every rib in my body! Imagine trying to keep our five-gallon water cooler, a full set of golf clubs and *me* up in the air at the same time! With them around we won't have to worry about the San Andreas Fault!"

Florrie had added that topper gag line for the Pacific Zone show and it got a small laugh from the out-of-towners and service-men who made up most of our usual audience.

Mattie Daniels came on mike, received her applause with a grin and a wave and took a short, sassy beat before her line. It came out at full volume.

"Mr. T?!"

"Shhhhh!"

"Oh, sorry, Mr. T. I was forgettin' the Stumblin' Bumbledums. They still sleepin' it off outside."

"But there's *ice* on the swimming pool, Porcelain. We're in the middle of a tropical freeze!"

"They're from the *Northern* part of Vulgaria, Mr. T. Tol' me they were *used* to actin' like polar bears. Or maybe it was *wolves*."

"I'll bet they are!" I said. "Heavenly days! Who's that?"

Music in and Under: Gypsy Dance

Fred Earl softly tinkled a couple of straps with sleigh bells rigged to them. The way he did it, they sounded like a troupe of Midway dancers.

"Mrs. T?" Mattie said, aghast,

"Lillie! Have you taken up the veil? What *is* this? What is *that*?"

Fred tinkled the bells.

"She's sayin'—look into my crystal ball."

"That's no crystal ball, that's the globe from the lamp in the hall closet! Wait a minute! I understand now! Those jugglers have convinced you to join their act!"

"Really, George! I'm appearing as a psychic with the Bouncing Borodins at the Shriner's Charity Carnival. This is my costume."

"Ah . . . Shouldn't you wear another costume over it?"

"How like the semi-veil-ed Moon, you seem, Madam, as you rise to greet the pearly dawn!" Sir Lionell was applauded on his entrance. "Rather like the Gypsy Queen in my famed production of 'Hamlet' at Stratford-upon-Acme."

"There is no Gypsy Queen in 'Hamlet,'" I huffed.

"Our costumes were left over from 'Carmen,' George. "Hamlet was dressed as a bullfighter—'Oh! What a roguish matador am I!'"

"What's for breakfast?" we said at the same time to Mattie.

"Well, Mr. T., you-all *know* about the meat shortage."

"Porcelain, Ronald Reagan is coming over this morning to rehearse tonight's program. Are you saying we're out of bacon, out of sausage?"

"Out of *ham*?" bellowed Sir Lionell.

The rest of us roared along with the audience.

"Cottage cheese *soo*-prize, ketchup on the side, comin' up. Oh, good mornin', Miz Rita. You mus' be dressed up for 'Hamlet,' too. De *Ghost*!"

"Good morning, Porcelain!" Rita, whose confidence had been shaken when she stumbled over my fluff on last week's show, got a good round of applause. She was looking forward to her solo spot, and her lines were better than usual. "This is my television makeup. Sir Lionell said it has to be *green* for me to show up at all."

"I think it's very *brave* of you, dear," said Lillie.

"Oh! Mrs. Typewriter! I didn't recognize you!"

"Lillie's joined the circus, and *you're* getting ready for *television?*"

"Embrace the future, Tirebiter! Be ready for the New Age. Come, my dear, speak the speech!"

"Romeo, Romeo . . ."

One of the sound crew rang the "Roll Out The Barrel" Madhouse door chimes.

Lillie ad libbed her threatening "George."

That prompted our running gag.

"Ben would be disappointed if we disconnected them so soon after Christmas," I ad libbed back. "That's probably Ron Reagan at the door."

Lillie backed away from the mike saying, "I'll let him in, dear." One of the sound effects doors opened and Lillie, now turned completely away from the audience said, "Come in!" and then screamed in mock outrage as the three AFRA acrobats, back for a second week of their "brother act," leaped off their chairs and surrounded her, gibbering and juggling. The effects crew jingled and juggled and jumped up and down. The audience loved it.

"Doople headstand!"

"Yumpp!!"

"Hoops!"

"Madame Lillie-ovitch! Yumpp!"

"Hoops!"

Lillie shrieked, "Look out for the door!"

With a slam, a glass-crash and a box of bouncing golf balls, the exit was performed. The actors actually carried Lillie off stage on their shoulders and got a huge hand for the unexpected touch of realism. Buzz gave us the "speed it up" sign from the booth.

Rita picked up the tempo smoothly. "What's this globe from the lamp in the hall closet doing on the breakfast nook table?"

"Oh, dear," I said. "Now I suppose Lillie will have to read palms."

"Rita," urged Sir Lionell, "your soliloquy, please!"

"What?"

"Your lines, my dear."

MUSIC CUE: IN AND SOFTLY UNDER.

"Romeo, Romeo, what's in a name? A rose is a rose is a rose and yet it smells the same . . . Oh, Sir Lionell, can't I just sing the words instead?"

She segued into a romantic novelty tune called "Romeo Smith and Juliet Jones," and I could relax for a moment and take a look at the studio audience. Monte Burke was sitting on the aisle to my right. Iris and Uncle Rickey were dead center. Ollie Tulley was not where I had planned.

Rita sang the last chorus and Ron Reagan came onto his solo mike. As Rita's applause faded, he stepped in: "Hello, George. The door was open so, wellp, I just came right on in. Where is everybody?"

"Thank goodness it's you, Ron Reagan," I said and cued another round of audience participation. "Lillie's been kidnapped by acrobats, Ron. Can I offer you some breakfast? It's cottage cheese surprise."

"I'm sure it's better than Army food, but I thought we were going to run though this part you've got for me, George. Is it difficult? I did used to be an announcer, you know."

"Dutch Reagan, all-American sportscaster, at the mike in Davenport, Iowa."

"That's right. W.O.C."

"Here's something I've always wanted to know, Ron. Is it true you once ad libbed an entire inning of baseball when the telegraph wire you were reading from went dead?"

"Yes, indeed. In those days the sports wire had just the bare facts, so to fill time, I'd squnch up my eyes and tell the listeners whatever I saw: 'The leaden skies threaten overhead as the UCLA Bruins in blue and gold huddle in the end-zone. Harvey squints at the determined Michigan line . . .' You know, George, it took me about ten minutes after I got my first radio job to see that people would believe whatever I made up."

"It's because you really do believe what you say, Ron, even if it's a figment of your imagination."

"That's how radio works, George."

"Let's get back to the game, Ron."

"Harvey squints at second base. He begins the windup, and . . . it's a hit! A hit! I think it's going all the way!"

"I thought this was the Rose Bowl Game, Ron!"

"Let's get a jump on the Series, George! It's over the fence! The crowd is on its feet as Greenberg rounds the bases. That's it! The Tigers win five to four . . ."

Amos Pitz, working on his own special microphone, cut in with the squelchy sound of an old-fashioned radio tuning away from Reagan's ball game and into the static between stations. Then he cut in and out of half a dozen broadcasts— "Who *was* that Masked Tenor?" he asked in the amazed tones of a crusty Western rancher—"This is Bob 'Air Transport Command' Hope in Prestwick Scotland, where the boys travel so fast they can have jungle fever and frostbite at the same time! But seriously . . ."

He began whistling in the Crosby style and then segued to the mournfully tuneless Theme from "The Whistler."

"I know many things, for I walk by night," Pitz said in a mysterious voice. "I know many strange tales hidden in the hearts of men and women who have stepped into the shadows." "Tell me, Amos." "What is it, Andy?" "What am de Statue of Limitations?" "Dat mean you cain't be persecuted for a crime you done seven years ago." "Whew! Am I glad 'bout dat! I been courtin' Madame Queen fo' seven years, an' my crime wave is ended!" There was a good laugh, and Pitz turned the radio dial again with a squawk.

"GoodeveningMranMrsAmericaanalltheshipsatsea! Flash! Unsolved Hollywood Mystery unravels as Killer strikes anew! Flash!"

Pitz stepped back, and Ben Bland picked up the Winchell rhythm with, "Glamorama Bath Soap lasts thirty percent longer!" and continued with the first commercial, out of which he introduced "Ray Knight and his Glamorama Goodtimers in an original up-tempo version of 'The Anvil Chorus Boogie!'"

While this was going on, I kept track of faces in the audience. Lillie had never come back from offstage, but she wasn't due on mike again until the end of the show. I hoped she was upstairs in our dressing room, alone with her baggage. I wrote, "Make sure Lillie's all right" on the back of a script page and gave it to Wally, our assistant director, who mimed "Why?" to me. I pointed to my stomach and my head and made a discreet expression of nausea. Wally shrugged and left the stage.

Thoughts had coursed through my tired brain like drifting leaves in a dark and roiling river as I lay on the floor of my office at six a.m. "The Anvil Chorus Boogie" did nothing to calm them.

If Lillie was returning with reels of film she had been planning to give to Basil Brewster, why were film storage boxes found in the motel room where he was murdered? They must have been planted by the murderer. That made it seem possible that there were two prints of the film. Two missing movies. Tommy Takasago had been trying to spook their location out of his former partners. One print turned out to be in a most unlikely place—the effects of Lillie's late mother. The other could have only been in Monte Burke's hands.

Monte had probably killed King and almost certainly killed Brewster, and tried to implicate Takasago and, if my suspicions were correct, Pegeen Gilbert and Muriel Albers, along with Lillie and any one else he could. It might be dangerous, I thought, but if I could make myself the target, maybe I could arrange to get pushed out of harm's way at the same moment the trap closed on Burke. I still had hopes.

The fourth invitation I had handed out for the evening's broadcast was to Lt. Whassissname of the Studio City division. Turned out his name was Wasserman and he gave me the impression he thought all actors were contaminated with radium and needed to be handled with six-foot tongs.

"Tirebiter? What have you got to offer?"

"I think I know what the Brewster murder is all about."

"This a confession?"

"No. An old killing. It happened at sea and it sank like a stone."

"If you're talking about the King case, why would there be any connection?"

"Blackmail. Smut."

"We're working on all the leads, Mr. Tirebiter. Have you any evidence you forgot to mention in out short conversation last Wednesday night?"

"Only suspicions. Miss Albers and I were doing some research."

"She told us about that. We're looking for the Jap. The evidence maybe could point that way. Chances're even it was some pansy pal of Brewster's. Anything to add, or was this a social call?"

"Actually, yes, Lieutenant. I'd like to save a pair of seats for you for my Friday night program. I'll promise you some laughs, and you promise you'll save my life."

"Why is it all you actors wanna be detectives? Now I gotta come back with something like, "Keep your nose out of police business, Tirebiter.""

"I promise to restrict myself to radio business, Lieutenant. Will you come?"

"Wouldn't miss it."

"That would be the biggest mistake of your career. See you on the radio, Lt. Wasserman."

Wasserman was up center on the aisle, with a view of all the actors on stage and in the audience. I could tell even from where I stood that he wanted to put his hat back on.

The "Anvil Boogie" came to a merciful close.

"Well, George old toot, how did you dig that voot?"

"Ray, you've done some serious damage to a favorite of classical music lovers everywhere. The Anvil Chorus is from a famous opera by Giuseppi Verdi. What do you think *he* would say if he could hear what the boys just played?"

"Verdi would turn *green* with envy, dear fella, old gate!"

Amos Pitz stepped in with a perfect duplication of my Old Man's voice: "I think not, but thank you anyway, Ray." Then, in Ray's Knightsbridge tones, "That concludes our programming for this evening. This is the BBC World Service. Goodnight." Then, a cascade of squeals and squelches in the manner of short-wave radio, followed by a mish-mash of foreign languages distorted by sun-spots. He cut back to English as Ralph Edwards: "Aren't we devils? All right, contestant, you did not tell the Truth so you must pay the Consequences."

Pitz tuned vocally through fragments of Artie Shaw's "Stardust" and the Ink Spot's "Dinah" to Basil Rathbone's "It's as plain as the nose on my face, Watson," and Nigel Bruce's "Huh, well, ah, mm, quite true, old boy, quite true." Pitz crouched over his microphone, his body changing its shape to accommodate his changing personalities.

"It *shall* be my duty as District Attorney," Pitz went on, in the ringing good-guy voice of Jay Jostyn, "not only to *prosecute* to the *limit* of the law *all* persons accused of crimes . . ." "The *weed* of crime bears *bitter* fruit. Crime does not pay!" John Archer's Shadow chuckled insanely. "Tirebiter knows!"

I could see that a good part of our audience was puzzled by the unfamiliar non-linear discontinuity. The on-stage cast was holding its breath, and off-stage the rest of the cast was assembled, peering out, shaking their heads. The bass member of the Knightsmen Quartet was moving his body in rhythm to Pitz' timing.

He drifted through a couple of bursts of FBI machine-gun fire into an exchange of lines between Lon Clark, Charlotte Manson, and Ed Lattimer, the regulars on "Nick Carter, Master Detective" . . .

"So how did you figure *this* one out, Nick?"

"That's right, Nick. How did you know *he* was the murderer?"

"Well, Patsy, Matty, he thought if he confused the evidence enough, no one would notice him, and he could escape as he did once before. When I dug through the confusion, *Monte* was the only choice possible."

Pitz concluded his Detective Variations with a thunderous foghorn blast and, "Out of the fog, out of the night . . ." then cut himself into a quick scat solo, followed by, "Good mornin' everybody, it's Arthur Godfrey Time and this ol' redhead wants you to listen to the Knightsmen and Ray Knight and the Orchestra with 'Seems Like Old Times.'"

It was over. The band started out the arrangement in the slow tempo at which Godfrey took the song, then swung into a jitterbug beat designed to get our audience's attention for the last part of the show. Although he had no applause, Amos Pitz gave a quick bow and walked back to his folding char, mumbling Arthur Godfrey-esque syllables and strumming an invisible ukulele.

The stage began to fill with our four additional singers, Capt. Reagan in full-dress uniform, a second percussionist for the TYMP UNDER, Manny, Moeski and Yackov and the rest of our augmented crew. Buzz had arranged to drop down an American flag behind the band, and there was a stir which crept over the auditorium and gave the jitterbug an extra jump.

The A. D., Wally, waved me over to the wings and whispered in my ear, "Lillie's not in your dressing room, George, and she's not in hers either, the one Reagan's been using. I sent the hairdresser into the Ladies and she's not there either."

"I have one thing to do, then I'll be offstage. Keep looking!" I had to get back on mike. The music was three seconds from ending, the cast was set, microphones had been reset, and everyone had an eye on Buzz in the booth. His palm was up for silence, then his finger raised and arced upward and finally pointed directly down at us with the authority of a Stokowsky.

MUSIC IN: A FANFARE. EIGHT RINGING TRUMPET CALLS. STRINGS ENTER AND UNDER.

I raised my script and entered on the beat, "Ladies and gentlemen, 'Hollywood Madhouse' would like to pay tribute to the brave men who are dedicated to making the Pacific peaceful once more—the B-29 bomber crews of our fighting Army Air Corps—as Captain Ronald Reagan stars in 'The Ballad of the Bombardier!'"

MUSIC: ENDS IN TRIUMPHANT CHORD. MYSTERIOSO TYMP UNDER INTO

Sotto March-Tempo Fading Under.

The stage lights dimmed and a spot hit Reagan, who stood, script in hand, with a deadly earnestness etched on his face, the picture of a brave officer on an enlistment poster. He began:

"The wind was an ice-covered gauntlet among the gusting clouds,
The moon was a ghostly battleship tossed between purple shrouds,
The road through the night-sky . . ."

The singers came in humming the march. When it comes to good old-fashioned simple-minded propaganda, I thought, we Americans can dish it out just as good as Dr. Goebbles ever could. And with that thought, I left the stage.

Lillie's suitcases lay open on my dressing room floor. There was very little in them. Unless an underwear thief had ransacked her bags, they probably had contained a couple of thousand-foot reels of 16 millimeter film. I ran to the greenroom where I found a romantically engaged teen-age couple from "The Aldrich Family," and Moorehead and Begley talking animatedly about where the plot was going on "Tomorrow Is Another Day." No one had seen Lillie.

There was a stage-door security man on duty, drinking coffee. He'd let one woman in who said she was "with Miss LaMont." She was "a real female woman shape-wise, bundled up inta black coat with the collar up." In his experience, "People come and go. They come and go. They're comin' and goin' in and out of this door all night. Terrible draft on me all the time."

There's a five-storey office building attached to the CBS studios. Lillie knew where my office was and how to get there. She must have hot-footed it upstairs to hide the film. A radio speaker in the ceiling in front of the elevator doors was broadcasting our chorus singing, "Fill the skies with eagles and fill the air with men, for we can see a world that's free when we come back again!"

Lillie sat at my desk, her face in her hands.

"Sweetheart?" I said.

She looked up at me with her eye makeup running down her cheeks. "Oh, George," she said. "I don't know what to do."

I switched on the desk radio and checked the clock. Ron Reagan was emoting brilliantly against a background of voices and orchestra:

" . . . There's one of every one of us aboard this flight tonight." The voices of the Crew were provided by the acrobatic trio in a variety of ethnic and regional accents and attitudes. "The Skipper hails from Bloomington!" "The gunner's from Baltimore!"

"Lillie, sweetheart!"

"I know, we have to be back on stage in four minutes." She rose wearily and grabbed a Kleenex. "Let's go. My things are locked in your closet."

I locked the office door behind us and we ran for the staircase.

The radio speaker in the lobby proclaimed: "Ah, yer hands're dirty, an' yer pants're filthy, yer oily behind the ears!"

As we exited in the lobby I heard, "Now the bombardier was flying the ship. He could see the target plain . . ."

We took a private hallway backstage and opened a door across from the greenroom.

We could hear the music on stage. The extra kettledrum man was earning his salary. The brass soared.

We saw him the moment he saw us. Monte Burke. He grabbed me by the collar.

"For heaven's sake!" said Lillie. "We have to be on stage in thirty seconds!"

"Twenty," I grunted.

"What the hell are you tryin' to do to me?" growled Burke.

"Let him go!" yelled Lillie and grabbed Burke around the neck and hung on, kicking his knees.

From the stage the stirring strains of "The Ballad of the Bombardier" built into a triumphant climax:

"Bombs Away!" sang the chorus.

Burke's thumbs were reaching for the core of my adam's apple.

A hardboiled gumshoe inside a girl's body shouted, "Let him go! Now! And reach!"

Burke did. I slumped to my knees. Lillie whispered, "You're on, George!" We ran for the microphone.

"Call it a day!" said Manny.

"We've done it again!" said Moeski.

"Direct hit!" crowed Yakov.

"Let's go home!" sang the male sextet.

"And the wind," spoke Reagan. "Wellp, the wind was a velvet slipper, and all the clouds were gone. The moon was a tropical island afloat in a deep blue dawn. The road through the night sky was homeward over the peaceful seas."

The singers hummed behind us as we said, breathlessly: "This is George—and Lillie—Tirebiter—with our very special guest—Captain Ronald Reagan. Until next week, when we'll—see you on the radio!"

The last four orchestral chords rivaled Beethoven's Ninth in their dramatic power, if not in sheer number of notes. Buzz held up his fingers in a "V for Victory" sign.

Ben stepped into his spot. "We're a little late folks, so goodnight, and don't forget The March of Dimes!"

It was one minute to eight o'clock. I had dark spots in front of my eyes. From offstage there was a gunshot and then two more in quick succession.

Chapter 32

Post-Mortem for Two

Lillie and I ended up, quite late, at the Cock 'n' Bull—a dark and usually crowded restaurant at the western edge of the Sunset Strip. We were seated under a framed playbill that I had never noticed before. There on the wall, in four-color lithography, clutching hands and staring into one another's eyes, were Monte Burke and Mary Maple Murray, starring in the premiere of *Passion For Two*, at the El Capitan Theatre, along with Orchestra, Organist, a Jazz Band, "International News Views" and Harry Langdon in *Feet of Mud*.

"Feet of mud is about right," I said, pointing out the poster.

"Who did you have in mind, lover?" She took a long sip of her martini.

"Oh, you, me—everybody."

"I'm sorry I could never tell you what I suspected. I learned to hide it over the past twenty-five years. Learned not ever to think about it."

"Nobody wanted to think about it until Tommy Takasago moved a cold pot back on the fire."

"You think he heard the broadcast tonight?"

"I told them to listen. It'll be in the papers tomorrow morning anyway. They'll be all right. They've been through a war."

She nodded. "George?"

"Yes, Lillie?"

"The young woman who started the shooting. Stella King. How did she happen to be backstage?"

"She gave your name. A friend of Miss LaMonte, she said."

"Really? But how did she know Burke was going to show up?"

"Did she?"

"Well, it doesn't matter. She saved your life—your professional life anyway. Buzz would have killed you if you hadn't been on stage for the close."

She finished the martini and lit another cigarette. It reminded me of the smell of burnt black powder that lingered back in the greenroom at CBS.

Lillie blew some smoke my way. "Do you think they'll catch the men who shot Burke?"

"They're probably passing through Phoenix right now, on their way to Chicago or Detroit or wherever they came from. What are you going to have?"

"Soup. It's celery-tomato."

I ordered. The waiter brought us two more drinks and an empty ashtray.

"You know, George, it was guilt that ate my mother up, and took twenty years to kill her. And she never had to feel guilty at all, did she?"

"Well, not very guilty. King would have recovered from the blow on the head Mrs. Murray gave him if he hadn't been pushed into the water. That was in the coroner's report back in 1920. Burke rolled him overboard as sure Tomorrow's Another Day."

"Mother decided to send me to Switzerland right after we took the seaplane from Catalina and rushed back to Chicago. When I came home six years later, Father was in that stupid affair with the figure skater, and Mother had turned all her energies to getting me on Broadway."

"Can you imagine those two women managing a rowboat in Avalon Bay on a windy night?"

"Mother said it was the last boat ride she'd ever take."

"You should have told me you were there, Lillie. It was lousy of you to leave me in the dark."

The waiter showed up with Lillie's soup and my Chef's Salad and coffee.

"They were very determined, you know," said Lillie when he had gone. "Mrs. Murray would have fought a hundred devils to get to King after she heard he had slept with all three of her girls."

"Not to mention filming them in the process, and I don't mean the process of sleeping."

"Meanwhile the cameraman was blackmailing King over the films."

"Burke put Tommy up to it. Burke saw a very lucrative business in making blue movies, and if he had to blackmail to get the seed money, he'd do whatever it took. But then Brewster stole King's print."

"Because Mary asked him to."

"In one of her sober moments, after she realized what a double-dyed cad King was, I guess so. It had to have happened that night, because Brewster passed the films on to Mrs. Murray, and she gave it to your mother to take away as quickly as possible."

"Her suitcase weighed a million pounds. They almost wouldn't load it on the plane out of Avalon."

"And then Burke stole the other copy from Tommy and claimed to know nothing about it. Until Tommy rattled Burke's cage twenty-five years later. Then Max Morgan leaned on him, I came out and talked to him . . ."

"Did you take your clothes off, and everything?" Lillie cooed like a character from "Private Lives."

"It was all quite modest, Lillie."

"I'm sure it was, what with Monte Burke leering at every dame who walks in the place. He probably had cameras hidden behind all the windows!"

I remembered how Burke had eyed the young refugee girl. Good works spoiled by rotten motives.

"The last straw was when Muriel called him with questions from *Screen Secrets.*"

"Muriel?"

"A writer I know. She discovered Brewster's body. I think Monte Burke called her from the Motel and imitated Brewster so as to confuse the time the murder was committed."

"Would you light my cigarette, please, George?"

I did. She looked around the restaurant and nodded pleasantly at Jo Cotten and his wife, who were leaving. She turned back to me with a plume of smoke rising above her head.

"About Stella . . ."

"Stella was on a mission to find her father's killer. Poor Pegeen was convinced that her own mother had done it. So were you. You chose to pretend it never happened. It drove Pegeen crazy, I guess."

Lillie looked at me with an arched eyebrow and a sarcastic turn to her lips.

"You bumped into Stella in the course of your amateur detective work?"

"Well, sort of. She understood all about you, Lillie."

"Unh huh."

"I let her know that her father's killer would be backstage after the show tonight. Thank God she got there early."

"She would have killed Burke herself, wouldn't she? If the two men in slouch hats hadn't taken over the opportunity."

"Rickey Villandros turns out to be a gangster after all."

We stopped talking for awhile and ate.

There had been an hour and of total confusion backstage as the police and ambulance crew arrived. Stella, gun still in her hand, was fingered for Burke's killing as soon as Lt. Wasserman, who had jumped onto the stage when the shots sounded, needed a suspect. Enough of us told him that he'd just missed the two medium-height, medium-built guys with hats pulled down over their foreheads and collars turned up around their mouths who had actually pulled the triggers, that he finally agreed not to book her for homicide.

Bill Gilbert showed up in the greenroom, had a private chat with Wasserman and took Stella away, probably to pick up Pegeen and retreat to the wide-open and very private spaces of the Antelope Valley. The men in white took the remains of Monte Burke away. Our cast drifted into the night one-by-one, after they had given their statements. Only the memories remained. I dwelt in them for a while, until Lillie tapped another cigarette out of her pack.

"Oh, George, I almost forgot to ask you. Did Ronnie ever say anything about that body you two found on Malibu beach?"

"Yes, Lillie, he did." I lit her cigarette, shook out the match and laid it in the ashtray. "He said it was the rest of him."

AFTERWORD

About a month after her byline appeared in *Screen Secrets* under a story titled "Closing The King Case: Murder Is Its Own Reward," Muriel called me to say she was moving back to New Jersey. Her old boyfriend had finally popped the question, and, she said, "We're going to look for the needle in the haystack of life."

"S. S. Van Dyke" published one more mystery book. I read it on the set of *Dixie Has Latin Trouble* after Paranoid loaned me out to Monotone to direct the second through the fourth of an interminable series of Dixie Cupps movies. In the novel, "Death Begins With Me," Stella recreated our assignation in her apartment, complete with the silly notes, the aquavit and the bubblebath. The difference was that her nameless detective took off his summer-weight grey pinstripe suit and got in the bath with her.

Ollie Tulley's career was resuscitated by "The Ballad of the Bombardier," (it was published with full-page illustrations in the *Saturday Evening Post*) and he went on to finally get his Oscar nomination after fifty years in the business for writing a one-reel short called "Athletes of the Saddle." Having seen him at work in *A Union Job*, the title seemed apt.

Ron Reagan ran successfully for President of the Screen Actors Guild in 1947. He was divorced from Jane Wyman in 1948, the same year she won Best Actress without speaking a line of dialogue. Of course, Ron ended up thirty-five years later inhabiting the White House. Jane, however, wisely plied *her* acting trade in "Falcon Crest."

"Hollywood Madhouse" only had one more season on the air. Mr. AAAcme decided he'd rather sponsor a show that was all music, and backed "Glamorama Bandwagon," with organist Ethyl Smith. Lillie decided to retire to Santa Barbara, leaving me more-or-less alone to direct comedies designed for the bottom half of drive-in double-bills.

I didn't get another network show until 1950, when I created a brand-new persona with hardboiled "Maxwell Morgan, Crime Cabby." After two years, sponsored by General Cigar and Bryllcreme, I sold it to television. They replaced

me with John Ireland.

Of course, by that time I was blacklisted and couldn't have gotten a job in Hollywood under my own name as a crossing guard. But that's another story.

GLT

GEORGE TIREBITER, UNKNOWN AUTEUR OF HOLLYWOOD'S GOLDEN YEARS

PART TWO: HIS LIFE AND CAREER HIGHLIGHTS 1941–1953

COMPILED BY FREDONIA COUPE
FOR *RADIO HERO MAGAZINE*, JULY 1988

1.

George Leroy Tirebiter began working as a child actor in the Chicago area and, after a stint with the Chicago World's Fair (1933-34) found steady radio work on top-rated WOP. As Tirebiter phrases it, "Poetry, commercials, prosperous young men-about-town, character roles, I did them all." He created a daily serial, "Young Tom Edison, Electric Detective," for WOP in 1936, wrote every show and played the title role until the program went off the air in early 1940. (Tirebiter's early years in show business—1930 to 1942—have been documented in detail by Freedonia Clinton and Langley Coupe in their article "Boy Wonder" in *Radio Hero Magazine* for October 1987.)

CBS brought GLT to Hollywood in 1941 to star in a new comedy-variety series, "Hollywood Madhouse." At the same time, he was offered a contract as a director by Paranoid Pictures. Tirebiter expected to be given a film series based on his radio show, but instead was assigned to direct, as he put it, "inexperienced young performers in the feel-good stories that spaced out the ballads, dances and swing band numbers in Paranoid's light-weight musicals." GLT was co-writer on such forgettable movies as *Babes in Khaki* (1942), *Dog Fights Over Broadway* and *Ruthless Combat* (both released in 1943) *Pardon My Sarong* and *Swing, Swing, Swing Shift* (both 1944), His run ended with *Pardon My Pinup* and *First WAC in Tokyo* (both 1945).

"Hollywood Madhouse" was on the air (CBS, Friday nights at 7:30) for its fifth and final season from September 1945 through May 1946. The cast included Tirebiter's wife, former "Vandals" star Lilly Lamont, teen-age singing ingenue Rita Monroe, vaudeville comic Phil Baines (as "Sir Lionell Flynn"), night club entertainer Mattie Daniels, and announcer Ben Bland, speaking for Glamorama Soap.

Tirebiter's final feature for Paranoid, "Three WACS in a Jeep," was released as

"First WAC in Tokyo" with new scenes added, in September 1945. Paranoid double-billed it with "Black Deborah," a pirate movie starring Jean Heather and Cosmo Sardo.

2.

Alas, in the Summer of 1946, Lillie and George split up. Lillie moved from their Toluca Lake home to Santa Barbara, where she became a long-time inhabitant of a bungalow at the El Encanto Hotel.

On loan from Paranoid, in August 1946, GLT directed "Dixie Has Latin Trouble," the second in a series of programmers starring former burlesque queen Dixie Cupps for Cameo International, produced by GLT's friend Derrick Darling, who ran the studio. It was released for the holidays billed with Cameo's "Ice Carnival of 1947."

In February 1947 GLT directed "Dixie In The Dark" for Cameo. Released in October with "Meet Mr. Hyde," a thriller starring Rock LaRouche.

During the spring of 1947 GLT directed six episodes of "Buffalo Bill vs. Sitting Bull" for RKO under the name "Elmo Yakima." As he explained it, "I needed to pay off some outstanding debts."

In November, 1947 GLT directed "Dixie Brings Down The House." This was the last film in GLT's loanout period at Cameo. His contract was not picked up by Paranoid. This last in the Dixie Cupps series was released in February 1948 along with "Bobbie Sox Beauty," a high school musical.

3.

In Spring 1948, GLT wrote "What A Family!" for Argyle Artists. In this seminal script, he introduced "Georgie" and the rest of the Tirebiter family and friends. In the film, Georgie's father, Franklyn Tirebiter, runs for Elmwood City animal control officer, but his son's shenanigans get him locked up in the dog pound for a night and almost cost him the election. Directed by George B. Selz, starring Brod Crawford, Spring Byington, Mickey O'Niell, Herman Hutton and Sammy Stone. It plays major showcase theatre dates with Spike Jones and his City Slickers and is popular enough to call for a sequel.

In the Winter of 1948, GLT became "The Sunkist Storyteller" in a 13-week series for Don Lee Radio Network. He narrated dramatized stories of cowboy life in early Southern California. Scheduled following the nightly 5-minute "Frost Warnings," the show did not prosper.

Also during 1948, GLT wrote the story and, replacing Brod Crawford, played

A still from Tirebiter's, What A Family!

Georgie's father in "What A Family Goes Hollywood!" In this script, Mr. Tirebiter moves the family from Elmwood to Glendale, so that everybody can get a job in the movies. Trouble is, the studio that hires them is run by a bunch of crooks. Released by Argyle in the fall of 1949, the film is a big hit, spawning a number of sequals, the best known of which is "Georgie and Jug Ears" (1950), starring Dave Casman and Joe Bertman in the title roles.

4.

From early 1948 until September 1951, GLT and Derrick Darling were partners in Flintridge Films, an independent production company. Aspiring to do only one important film a year, the team manages to release two films through Cameo International. They were:

"Morgan For Hire," with a screenplay by GLT based on the hard-boiled novel "Night Rides" by Conrad Wyrich. Directed by Darling in the fall of 1948 and released in May 1949. Morgan was played by Scott Brady.

"Lust For Light," with a screenplay by GLT based on the popular novel about the painter Gaugin, directed by Darling and starring Lee Marvin, was released for the holidays in 1950.

GLT wrote an original screenplay based on "Gulliver's Travels," but Flintridge never delivered its promised third film.

In 1949, GLT developed a radio series for NBC, "Max Morgan, Crime Cabby," based on the cab driver character in "Morgan For Hire." It was scheduled to run in the prime slot following Talullah Bankhead's "The Big Show."

In January 1950, "Max Morgan" premiered on the air, starring GLT, running through May and continuing for a second season in September.

In March 1950, GLT dated Marilyn Monroe and, as a result of the publicity, Lillie began divorce proceedings.

In late 1950, Lillie denounced GLT as a fellow-traveller in order to clear her own name and make way for her comeback role in "Yesterday's Sunset." She portrayed Baby Heather, a psychotic former Follies star whose power-hungry understudy Eva (played by Marie O'Saint) steals the affections of Baby's voice coach and young lover, "The Professor" (William Holden). Baby's jealous butler (Brod Crawford) shoots Eva as she decends the staircase to the swimming pool, ending her threat to Baby's already failed career. Released by Paranoid in 1951, this film got six nominations, but no awards.

"Max Morgan" was cancelled and off the air in June 1951. GLT sold the television rights to Dumont and the series ran from the 1951 Fall season through May 1954. Scott Brady played Max.

5.

Early in 1951 GLT sold their Toluca Lake house as a part of the divorce settlement with Lillie. After several months living in Darrick Darling's guesthouse in Woody Glen, GLT bought the Rose-Bud Court from screenwriter Oliver Tulley. Located south of Downtown Los Angeles, in the University of Southern California area, on 30th Street just an alley away from Adams Boulevard, the Rose-Bud had been built in 1926. Tulley had picked up the attractive nine apartment court from its long-time owners, Rose and Bud Levy, in a 1948 real estate swap.

GLT bought the court and moved there in September 1951. Eccentric ex-sailor Seaman O'Toole and elderly sun-bather Mrs. Whitmer were living there at the time, and had been for years. The Perry's, Will and Sally, moved in just before Litttle Joe was born in December 1951. Will Perry was about to become a famous scifi illustrator and turned GLT onto the science-fiction "scene."

Gideon Selz, brother of the director and a Movietone News cameraman had rented another of the bungalows for years, first because it was convenient to a job with the USC Photo Lab, and later as a retreat. When he retired to the Motion Picture Home in 1952 he passed it on to his twin daughters, Sappho and Sabina. They moved in October 31, 1952, confusing GLT into thinking there was only one of them, a USC student he nick-named "Silly Sally." Two of the other bungalows remained rented to a regular turnover of USC students.

GLT was out of work for the rest of 1951. He decided to write a novel and began work on "Street of Broken Glass," a semi-autobiographical *noir*. In 1952, after seeing "Destination Moon," he wrote his first scifi story and quickly sold two novellas, "Nomads From Neptune" and "How Time Flies" to *Astonishing Science Fiction*, both under the pen-name of Ty Pritter.

GLT played the crippled evil genius Doctor Loco in a Mexican language version of "Frankenstein," in which "Frankenstina La Monstra" was played by a very drunken Dolores Del Valle. This was a guest spot GLT promoted for himself while beachcombing in Puerto Airto in October-December 1952.

6.

In early 1953, GLT was still working on his *noir* novel and had landed several jobs—scripting a film version of "Nomads From Neptune" and writing and directing (as Ty Pritter) one of the first 3-D scifi films, "The Beast From Under the Bed." As "Dixon W. Franklyn" he wrote the 14th installment of the famous "Smartee Boys" series of novels for youths, in which the brothers Smartee encounter the "Mystery of the Flying Saucer." Busy in Hollywood once again, GLT landed a writing job at Metro—additional dialog for the sensational new wide-screen movie, "Quo Vadis," and thirteen episodes of the last Western serial, "Buffalo Bill's Horse" (based on a Mark Twain story) for Columbia. Later in 1953, he wrote additional dialogue for "Julius Caesar."

Kat Musik moved into the Rose-Bud Court, across from GLT's bungalow in the Spring of 1953, two years after her husband was MIA in the Korean war. A young television producer, Kat introduced George to the hot new medium and a new phase in both his love life and his show business career.

Reprinted by permission from *Radio Hero Magazine*

ADVENTURES WITH GEORGE

A MEMOIR AND APPRECIATION OF GEORGE TIREBITER

BY DAVID OSSMAN

I was just a kid when I met George Tirebiter. For one thing, I was his paperboy, and delivered him the *L. A. Daily News* back in the days of the Korean War, Atom Spies, and The Big Red Menace. George lived in a bungalow court—I guess he owned it—a block north of Fraternity Row on the fringes of U.S.C., around which my route went.

I recognized his name, of course, and to me it was like collecting a dollar-fifty a month from Fibber McGee or The Great Gildersleeve. Tirebiter had one of those instantly recognizable radio voices, like Parley Baer or Karl Swenson, John McIntyre or Olan Soule. He had recently played Max Morgan, a radio detective who was really a cab driver, and I had listened to that show pretty regularly, so I was a fan.

(When my family had lived with my aunt and uncle in San Francisco back in 1946, Tirebiter's Friday night radio program, "Hollywood Madhouse," played opposite my favorite, *The Lone Ranger*, so I hardly ever heard him then, except when one of the many adults in that overcrowded household switched the Philco to CBS.)

I knew he was a sci-fi writer in those later days, early 1952, and out of radio. I said something to him once like, "Sorry you're not on the radio anymore, Mr. Tirebiter," and he looked over the top of his glasses and replied "Not half as sorry as radio is, Dave."

I didn't know he had been blacklisted in Hollywood until a couple of years after that. By then I had joined the Los Angeles Science Fantasy Society—a fan club where published writers and artists, and Hollywood people too, would gather for a prepared program and then engage in heavy socializing.

Tirebiter had sold both of his first two published stories for films. Outer Space, 3-D, Invaders From Wherever, Tirebiter was there at the first explosion of science fiction movies.

David Ossman and Ray Bradbury, 1954.

He came to a LASFS meeting one hot summer Thursday night, in the company of Ray Bradbury. It was some sort of special anniversary, and the ranks of the sci-fi readers had been swelled by the writers—A. E. van Vogt and Anthony Boucher and Gerald Heard were also there.

I re-introduced myself to Tirebiter, who introduced me to Bradbury (who later introduced me to Norman Corwin!) by saying, "This was the only kid who could hit my front porch with a flying tabloid five times out of six. And you quit!"

"We moved," I said. "To 56th and Vermont. I'm a senior at Manual Arts High."

"Ray," said Tirebiter, "meet Georgie."

I didn't get it, because I'd never seen *What A Family!* a pretty popular movie Tirebiter had written eight or ten years before. "Georgie Tirebiter" was the kid role, played by Mickey O'Neill. Spring Byington and Brod Crawford were his parents.

Tirebiter came along after the meeting to a French-dip sandwich place—Milani's on Santa Monica Blvd.—where we all sat family style at a long table and dipped the thick roast beef sandwiches in high-caloric jus and drank Cokes or coffee. I was just a teenager—the rest of them should have known better.

I was there with my friend who drove—Bill Mosely—(who'd help me publish, by mimeograph, my first book of poems and shortly thereafter would kill himself—scary stuff). Bill was sitting to my left and almost across the table from Tirebiter and engaged him in a conversation about whether it was more interesting to write for movies than for magazines.

Tirebiter got a big kick out of that, and said, "I don't write pictures because it's interesting, I do it because it pays better than anything else. Writers have to write every day. Have to write something. Anything. I used to write with four other comedy writers in a smoky room together four or five days a week, and that was one of the inner circles of Hell. But it was also a hell of a way to get down to the essence of those really unforgettable laughs. My guys re-wrote each other until the script was funny. Then I re-wrote them until I was funny. And re-writing is better than not writing at all."

"I try to write a poem a week," I volunteered.

"Don't try, do it," said Tirebiter. "If they let you. They won't let me, you know. They don't want me to infect your young minds with my un-American sympathies."

"Do you have any?" said Bill.

"Misplaced, maybe, but un-American never," he answered, and shook his head. "I'm just scared of 1984 settling in about 1958."

I ran into Tirebiter once again when I was working at KPFK radio in the early Sixties, when he came in to the studios for an interview after his novel *Street of Broken Glass* appeared from some local press. Re-written, I guess it had been, and re-printed.

Because the book's story dealt with the blacklist, our public affairs guy, Fred Haines, did the interview. (Fred was always planning a definitive documentary on the Hollywood Ten, just like I was "working on" the definitive documentary about the California Indians.) He asked Tirebiter what he did to survive during the blacklist.

"I wrote additional dialogue for Shakespeare," Tirebiter said. "And I'd do it again."

Ossman in the studio

I realized that's what he had been doing ever since back in the bungalow court days—surviving.

A few years after that, in 1967, Tirebiter popped up on the L. A. political scene, running for City Council in Glendale, on the Peace & Freedom ticket. He was "around" a lot, had a regular column in the *Free Press*, was seen to schmooze with Tim Leary and Ken Keasy, show up at Zappa concerts, avant-garde art exhibitions, and private screenings of *Easy Rider*, *Zabriskie Point* and *Head*. You could tell by his groovy love-beads that he was on Our Side.

That's when the whole Firesign Theatre met Tirebiter. Peter Bergman had him on "Radio Free Oz" as a guest-guru one night over KRLA, some time after the first Love-In.

I told him, "Pete, get George Tirebiter on the show, and ask him about flying saucers."

"Groovy," said Pete, and he did.

We actually wrote an "old radio script" to do live on that broadcast. It must have been one of the first pieces of group writing we ever did. Tirebiter mesmerized the Magic Mushroom audience, and especially Peter, with his tales of Alien Communications kept Top Secret by the Thought Police.

Phil Proctor heckled him in a mock-Deutch accent: "Come clean, Herr Rieffenbissen! You've been brain-washed!" Then, in a quick switch to a close aproximation of Peter Sellers' Bombay dialect, "Goodness gracious me, de Aliens vere only looking vor his Turd Eye. Dot is vy he looks flushed"

George took it all very well. He did not, however, win the election.

When the Firesign Theatre wrote George Tirebiter into their *oeuvre* in 1970, (even as the unlucky Apollo 13 guys were improvising to stay alive in their own personal Module of Aquarius), he was already "catching on" among film buffs. I remember a screening of two of his pictures—"First WAC in Tokyo" and "What a Family!"—at the Midnight Movies on Western, and later on, he and I were both judges of an "underground movie" festival. There was a major interview with him as an anointed *auteur* in ***Film Culture***.

Firesign was On Tour for the first time that year, and, after a surprisingly full house at Columbia University's McMillian Theatre, (where I myself had seen both e. e. cummings and the Budapest String Quartet perform) Bob Grossman, artist, cartoonist and Yale-pal of Peter's threw us a welcome at his loft.

A swing hung from a beam in the middle of the loft, and I recall sitting on it, swinging, in the midst of the kind of brouhaha you can get only at a party in NYC, when Phil Austin handed me something and said, "I think George Tirebiter should star in the next album."

"I thought it was my turn."

"You play George."

"That's an idea. It's a great funny name, whether he knows it or not. He's a great guy. What exactly were you thinking about?"

It was in the Firesign Code of Hippie Conduct never to get permission for anything we stuck into our evolving collage of Americana. It was all in the name of Art. So we—I—never called or wrote Tirebiter. We ended up ripping off his teen-ager, whom we dubbed Porgie Tirebiter, and some of the plot of "What A Family!" which we called "High School Madness." We also made reference to George running for office, and stuck him in a game-show where he got a wifely "Stab From The Past!" I copied his "elderly voice"—the one he had used to disguise his youth at the beginning of his career.

However, the Tirebiter who shows up on our third Columbia album, ***Don't Crush That Dwarf, Hand Me The Pliers***, has a lot of other clean-cut young men in him too—Andy Hardy, Archie Andrews, Henry Aldrich—and, of course, he plays the Sterling Haydn character in "Parallel Hell." But the blacklist, the acrimonious divorce, his old movies on late late night tv, even the fact that his phone had started ringing again, with job offers, all crept into our evolving story.

Later on, when we had adapted *Dwarf* as a stage piece, I played the part of George as a "former celebrity." I kind of felt that way myself—sometimes the Wheel of Life has us on Top, sometimes the Bottom. He'd been there and back again, a survivor of his hungers, and I felt that *that* was the most important thing about him then, in the early 1990's. I played him as a much thinner Orson Welles, or King Vidor, or Francis X. Bushman—an old-timer, wondering why his career is behind him, when he feels as young as he can still see he is, on the tube.

The real George Tirebiter never got wind of the album parody. I had to tell him about it when I met him again—he was running for Vice President on the Nat'l Surrealist Party ticket in 1976. The Firesign was involved, in various un-coordinated ways, in that year's Bison-tennial Papoon for President "Campoon."

Tirebiter showed up at a Hollywood "fun-raising" party, signed on to the "Not Insane!" slogan, and finally announced his candidacy at the Surrealist Party Convention that I'd organized (with tremendous Grassroots support) in Santa Barbara. He was vigorously opposed by a local right-winger, "Senator" Boron, but won in a landslide vote from the many and varied organisms present.

At the party after the Nomination, I showed George the *Dwarf* album, and asked him if he'd ever heard it.

"I don't believe in astrology," he said.

"This is a comedy record. I play you on it."

"Me?"

"Well, a guy with your name."

"The U.S.C. football mascot was named after me," he mused. "And he was an Airedale. I consider it an honor to be played by you, Dave, a fellow human being. Who won?"

"Won what?"

"You, playing me. Who won?"

"I'll give you a record, you listen and tell me. It's really about growing up and resisting authority, so a lot of people who've been growing up and resisting authority recently really like it. You get control of the Channel Selector of Life."

"Not Insane!" George said.

Then came all the scandals of the Campoon, which I dutifully reported for *Crawdaddy*, after which, after Papoon's re-election, George Tirebiter declared himself bound for Washington D. C., determined to be an even more surreal Vice President than Walter Mondale.

We did some terrific audio theatre in the Eighties, George and I. Producer Judith Walcutt (my wife) coaxed him out of semi-retirement to host WGBH's

"Radio Movies" with me. He had a great time spoofing "Doc Savage," explaining sound-effects, and getting me stuck in a time-trap during an intermission in "Lady In The Lake."

I cast him in guest spots in most all of our big productions, like "The War of the Worlds 50th Anniversary" show, and Norman Corwin's "We Hold These Truths." You can also hear his voice, among those of other media heroes, in my play based on the history of radio, "Empire of the Air."

Maybe the most fun we've had together, now that we're both way over 50, was during a Midwest Radio Theatre Workshop. George had been invited out to Missouri do an acting class, I believe. He'd asked me if I'd care to adapt a little entertainment from his mystery novel, *The Ronald Reagan Murder Case*. I roughed the first couple of chapters into five heart-stopping, cliffhanger serial episodes. To our surprise, because one of the other plays scheduled for production crashed, as they say, and burned, we ended up doing the show live on the air, with George playing himself, with Richard Fish as all the rest of the Hollywood Stars.

✿

Don't Crush That Dwarf has stayed pretty much in print for thirty-five years now. Pretty good for a comedy record.

The real George Tirebiter remains nonplussed about the Firesign album, but he has been in the theatre when Phil and Phil and I have done the now-legendary "Breakfast Scene," and he has heard the laughs his namesake provokes.

He told me once, "Dave, that bit is funnier than anything I ever wrote for a Hollywood movie. And *that* was when they'd let me write."

"George," I said, "That was when they'd let *us* write. And, thanks for the use of the monniker!"

ANOTHER CHRISTMAS CAROL

A GEORGE TIREBITER ADVENTURE

BY DAVID OSSMAN

1.

The Eighties were about to become the Nineties, and there wasn't anything we could do about it. I was coasting back into work—some personal appearances, the occasional cartoon voiceover, classes in radio history, writing and acting—and a guest spot in or somewhere near Kansas City, playing Mr. Scrooge in a Community Radio presentation of the original Old Chestnut, a tear-provoking horror-tale that always proves to be just what the Season needs.

A nice, clean Town Car limo came to pick me up at the KC airport. A Slavic gentleman in a nice, clean black suit had my name on a card. I said, "That must be me!" and he escorted me out.

"The Imperial Limousine Service welcomes you to Greater Kansas City, sir. I am Vlad."

"As in Vlad The Impailer?"

"Is who?"

"Count Drack-ulaaa!"

"No, as in Vlad To Meet You!"

"Well, you too. This is a wonderful surprise! Most of my airport pickup cars usually have only one clean seat."

It really was comfortable. "I'll just stretch out on the blue velvet back here, quiet the nausea, and you take the scenic route wherever we have to go."

"I'll do my best to be scenic, sir. You are feeling sick, sir?"

"It's nothing. Probably the Foodless Airline Snak I ate. Laughing—semi-hysterical, really—Cow's Cheese, Melt-O-Mints, Carter's Little Packing Peanuts. Honey roasted, I believe they were."

"You are a Visiting Celebrity, Mr. Tirebiter?"

"I think I'm what's known as a flash-from-the-past. I'm promoting a preposterous musical movie I made nearly fifty years ago, and playing the occasional Guest Star on the radio theater circuit. This week, Scrooge. Next week, God—featured part they tell me. Where are we going?"

"Kansas, Mr. Tirebiter, sir. Westward the course of Empire."

"Kansas? Not Missouri? I was looking forward to being in the same state as George Papoon. Well, no. No one could be in the same state as dear George. He was a Surrealist, you know."

"Like Gorbachev?"

"Only more so. I was Quale to Papoon's Bush back in '76."

"Is this a strange-twist-of-fate in American Politics story, sir? They are favorites with us who have come from the Soviet Union here."

"Yes, you see, after the resignations of Pres*Ididn't* Nixon and Vice Pres*Ididn'teither* Agnew . . ."

"I didn't know."

"Then Ford became the first unelected Pres*Idon't*."

"And everything I know . . ."

"You're right! Rocky Kissafeller was Acting Vice-*Preci*-dent. Republicans love an unelected government the best."

"At that time I was trying to grow marijuana in Siberia."

"Keep following. The way was then clear for a Surrealist takeover. Children and pets were given the vote and they swept George Papoon and me into office. Unfortunately, we were swept out of those same offices by the Gang of Two—the Casey/Meese Counter-Revolution."

"Them I understand."

"Don't we all! What time is it?"

"Digitally speaking, sir, 7:42. Your plane was twenty minutes late."

"Is wherever we're going a long way? Maybe I'll look at the TV back here. It's the Syndicated Hour."

"Remote control on jump seat."

It was. I picked it up and discovered it also controlled the bar. I got the Brandy Channel. There was a hair-dryer in case the brandy missed the glass and hit your pants. Oooops! Moon Roof! Very warm for May. An up-to-date Fax machine and . . .

"It says Jacuzzi."

"No, sir. Don't press button. Hot tub is for couples only. Next time, bring a friend."

"At least an acquaintance. Here's the TV. I'll keep the sound off and describe it to you. Here's 'Family Feud.' You do know all those so-called families are actually completely unrelated actors?"

"Not nuclear?"

"Not even best friends. Here's 'Wheel of Fortune!' There's Vanna—she has those big . . ."

"Big letters, yes, I know, sir."

"The Host is still that Cookie Man. I thought they should have replaced him with Morton Downey. Would've pepped the show up considerably. Did you know Mort's father was an Irish tenor?"

"Not Pat Sajak?"

"Look! No, don't look, it's Jacques Cousteau. He's saying, Ah, merci! Oui, oui, le même chose. Ques-que-say? They are eating the dolphins? 'Urry! We will attack 'Onolulu! Then he flips off the boat. Now, something new, Entertainment Tonight! I think they're reviewing my film . . ."

The sound bumped up to "Fans of George Tirebiter's will be happy to learn his best-known movie, 'Babes In Khaki,' is about to be released in a colorized version. This legendary classic . . ."

"I thought I recognized you, sir. You are in TV Guide."

"Yes, I am. Selling '40 Unclaimed Melodies.' Shhhh . . ."

" . . . however, there are moments of sustained brilliance amid the equally sustained implausibility of the musical numbers . . ."

"Enough of that. 'Babes' does look wonderful in color. The original was in sepia-tone. That was the closest we could get to khaki. Colorized, you can get the full impact of those Army tanks. I had them painted red-white-and-blue for the big dance number . . ."

It was fifty miles to Lawrence, Kansas. I watched the dance number. The tanks were impressive. I slept the rest of the way.

2.

College campus at night. Never the best time to find a rehearsal studio. Vlad let me off in front of a building that looked sort of like a top-secret government laundromat, maybe.

"In America, sir, culture is not always gaudy. Call my number, I will pick you up and take you to Hotel. It is my non-profit donation for free radio. Break a leg, sir."

The lobby tried its best not to look like one, which made it hard to find anything. What was I doing here? Was the radio world really waiting for yet another production of "A Christmas Carol?" You'd think they'd play the one Lionel Barrymore did, or Ronnie Coleman's. He was marvelous—'There's more of gravy than of grave about you, whatever you are!' I was Second Boy in that one.

I looked around for some basic information. I could tell that the windows were all fakes. This was the first floor and the doors to my right were numbered 605, 608, 609/611. Maybe this was the parking garage . . .

The second time I passed an Exit sign I was walking the opposite direction. So, if I go left instead of right next . . . Woman's Room, Men's Room, Green Room. Ah! "I must be near the stage door . . ." I said.

"Don't count on it." A guy who looked like a junior high bowling league coach in a brownish uniform came up behind me."

"Wonderful! Security at last."

"I wouldn't count on it."

"Maybe you're CIA?"

"Nope."

"Tell you what, I'm looking for the Little Theater. Maybe you have a compass? A map?"

"Wouldn't count on that. I got blueprints, tho. You lookin' for Communications or Fusion Lab?"

"I'm George Tirebiter and I'm due on stage for a radio drama rehearsal."

"OK, then. Go right on thru that door marked Exit, take the staircase up to the dressing rooms, straight thru, two sharp lefts. Backstage."

"Go out the Exit? Right here?"

"I wouldn't count on anything."

"Glad to hear it."

Yes, there was a black-box theater room off to the side of the main house, and as I got close, I could hear the rehearsal going on. There was a burst of jolly laughter and "Bob" said, "And now I give you Mr. Scrooge, the Founder of the Feast!"

"I've only got one glass here, Don. No amount of clinking it will sell a crowd."

"Make a note. Go on."

"And now I give you Mr. Scrooge, the Founder of the Feast."

"The Founder of the Feast, indeed! I wish I had him here. I'd give him a piece of my mind to feast upon!"

"And that would be Mr. Tirebiter's cue, if he were here."

"But I am here, at last, Mrs. Cratchit."

The safety door slammed behind me, the way they do.

"Mr. Tirebiter. Hi, I'm Don Brophy, the director. Did you get lost? Everybody does."

"We all do," said Mrs. Cratchit.

"The audience does," said Tiny Tim.

"Lost? In the M.C. Escher Communications Center? A wormhole in Space, where outside and inside are in parallel universes? I wouldn't have missed it. Unless I did."

"No, you're in the right place. Hope you don't mind, we started without you."

There were about ten actors, a sound-effects guy and a couple of additional voices to help out with the verses of Carols, which when sung made for cheerful transitions. I knew I wouldn't remember anybody's name, so I nodded happily and said, "Glad to be here, everybody."

"You ready to go on, Mr. T? You look a little woozy."

"Whipsnade's Complaint. It can strike in many ways. Suddenly, no matter where I am, I'm certain I'm in Philadelphia. Also, when in Kansas, Christmas comes in late Spring."

"We have to have time to market the program, and with you playing Scrooge, Mr. Tirebiter, we could get maybe fifty stations, more maybe to broadcast it."

"Well, then, on with the show."

"The pizzas will be here anytime," offered Tiny Tim.

"I took the Snak Flite."

Don, the director, said "If you're vegetarian. Mr. Tirebiter, we got the Tufu Special and Three Cheese with Lox. They're a contribution."

"I ordered Chorizo with peppers and hot sauce," said the sound-effects man.

"We usually get a Hawaiian one. Pineapple and poi."

"Cajun with Cornbread crust and Crayfish is better 'n that!" said a Ghost of Christmas Whenever.

The pizzas arrived and slices were eagerly devoured. I wondered what had brought me to do a Christmas play in May? Promotion! That's what! I stepped inside the engine of hype that runs the American Bozo Bus! A small photograph in *People*, awkward questions abut my past on morning talk shows in major markets. Autographs for young people in shopping malls who never heard of me. Getting to pick the big winner on 'Dialing for Dollars' in Dallas. Mother invited on Oprah . . . No! Mother, you wouldn't!

3.

"Let's pick up on page twelve. Your line, Mr. Tirebiter."

"How now! What do you want with me?"

"Much!" Oh, God, it's Mother! "Ask me who I was!"

"Who were you then?"

"It's Mother, Georgie, dear. I'm here on Oprah!"

"Don't tell her anything!"

"I'm on Geraldo, too!"

"Stop!"

"Oh, yes, Oprah! Georgie was such a talented little boy. My only child. His stepfather always frightened him. He was a butcher, Geraldo. Probably a Nazi spy, Oprah. He could have been a child molester, far as I know. He was a butcher in East Daileyville until the end. I became a Stage Mother in self-defense, so he couldn't abuse me anymore. I've never told this anywhere before, Oprah! I've never shared it with anyone, Geraldo . . . Little Georgie never knew his real father . . . I hardly knew him . . ."

"Mother!"

"He was the famous British detective, Sir Hemlock Stones. Georgie was our love-child."

"Oooooooooo! . . . You will be haunted by Three Special Effects . . ." said an Kansas-inflected actor.

"Chains, please. Come on microphone, Ghost. More chains!"

"I was hoping to go to sleep early, Mother."

The sound-effects man crashed the chains and Mother vanished.

"Look to see me no mo-o-o-ore!" said the Ghost.

"Now, sound of unlocking the door," said Don. "You want to sit down for a moment, Mr. Tirebiter? You were looking a little green in the middle of that."

"Yes, well, the strangest thing. I thought I saw my dear Mother for a moment. She was right there—plain as the nose on your microphone. Funny touch by the way, Dan. Let's just go on with my scenes, I'll be fine."

"I brought you some coffee, Mr. T," said a young thing with red braids. "It's butterscotch decaf."

"Cajun crawfish and candy coffee. Everything's up to date in . . . where are we?"

"Let's rehearse the snowstorm bit," said Don and the soundman wound an old-fashioned radio effect, with a strip of canvas sounding like heavy wind going around and much blizzardy blowing across the microphone. "Now let's hear the snow stopping."

"Say what?"

"The sound of snow stopping."

"Can't wait to hear that," I said.

The wind stopped.

"Too quiet."

Wind chimes proved serviceable. There may have been some broken glass in there too.

"Just serviceable. Let's think about it. OK, now, you, Scrooge and the Ghost of Christmas Past walk along in the snow . . .

"Would that be one or two pairs of feet?"

"Use your imagination."

He tried out two pair, using rubber boots and leather brogans. "Nope," he said. "Ghosts don't have feet. I'll use the cornstarch."

"Wind, please."

I set out as if walking in heavy snow, puffing with the effort, the steps crunching into a box of cornstarch like the old radio days, Scrooge's thoughts coming in short bursts.

"I feel as . . . as if I were really there . . . but, strangely, not cold . . . the snow isn't cold because . . . it is really . . . cornflakes . . . it's the backlot of Paranoid Pictures, and I'm not alone . . . I am . . . arm-in-arm with . . . a bit of undigested artificial reality . . ."

"Naw! It's only me, kid. Oliver Tulley? I was yer partner on that first hit picture of yers, don'tcha remember? *Variety* said, Oater Scribe Joins Radio Wonderkid for All-Star Babes."

"It's really you?"

"How about that? I'm a Special Effect now. I mostly do trade shows."

"Sorry to hear that, Ollie. I know we lost touch . . . I always meant to get together with you for lunch. I was such a green kid in those days, Ollie."

"It was a winter day like this on the set, remember, Georgie? The Big Finale. Red, white and blue tanks! Gals in uniform. Fireworks! I wrote it, kid. I wrote it and you got the credit."

"It was the Writers Guild, Ollie . . . the producers . . . I didn't know. I came out to Hollywood to do serious work."

"You gotcher break, kid. I went back to Majestic for a Hoot Gibson. And a lot more Gibsons after that, until I didn't give a hoot!"

"Don't fade, Ollie, don't fade! Wait! 'Babes In Khaki' is coming out again."

"Re-issued?"

"On TV, tinted in color, your finale with the tanks!"

"What a scene! Wasn't it Pat O'Brien?"

"George Murphy, I think. My wife Lillie was the wounded nurse. She only had that one line, 'What is an American?' but she listened very expressively."

"To Pat O'Brien."

"George Murphy,"

"Couldda been Dutch Reagan."

"You could be right."

"I remember it like yesterday . . . He said, "What Is An American?

"He's a Broadway Zip, with a flask on his hip,

He's a bum from Baltimore. And yes, what's more—

He's blonde as a Norwegian or black as Alabam'—

He's a copper, he's a cooker, he works for Uncle Sam!

He's Joe or he's Giuseppi, he's Pete or even Pepe—

His name? It doesn't matter. Call him Boulder Dam!"

"You deserved the Oscar for that, Ollie."

"He's an American . . .

Like Washington on the dollar bill,

And Injun Joe on the Ol' Mizzippi,

Like Dan'l Poon, who could not kill—

Or General Ike, who's ready and will!"

"They all shout Yippee when they see that flag go by!"

"And when you're at War and the going gets tough,"

"And you don't have the sense to know when 'nough's enough!"

"It's not dying you mind,"

"It's just one more bluff!" We chorused together. I still have no idea what Ollie's lyrics meant, but the tanks looked great.

"Remember my Oscar! . . ."

4.

"I cannot bear it! Leave me! Haunt me no longer!"

"Great, Scrooge, great. Now it says 'exhausted by an irresistible drowsiness he sinks into a heavy sleep."

"I will, Dan. You just go on with the Cratchits."

The soundman cued up a tinkling carousel. It reminded me of Christmas Day,

London, 1850. No! July, 1950, the Santa Monica Pier. It's a scene from my novel. Better yet, it's my screenplay, based on my novel . . . a pan shot . . . I'm the psychotic Hollywood writer, and I start to narrate, 'The Pacific Ocean is a sea of broken glass. I was here with Lillie once. My ex-wife. We listened to the carousel . . .'

"Listen, George. Musical ghosts," said Lillie. "The Voices of all our Christmases Past."

"Why did you do it, Lillie? Why would you tell them anything?"

"They wanted names. I gave them the ones everybody knows about. But they wanted more, George. They wanted fresh meat. I don't know why, George, but they wanted you."

"I'm finished, Lillie. You know that. Once the Committee has your name . . . Why?"

The carousel began spinning faster. The horses rising and falling.

"Billy Raymond wants me for 'Wilshire Boulevard' at Paranoid. If I gave them your name, the job would be mine. You can understand that, Georgie."

The horses spinning, the music gone out of whack!

"I called Dick at NBC about my contract. He says radio is going to be hit songs played all day in rotation by robots! Nobody wants theater anymore, he says!"

"Say you'll forgive me, George."

"I called Sam at Paranoid and he said I should call my agent. I did. 'Mother, what's going on here?' I asked. She said they said it didn't matter if it was a 'Roscoe The Dog' serial, if I was a Red, I was off the picture. I said, 'Mother, you know I'm not a Red. Lillie put my name on some petitions.' Mother said, 'I wish your father were here to see you at times like this."

This dream had theme music. As Mother screamed, 'Forgive me, Georgie, please!' the carousel vanished and the Announcer came in over the pulsating chords:

"This week, Brew 102 Television Playhouse presents, 'Street of Broken Glass,' adapted from George Typewriter's hard-hitting novel of murder and desire in a Hollywood full of hate, starring Mr. Typewriter and his beautiful new discovery, Annabelle, as . . .'"

OK, so it's not a Feature, it's not in Cinemascope. It's better! It's live. Black-and-white. Hard-hitting. My own personal disaster, turned into Play of the Week—just like Ollie North and Baby M! Who wouldn't like that? It would be a come-back, even if I had to use an assumed name. Lillie! Why are you haunting me?

Lillie echoed, "I need your forgiveness!" as all the clocks struck twelve.

"For giving me up to the Brain Police? Along with Larry Parks and Gale Sondergaard? Poor Zero Mostel! Never! Besides, you're only a character in my novel. Why should I forgive you? You're out-of-print! I could even kill you off!"

"Didn't you, George . . . didn't you . . . ?"

"I don't know . . ."

Her echoes faded away with the last clock chime.

"OK, folks, maybe we should take a little break here. Ah, er, Mr. Tirebiter, you got a bit edgy there when the Ghost was vanishing."

"Jet lag. A brief hallucination. Whipsnade's Complaint! It's nothing. Let's go right on. This is my favorite line: 'Lead on! Lead on! The night is waning fast, and it is precious time to me, I know. Lead on, Spirit!"

I wasn't surprised when the phone rang and the Spirit's voice said, "Typewriter! Listen to me. Yuh wanna know what's in store for ya, Futurewise? Shaddup an' listen! I'll meetcha at the Hall of Mirrors. Midnight. An' don't be late!"

When the driving Eighties TV series theme music came in, I knew I was in one, getting an anonymous phonecall in the middle of the night, right when I was dreaming of a White Christmas, too. The Main Titles are rolling. My big sports-car whine builds to a roar. Ah, I love the way each one of these dynamite action sequences fantasizes me, the author, as a rich, successful hero. It's all in my head!

Running feet in a dark, wet alley! Gun shots! Typing! That's me, finishing another page! Theme goes out . . . I come back after the commercial. I'm looking over the Medical Examiner's shoulder. The cops are talking to the witnesses. . .

"I don't know much about it either way. I only know he's dead."

"When did he die?"

"Looks like last night sometime," says the M.E.

"What was the matter with him?"

"God knows."

"I thought he'd never die."

"What'd he do with his money?"

"Didn't leave it to me, that's all I know."

"Smart guy, huh?"

Scrooge's body has been stripped. Cut away to a couple of street-people. They have his clothes, there, under a freeway overpass down by the L.A. River. They're laughing . . .

Swish-pan to the Hell of Mirrors . . . irrors . . . full of echoes . . . my face is reflected . . .ected . . . ected . . . a thousand times . . . imes . . . imes . . .

"Yo, Typewriter! . . . iter . . . iter . . . iter . . .!"

5.

"Yes? Who?"

"Me, Freddy Rambo, Typewriter. International Artists. Good to meetcha. I'm a big fan, Typewriter. Those old 'Joe From Mars' stories back in the Fifties? Great! How about somethin' Lite?"

Freddy was from Chicago and spoke Middle Western. We were at the Bel Air. The waitperson was from somewhere south of the Mason-Dixon Line.

"Ready? We have Lite Japanese Beer, Lite Peach Wine Cooler, Lite Italian Water, butterscotch decaf and complimentary packing peanuts."

"Perelli with lime," sez Rambo.

"What about you?" Like I was Scrooge or something!

"I think I'd like a Martini," I said.

"I'll have to see if the barperson knows how to make one. Thank you." Waitperson vanished.

"Let's cut to the chase before I wake up, OK, Freddie?"

"It's Joe From Mars, George. My people, your people, we all like the idea. The Alien Next Door. Average blue-collar family outta Rosanne or Married With Chiuldren. Duplex in Cleveland, Pittsburgh maybe . . ."

"Philadelphia?"

"Better numbers in Cleveland. OK, they share the duplex with Joe—he's a Tom Hanks lookalike, OK? No antennas or anything. He's thirtysomething, if you get what I mean. Like, if this Joe was human, he'd be staring fifty in the face and he's still a lost boy, can't make up his mind about anything, but he's really from Mars. Don't we all feel like that?"

"Sometimes, I suppose . . ."

"So, follow me, only the kids know about Joe—somethin' like ET, but better. Oh, yeah, he is tryin' to get home, but he also gets involved, ya know, mixed up in people's problems, like the Equalizer, sort of, but more Quantum Leap, you grock?"

"I'm grocking as fast as I can, Freddie."

"So, keep up—what we got here is a sort a Hulk/Fugitive/Lost In Space thing with good, healthy Cosby-type laughs. Plus strictly contemporary headline stuff—this is the Nineties, Georgie. Joe saves a homeless family from crack pushers. Joe saves the schoolkids from a maniac with an AK-47. Joe finds a terrorist bomb in the wife's van . . . Hasn't been anything like it since Mork & Mindy!"

"Wow! Joe? I must be dreaming! I don't know . . ."

"George! Let me demonstrate the awesome power of my company, George. We're the ones developed the 8.3 quake on the Universal Tour."

"I knew that."

"We can give you the same treatment in your own home,"

It was a good demo. Eight-point-three.

"Impressive test numbers."

"And here's a bonus you can't turn down, Typewriter. How about a gig as a celebrity murder victim on the next Nightmare flick? You'll be criminally insane, gut a couple of good-lookin' teens, then get turned into fettucini marinara by a berserk pasta slicer. Lotsa gore! Like it?"

"Where do I sell out?"

"Sell out! Sell out! That's great, George! On the dotted line. Use my pen—it's already filled with your blood!"

"How do you do that?"

"It's a Stephen King bit. Ha ha. Just kidding. Red ink. Means it's a business expense."

"I must remember that one. Well, why not?"

"Merry Christmas, George!"

"Yes, yes! God bless us everyone, eh?"

"Well, Typewriter," sez Freddie, "I wouldn't go that far."

"Deck the halls," sang the chorus.

"And it was always said of him that he knew how to keep Christmas well, if any man alive possessed the knowledge," said Bob Cratchitt. "May that truly be said of us, and all of us. And so, as Tiny Tim observed . . ."

"Great, great! Unlucky to say the last line before the broadcast."

Just as I was about to sell out to the Agent of Xmas Yet To Come!

"Credits go over the music and we're out. Thanks everybody. Thanks, Mr. Tirebiter. You were great. Just go ahead and use those ad libs you did for Scrooge. Really funny. OK, dress at four and broadcast at seven-thirty tomorrow. Don't worry about a thing—it's gonna be great."

They all left, knowing where they were going. I borrowed the office phone, called Vlad.

The director was next-to-last to leave. He escorted me through the gray maze of Communications to what was, at least on this side, the front door.

"Have you had enough to eat, Mr. Tirebiter? You could go to Johnnie's—he stays open late. Good burgers."

"No, thank you anyway. I'll have Vlad take me to the hotel. Which one is it?"

"The Angst. Downtown. Very historic. The rooms're named after famous characters from Kafka, Sartre, Woody Allen. I think you're in the Montressor."

"For the love of God, really? I'll just watch a little TV and drift off to sleep."

"Sorry, there's no TV at the Angst. Not historic."

"I see."

"Family dining, though."

"Maybe room service?"

"Restaurant closes at ten."

"Lounge?"

"Upscale sports bar with loud music until two. They give you two sets of earplugs in the bathroom."

"Two sets. How generous."

6.

The House of Usher suite had something called a reversible shower and a Murphy bed. Perfect decorator touch, I thought. It swung to the floor with a clang. There was a radio. It was tuned to the same New Age music that seemed to be playing everywhere those days.

I lay down to the squeeking of historic springs. The music of Dickens played on in my mind. That guy could certainly write dialogue. A few laffs, a few tears, some spooks. Can't miss. Those hallucinations, though. What were they all about?"

"Come, come, Tirebiter! Can't you guess?"

It was Scrooge, perched on the foot of my bed.

"Well, Scrooge, you were about greed. Also, you were not exactly a party animal."

"Not at first. I loved the money more than my fellow man."

"Person, Scrooge. Fellow person. Also child-care-provider and flight attendant. Nothing's the same."

"We're the same, Tirebiter. Think about it. Think about the past, the present and the future, sir, and the lessons that they teach. And then, be jolly! Raise someone's salary and buy a second coal-scuttle before you dot another 'i'!"

"I will honor Christmas in my heart, and try to keep it all the year, eh, Scrooge? A kinder-and-gentler Scrooge."

I faded then. Scrooge faded.

He's gone, but he'll be back. Every year. Until next time, let's join those Kansas radio actors and toast Mr. Dickens and his snowy Holiday once more.

"God bless us, every one!"

"Another Christmas Carol" © 2016 by David Ossman

We won't judge you
for not having all the
8-tracks.

We don't have them
either.

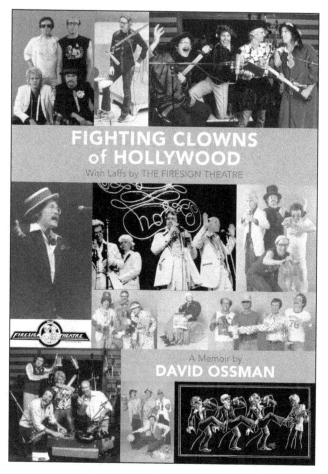

FIGHTING CLOWNS of HOLLYWOOD
With Laffs by THE FIRESIGN THEATRE

A Memoir by
DAVID OSSMAN

DAVID OSSMAN's memoir of THE FIRESIGN THEATRE's rapid response to the on-coming Reagan Era recounts the quartet's uneasy transformation from writer-performer-producers of in-studio comic audio masterpieces to theatrical hopefuls and Movieland script-writers. FIRESIGN goes Hollywood with a million $$ MGM movie deal and a string of big stage shows, featuring all-new hot comedy material, performed at the Roxy, premiere rock-club on the Sunset Strip.

Here are FIRESIGN's new sketches from the "Owl & Octopus Show," all the words to the full-frontal musical revue "Fighting Clowns," and the one-act play, "Joey's House." Nick Danger, "America's only detective," re-appears in three confusing episodes and Old Time Radio fans will also dig "The History of the Art of Radio," and "The American Pageant," both of which turn American history over in its grave.

www.bearmanormedia.com

CPSIA information can be obtained
at www.ICGtesting.com
Printed in the USA
BVHW061949010519

547075BV00008B/264/P